The Portrait

by

Louis Ryman

DORRANCE PUBLISHING CO., INC.
PITTSBURGH, PENNSYLVANIA 15222

ISBN # 0-8059-5403-1
Printed in the United States of America

First Printing

For information or to order additional books, please write:
Dorrance Publishing Co., Inc.
643 Smithfield Street
Pittsburgh, Pennsylvania 15222
U.S.A.
1-800-788-7654
Or visit our web site and on-line catalog at *www.dorrancepublishing.com*

In loving memory of my daughter, Linda, a courageous and beautiful lady whose thoughts and concerns were directed toward the welfare of others.

DORRANCE
PUBLISHING CO.
INC.

643 Smithfield Street • Pittsburgh, PA 15222 • (412) 288-4543 • FAX (412) 288-1786

Dear Program Director:

We have enclosed for your perusal a complimentary copy and some descriptive material regarding *The Portrait* by Canton, Ohio resident Louis Ryman because we know that the public looks to you to keep them abreast of what is new, interesting, and significant in your area. In a time of social disintegration, freelance artist Peter Grant overcomes many conflicts and personal danger to create an awe-inspiring painting which renews man's faith in God in this moving novel.

Please feel free to contact Dorrance by mail or phone at (800) 788-7654 if you have any questions, would like some additional material, or would be interested in arranging an interview with the author.

We look forward to hearing from you.

Sincerely,

Jessica Cunningham
Promotion Manager

Enclosure

Contents

Chapter 1
The Encounter

Security made it clear their taxi would arrive precisely at 10:30 P.M. and it would be marked with the number seventeen. With both specifications met, young Wesley climbed into the warm taxi, followed by his mother and his father, Peter Grant.

As they eased onto the icy streets of Washington, D.C. the cabby snapped a dashboard switch causing protective cushions to slide into place. The snow-covered ground reflected millions of tiny diamonds soon to fade with the intrusion of westerly clouds. On this New Year's Eve, more than the usual excitement prevailed.

The drive to the parish would take longer due to the weather, but the cabby assured them they wouldn't be late. He would take the rural route to avoid the heavier residential traffic. Confident but aware of the danger, Peter Grant and his family felt a tinge of solace seeing the gaily decorated Christmas trees in the windows of homes spotting their path.

They were not Catholic but it didn't matter. Tonight, St. Michael's Parish would be overflowing with many faiths and denominations. The approach of a new year, normally welcomed with joy, made this moment stand out. This moment was far from normal.

They sat in silence as the warm taxi began to relax them. The moon disappeared behind clouds and the sky turned black, prompting the cabby to initiate a smooth transition from lunar to liquid fuel intake.

For security reasons, Peter Grant hadn't seen Tracy for over two months. The uncertainty which lay ahead compelled him to lightly kiss her forehead. She unbuttoned her coat. "Darling, will you please lower the thermostat?" she asked, resting her head against his shoulder.

Grant complied, knowing her discomfort stemmed mostly from apprehension. Her oval face, cushioned with blonde velvet curls, showed signs of tension. He kissed her forehead again, causing her to smile faintly.

Gazing out the window, Wesley's eyes followed a soft falling snow highlighted by passing headlights. Grant glanced fondly at his son. Until eleven weeks ago, he hadn't seen Wesley for two long years. Now the boy was eight, handsomely tall and mature for his age, but not ready to grasp the significance of the huge portrait hanging in the parish sanctuary and demanding world attention. Within two hours it will be unveiled at a special Midnight Mass.

Except for a small copy, Wesley hadn't seen the portrait since its completion eight months earlier. Tonight he and millions of others would see the original. A wave of love passed through Grant, knowing he would share this memorable evening with his wife and son. They would have more to share later. By then, Wesley would more fully understand their joy and share it with them. They needed only time.

Grant checked his watch. It was 10:35 P.M. The year was 2027 A.D. and on this night world peace would begin to unfold. The vestiges of war would end, climaxing one of history's bloodiest eras. Despite giant technological strides that harnessed ecological and population needs, refined synthetic foods, produced human genes, established the first Deep Space Station, and eliminated all cancers except the T-cell leukemia virus, world peace would be mankind's supreme achievement.

How would man's dream be realized? Scratch the UN, NATO, heads of state, and all international humanitarian bodies. Oddly, peace would prevail through the efforts of a single man. Within the confines of his studio and without fanfare, an artist would paint a portrait of Christ the likes of which had never been seen. The portrait would pave the way for peace.

What manner of man was the artist? Ordinary. He was an average craftsman with a passion for painting and for living. He was no Michelangelo, Rembrandt, or Picasso, yet his portrait would open new avenues for human dignity and narrow the gap for greed. Throughout history no work of art would do so much for so many. Grant withdrew his billfold and removed a reproduction of the portrait, as if to reassure himself it was reality and not a madman's fantasy.

Peter Grant painted the portrait and he did it despite his nemesis, John Baxter. The two men had a strange relationship, one which Grant finally understood after two years of living hell.

Grant's eyes turned from the hypnotic windshield wipers to the massive shoulders and stubby neck of the taxi driver. A man of considerable strength and a source of comfort, should trouble arise, thought Grant.

The artist knew he was a target hunted by killers. Yet those responsible for his safety, especially head of security, Dr. Judith Gillespie, had his utmost confidence. Peter Grant's two hellish years were about to end, but they first had to start. It all began when Peter Grant encountered John Baxter. It was April 20, 2025, two months into the American civil revolt.

Δ Δ Δ

Rain pelted Chicago's Northside all day as a lone man forged his way north on Ashland Avenue.

Night had fallen and Peter Grant's progress was slowed by winds sweeping off the lake. He felt confident a hotel or an apartment would be nearby and he proved to be right. Just ahead he had spotted an apartment for rent and with a skylight. It looked ideal for his needs.

As he approached the lighted apartment, his attention was caught by a speeding car coming toward him with automatic gunfire, wildly spraying his side of the street. Grant dropped to the sidewalk belly-down as the car passed him. His relief was momentary as the car made a U-turn and returned, causing Grant to run the side streets. When exhaustion set in he dropped behind a hedge.

Thirty minutes later Grant relocated the apartment after losing direction in his confused state. He mounted the steps and pressed the door buzzer. After a second try the door opened. In the doorway stood a man of Grant's dimensions wearing soiled pajamas and smelling of stale whiskey.

Before Grant could speak, the man grabbed his arm only to release it quickly. The man's face paled with fixed eyes and mouth ajar. "I...thought you were the devil," he muttered, barely above a whisper. "My mind...my mind is misbehaving. It's.... His voice trailed off but his eyes remained fixed upon the artist.

Grant remained unruffled. "Good evening, I'm looking for an apartment and...."

The artist continued to explain but he wasn't heard. The man was still surveying the intruder, noting Grant's frame to be much like his own except more erect. But that face. Those eyes. By God they could be his own, the man was thinking.

"...and I thought your apartment might still be vacant," Grant was saying.

"Vacant apartment?"

"Your upstairs apartment. It has a skylight and—"

"Come in, come in," interrupted the man. "One could drown in this damn Chicago weather."

Once inside, the man introduced himself as John Baxter.

Grant removed his wet raincoat, and they seated themselves before a crude fireplace. The artist was quick to notice Baxter's afflictions—limp right hand and a right foot that dragged when he walked. With some effort, Baxter hastily rekindled the flames, causing shadows to bounce off their faces. The brick building was old and damp but sturdy. Scant rays of light filtered under pulled blinds, providing an air of seclusion.

Baxter half-heartedly apologized for the room's disorder, saying he had taken the apartment only a week earlier.

"So, you need an apartment with a skylight," Baxter finally uttered. "Damn scarce these days." With slow deliberation he pawed the stubble of whiskers on his chin. "Mister, don't think I caught your name," he mused.

"Grant, Peter Grant."

"Yes, of course. Grant. It has a familiar ring," he reflected as he sat back shaking his head. "Mr. Grant, you must understand I'm sick. Sick as hell. My mind...it plays tricks on me." He closed his eyes. "Memory comes and goes. Presently, I'm in one helluva fog. Swear I've heard your name before."

Grant was beginning to feel uneasy. He checked his watch. "I'm an artist of sorts," he volunteered.

Baxter's eyes widened. "God almighty! That's it! Grant, the painter!" he blurted, slapping his knee with his good hand. His voice suddenly lost its softness and his face became hard. "The Vagabond. A fair piece, Grant. Only fair. Structurally sound...like this old building," he gestured with a sweep of his arms, "but badly in need of refinement. Don't you agree?" he asked bluntly.

Grant's brows lifted to Baxter's criticism, which he considered to be without validity, but he passed it off. "I take it you're a connoisseur of art?" the artist asked with a hint of sarcasm.

John Baxter's eyes glared as he staggered to his feet. "Art! Ha! A dirty word, painter. I detest the word. Most damnable fraud ever contrived by man." His head lowered and he began a slow drudging pace before the fireplace. "As a form of expression, it is superficial. Doesn't touch man's soul. Doesn't convey gut feelings. Doesn't reveal man's hideous conflicts," he concluded, returning to his chair. Baxter covered his face with a hand and began to tremble.

Grant glanced at his watch once more and rose abruptly. "Mr. Baxter, perhaps I caught you at a bad time. I'll come back another day," he said.

"No! No!" Baxter pleaded, slipping between the artist and his raincoat, which had been draped over a nearby couch. "Don't go!" he demanded. "You can't dammit! I mean...." He groped for words, nudging closer to Grant. "Look...you're still wet," he observed. "And my upstairs apartment is vacant. Painter, the apartment is yours if you'll stay a bit longer."

Grant paused, trying to analyze the man. He turned to the fireplace and leaned against the mantel with outstretched arms. By now the fire had taken hold and his brown suit shimmered in its warm reflection. Stay! Stay! Stay! John Baxter's word peppered Grant's mind until it mellowed into the gentle voice of Kay Allyson.

In the leaping flames, Grant saw her sad face as he remembered it last summer. She had asked him to stay and freelance in Chicago, but New York

City offered a challenge he couldn't resist. Kay's image faded and Grant turned to Baxter. "But why? Why do you insist I stay?"

Baxter worked his way to Grant's side. "Need your help, dammit! Without it, I'll break! See?" he said, extending his good hand, "Nerves shot to hell."

"Perhaps you need a doctor?"

"Headshrinker, you mean. Got one but he's a quack. Can't be trusted. None of them."

"Why should you trust me?"

"Because you're here, dammit! There's no one else...no one."

"Mr. Baxter, how can I help you?" Grant asked flatly.

"Answer some questions," Baxter shot back. "That asking too much?"

Grant returned to his chair, causing Baxter's whiskered face to brighten. "Good!" Baxter said as he shuffled to a desk and retrieved a half-empty bottle of whiskey. He took a gulp and wiped his mouth with a pajama sleeve. "Look at me," he demanded, as he squatted on the edge of his chair while nudging it closer to Grant. "Look at my face, painter!"

"I know," said Grant, his eyes returning to the leaping flames. "Our features are similar but commonplace. I see my face in many men."

"Where's you car, painter?"

"Car? Haven't any. I came by foot."

Baxter emptied the bottle in two more gulps and tossed it onto the nearby couch. He slumped back in his chair. "I had a car once...but it was totaled."

He related a brief account of the accident, much to Grant's displeasure, as it reminded him of an earlier disaster which had claimed his parents.

"Sorry," Grant said finally. "I'm sure you'd rather forget it."

Baxter appeared preoccupied in thought and didn't respond.

During the lull, Grant lit his pipe and checked his watch. "Time is pressing. May I see the vacant apartment?"

"Painter...how did you know my apartment was vacant?"

"I didn't. I accidentally came upon it."

Baxter ignored his answer and changed the subject. "I have a damn headache. The pain started a week ago. Hasn't let up."

He opened his eyes to the empty bottle on the couch. "I drank and took pills, but nothing helped."

"Did you phone your doctor?"

"Doc Wells? Had to. I was desperate and still am. Doc said he'd be here in thirty minutes and he's already two hours late."

"Your doctor makes Sunday house calls?" Grant asked, concluding the man wasn't making sense.

"Today is Sunday? Damn! Did I lose a day?"

"It's easy to become confused when you're not well," said Grant.

After a moment, Baxter maneuvered to the fireplace, his back facing the artist. His dark eyes widened and his body began to tremble. He suddenly whirled awkwardly toward Grant. "Painter...you're a stranger, yet I hate your pigmented guts! Ha! Look at you...dressed like a proud peacock and masquerading as a Christian gentlemen!" His excited body stiffened. His lead lowered and he steadied himself against the mantle. The outburst had subsided. He was exhausted and breathing hard.

Peter Grant leaned forward in his chair, fondling the stem of his pipe. "Mr. Baxter, perhaps it is yourself you hate because of your past troubles. I may remind you of yourself at an earlier, happier time."

"When I was well?" offered Baxter in a subdued tone, still facing away from Grant. "Before the accident. Before I lost everything. My wife...my livelihood...my hand that painted so effortlessly." He turned to Grant. "Before I lost my mind?" he muttered.

A gust of wind shook the bay window to Grant's rear. The artist checked his watch again, then stepped to the fireplace and knocked the ashes from his pipe.

Baxter grabbed his arm. "Painter, one more question?" His long fingers dug hard into Grant's wrist. "For six ungodly days," Baxter persisted, "I was tormented with a headache that burned with the intensity of those flames." He gestured toward the fire. "Yet tonight, when I opened the door and saw you, the pain stopped! I ask you...how in God's name could that happen?"

Grant slipped into his raincoat. "I take it, Mr. Baxter, you're an atheist?"

"So what?"

"It's enough to know that with God anything is possible. It isn't necessary that we know how."

Grant stepped to the door. "Mr. Baxter, you are the proprietor of this apartment building?"

Baxter nodded. "It's all I have left," he said soberly.

"I would like to take the upstairs apartment sight unseen and with a three-year lease," suggested Grant.

"I'll write up the contract tonight on those terms," Baxter countered.

"Good, Mr. Baxter. With your permission I'll move in tonight," he said with a sigh of relief.

Chapter 2
A New Beginning

Heavy winds whipped into the nation's capital, causing the snowstorm to worsen.

Wesley worked on a crude landscape at the steamed rear window while his mother gazed beyond the windshield wipers, her head still resting against her husband's shoulder. The dashboard clock read ten-forty. If all went well, they would reach the parish in fifty minutes. Security was strict with time schedules.

A light flashed at the dashboard, prompting the cab driver to reach for a transmitter-receiver.

"Big Bear twenty-two here. Over," he responded.

"Zebra two here. Over," came a man's voice from the other end.

"This is Big Bear twenty-two. Forty-two, fifteen. Over."

"This is Zebra two. Okay at cloverleaf. Twenty-three, eleven."

The cabby replaced the instrument and glanced over his shoulder. "Everything's under control," he assured them.

"Good," Grant replied.

It amazed Wesley how such talk could be understood by anyone.

His mother responded with a sigh of relief.

The artist slipped his arm around his wife's shoulders and gave her an assuring hug. As he did so, his eyes caught the headlights of a car to their rear. He wondered if he had seen those headlights earlier while being mindful one's imagination could magnify things in potentially dangerous situations. Grant tried to relax. He closed his eyes and began to breathe slowly as his thoughts, drifting back, eventually returned to 2025 and his Chicago studio apartment.

∆ ∆ ∆

Grant had just stirred from a light sleep. Lying on the cot at the south wall of his studio, his eyes surveyed the room with approval. The studio's high ceiling was bisected and sloped to either side with the south slope housing the skylight. The north wall separated the studio from a kitchenette, bedroom, and half-bath. A fireplace adorned the east wall and a door bolted on both sides led from the kitchenette down a stairwell to the exterior.

Four days had passed since he had moved in and his meager furnishings were in reasonable order. Risers still needed to be placed against the north wall where shelves would be installed to accommodate his canvasses, oils, brushes, and miscellaneous supplies. The cot would do until his bedroom furnishings arrived.

It had been almost two weeks since Kay Allyson broke their relationship. She had been working in Chicago as a field photographer for Reed & Lambert Publishers and he was freelancing in New York City. The day had started badly when Grant barely missed a good assignment and had nursed his ego with alcohol. By evening, the drinks and his oils had difficulty mixing, yet his deadline had a mere twelve hours.

Despite his condition, Grant's model, Tracy Duvall, had posed patiently, considering her inexperience. When she walked into his New York studio last September, she offered to model for him at any pay scale. Recognizing her potential, he hired her above the going rate.

Grant had sensed her fondness for him at the outset but he made no advances. Even on this occasion, he had resisted. He was determined to meet the deadline, and he would have had Kay not phoned.

The long distance call came shortly before midnight, just as they had finished three hours of painstaking work. Now, with his concentration broken, Grant had decided to break and gestured for Tracy to take the call.

He mistakenly assumed the caller was a local prostitute who somehow had gotten his phone number.

"Tell that meddling whore to peddle her ass elsewhere," he grumbled, as he scraped paint from his fingers with a palette knife.

Unfortunately, Tracy had relayed his message verbatim.

Grant grabbed the phone to explain but his words were jumbled and a bad connection had caused him to have difficulty hearing Kay, except for her final words: "I'm sorry, Peter. Please let this be the end for us."

The line went dead and with it part of him. Hurting and hating himself, Grant tossed the canvas aside, sent Tracy on her way, and dropped onto his cot. As he lay there, it occurred to the artist something was totally wrong between Kay and him. It was something beyond her telephone call. She had been distant with him recently and the phone call only surfaced the matter. *To hell with the deadline. Kay is more important,* he thought.

At that moment Grant had made the decision to dump New York in favor of Kay. He would pull up stakes and return to Chicago. He would apologize to Kay for his crudeness and explain Tracy Duvall was his model and nothing more. Most of all, he wanted to make amends in person.

However, Kay was gone.

Reed & Lambert had rushed the little photographer off to Brazil on emergency assignment, snapping jaguar along the tributaries of the Amazon. Grant reasoned the unexpected trip was her purpose for phoning him. Now there could be no phone calls for two months, even if she wanted. She had been there before and the artist knew the dangers she faced in that Godforsaken jungle. The thought of it troubled him. Given the chance, he would make up for his callousness and prove his love for her.

Grant rolled to his feet. The cot had served him well as a retreat from weary hours at the easel, however during his recent New York stint, it had been neglected. Kay was right. He should have freelanced in Chicago where his reputation as an excellent figure painter had been established. Nine months in New York had produced a modest clientele, but the struggle had been slow, with the hiring of Tracy being the only good to come from it. Most of all, he had lost the closeness of Kay.

After showering, Grant prepared to shave. Drawing closer to the mirror, he detected tiny blood vessels in both eyes. It was a reflection of soft living. His childhood and adolescent years had not been characterized by softness. Those had been difficult and lonely.

Peter Grant's sixth birthday was marred by a head-on auto collision which had killed his parents. Until then, his childhood had been happy. His father had taught him to swim and would take him to the Cleveland art institute, but it was his mother who had nurtured his creative instincts. She had often spoken of talking lessons from him, "...after you become a real artist and open your own studio."

All this had vanished on Grant's fateful birthday. His parents had driven to pick up a trainer bicycle as a gift for him when the accident had occurred. Young Grant felt responsible for their deaths and the unjustified guilt had lingered through the years.

Following the tragedy, Grant had been placed in the custody of his only living relative, demanding Uncle George, where the boy remained for twelve years. This compounded his misfortune but, thanks to strong roots, he had managed to survive.

After shaving, he trimmed his brows. The artist had sharply cut features and a fair complexion to contrast with dark hair and eyes, providing a youthful thirty years. Lately he felt much older.

He disengaged the towel and dropped it over a chair. The only other bedroom furnishings were a telephone and a dresser from which he pulled an assortment of shirts. His tall frame easily handled one hundred eighty pounds and, while well built, his only claim to athletic prowess was having swum for Euclid High in state competition. The swimming had developed broad shoulders and long-muscled arms that squirmed into a chartreuse shirt.

A white scar at his rib carriage was the result of an accidental bayonet stabbing he had received during his army volunteer training in the jungles of Hawaii. He had enlisted for a three-year hitch following high school primarily to escape his uncle's domination. The scar reminded him of his dislike for the tropical wastelands, especially now with Kay immersed in one of the most treacherous jungles of all.

Grant stepped into lemon slacks, then dialed his former employer—Glick Publishing Company.

While being put on hold and awaiting transfer to the PR department, he momentarily recalled the day he had joined the company in March 2019. He just received his B.F.A. degree from Chicago School of Fine Arts and the school director, Doctor Ancel De Breau, was bidding him a fond farewell.

"Peter," he advised, "our country is passing through a dark tunnel. America is being tested. You, too, will be tested many times, especially your courage and faith. As you face up to professional standards and ethics, you may become discouraged. Don't despair. Have faith in yourself, in your abilities, in your future. Above all, have faith in your God." With that, he presented Grant a gift—a gold anchor encased in a gold ring. It fit snugly in the inside pocket of his jacket where it would remain. It was a token of faith which would serve the artist as a source of strength thereafter.

It was a proud moment. However, he was not proud of his actions only hours later.

He and a fellow student had visited a local tavern in celebration of graduation. Grant seldom drank, but this day was an exception. After an hour of imbibing, his friend had to leave and a young brunette had slipped onto the vacated bar stool. Later she had slipped into bed with Grant.

Now, his memory of it was foggy. He remembered she was tall and attractive, but little else. He couldn't recall her name or if he had used protection.

Grant was twenty-four at the time, and he clung to the belief sex was meant for a mate or loved one. Because the attractive brunette didn't qualify, he remembered the venture as being tasteless, without feeling and ending prematurely. He still harbored the shame of it.

"Pete! Where've you been? I've been trying to run you down for a week!"

It was Preston Thomas, an Afro-American and Glick Publishing's top publicity man at the other end.

"Slow down, ol' buddy, I'm only thirty minutes from your office," said Grant.

"You're here? In Chicago?"

"Right. Got in several days ago."

"Pete, why didn't you check in sooner?"

"I meant to, Press, but I've been feeling out-of-sorts lately. Also, I've been busy getting my apartment in order."

"Your apartment?" Press asked after a pause.

"I found an apartment on North Ashland and moved in last Thursday," Grant explained.

"My Lord!"

"So, you've been looking for me? What's up, Press?"

"Plenty! Can you run over?"

Within the hour they were seated in a booth at the company's coffee shop. The dining room was replete with the latest interior innovations and nearly empty of patrons due to the early hour. A waitress responded to their needs and Preston Thomas was soon sipping his black nectar. Thomas was pudgy, prematurely gray, and a model of personal grooming, always clean shaven and good smelling. His light gray suit contrasted with dark eyes that approvingly surveyed his friend.

"Glad you're back, Pete. Never should have gone, you know." A dozen years Grant's senior, Thomas had taken the young artist under his wing since Grant's first day at Glick almost six years ago. Little escaped his notice, and Grant wondered if news of Kay had prompted their meeting.

Thomas adjusted his eyeglasses. "So, you've located up on North Ashland. Nice strip for robberies and muggings. Still don't carry a gun, Pete?"

Grant smiled faintly. "Press, I create, not destroy."

"But you need protection!" Thomas objected. "Dead men don't create a ripple."

"I know. Only a stink or two," said Grant in a light vein.

Preston Thomas's face reflected the concern of a father.

"Press, I appreciate your interest in my welfare but I can't compromise my feelings about killing. The moment I pocket a gun, a terrorist or roving rebel will force my hand. Besides, didn't I survive New York?"

"Yes you did, but I feel something has happened since your return. I can smell something."

"You're right, Press. It must be my landlord you smell."

Before his friend could respond to the offbeat remark, Grant revealed his encounter with John Baxter five days earlier.

Press had listened intently as he slowly sipped his coffee. He leaned back and readjusted his eyeglasses. "I must say, Pete, Chicago didn't welcome you with open arms. This Baxter fellow comes across like a page out of Poe," he said, looking uncomfortable.

Grant grinned and emptied his cup. "If you think the man could commit mayhem, forget it. As I see it, he appears to be a has-been artist who is bitter with the world, not me."

"Hmmm...possibly a misanthrope," said Thomas.

"His bitterness may be justified," Grant continued. "His wife died tragically. Baxter rammed a steel hauler on Interstate 60. His wife was decapitated, while he came out of it with a lame leg and a paralyzed painting hand."

"Those ill-brained maniac drivers," sighed Thomas, a widower through natural causes.

"I think Baxter is more sick than dangerous," the artist went on. "He went to Evanston four days ago to see a psychiatrist, Doctor Wells. He has yet to return.

"So? That sounds rational, Pete."

"Except there is no Doctor Wells, Not in Evanston. I checked."

Thomas sat back. "So, what do we have here?" he pondered. "Your landlord may be a mythomaniac. Obviously, he's sick. He hates the world, has wide mood swings...."

A waitress interrupted, giving them coffee refills with a smooth motion.

She provided the opening Grant wanted. "Okay, ol' buddy, let's get to the issue. What's the news you have for me? Is it Kay?" he asked with apprehension.

Thomas stirred uneasily. "In part," he admitted. "Pete, she phoned me from O'Hare just before takeoff."

Peter Grant leaned forward, pawing the rim of his cup. "Then you know about her new assignment and our break-up?"

Thomas removed his eyeglasses and eyeballed his friend. "Only this much. Kay asked me to tell you she was sorry for what she had said to you. That's all I know, Pete."

The artist slumped back. "That's a relief," he sighed, brushing a hand through his thick hair.

"Pete, whatever happened between Kay and you, I hope you make up with her."

"That's my only reason for returning to Chicago," Grant countered. "Reed & Lambert was brief with me. Only that she was snapping jaguar along the Amazon. God!"

"No pussycat party," admitted Thomas, "but she's more than capable, Pete."

"Last time it was gorilla, but cats! Press, they're so damn unpredictable, especially the Amazon variety." Grant absentmindedly added sugar to his already sweetened coffee. "Could there be a more perilous place?" he lamented.

"Sure. Try highways, schools, and hell. By the way, Pete, did you know Kay will have Ben Hollingsworth as her guide again?"

"Good. That's a plus," Grant reflected. "You're right, Press. Kay is more than capable. She'll make it. The question is, will I?"

Grant stared into his half-empty cup. "Press, I'm disjointed as the devil. I need to paint. I mean something big. Something I can pour my guts into."

Thomas leaned forward, almost spilling his coffee. "You artistic ape! Why do you think I've been tracking you down?" His dark eyes narrowed. "Pete," he continued, "you've heard me speak of Ambrose Thorne? Nelson-Faust Advertising Agency in New York?"

Grant nodded, his face a mask of concentration.

"Thorne phoned me last Wednesday, six days ago. He had been trying to contact you at your New York studio, thinking you may be interested in a big job out of D.C. Thorne's agency is handling a special assignment for Saint Michael's Parish."

"A religious theme," the artist concluded.

Thomas nodded. "Pete, it could be dangerous."

"Go on," Grant urged.

Preston Thomas wet his lips and continued in a lowered voice. "The assignment will be a huge portrait depicting the crucifixion of Christ, the purpose of which is to commemorate the parish's sesquicentennial."

"God. The crucifixion," Grant reflected barely above a whisper, his eyes gazing into space.

"Thorne didn't talk commission, but it would run into several digits."

"Commission?" the artist finally responded. "That doesn't concern me, Press."

Preston Thomas leaned even closer. "The painting will be a gift of a Louisiana oil man. The deadline is April, 2027," he went on.

The carotid artery at Grant's neck was visible pulsating. "Only two years away," he mused, pawing his chin. "Press, how huge?"

"Eight feet by twelve feet."

"My Lord!"

"Thorne said a number of outstanding figure painters are in the hopper, including Gravelli, Osmond, Pelty, and Gruenwalt, to name a few."

"Good competition."

"Pete, the assignment is taboo, you understand. No publicity. If the revolutionaries get wind of it, they would rub you out in a minute," Press warned.

"Mum's the word."

"Well, Pete, what do you think?"

The artist finished his coffee with a gulp and got to his feet. His stomach was churning. "This is what I've been waiting for. Good Lord...the crucifixion." His dark eyes measured his friend and he placed both hands on Press's shoulders. "Thanks for everything, Press."

Chapter 3
The Interview

A week later, Peter Grant was on a flight to New York for his interview with Ambrose Thorne. Prepared and confident, he scanned the morning paper. "President Warns U.S. Rebels," read the headline. He found in smaller print: "U.S. Forces Withdraw from Nicaragua." This military action was in response to a need for stronger security at home to counter the current American revolt.

Grant reflected upon the similarity between the earlier Vietnam conflict and America's present involvement in Central America. He put the newspaper aside and gazed out the window. He perceived the scene below as a beautiful pattern of green earth, which some of his countrymen had set about to disrupt.

It was difficult for the artist not to be saddened by the cries of a wounded democracy. He believed the mistreatment of the American Indian and especially black Americans had been his country's greatest shame. Yet he loved his country and had always believed she was destined to survive all obstacles, including the present revolt.

Grant had read in history books about Russia's about-face in favor of more democratic policies, but Asia was still a mess. The Middle East turmoil had been a constant thorn in the belly of the world, resulting in a continual escalation of terrorism throughout the world. However, subversive activity had been making inroads in America long before this. Sabotage and spying at high government and military levels in the form of selling classified information to Middle East adversaries had become common. Also, there was growing corruption in business, labor, law enforcement agencies, and finally the courts, as they had become controlled by big vested interest groups, causing their interpretations to lack consistency.

The undermining of America's institutions had been given impetus by a judicial eclipse, mainly the failure of the congress to update out-moded laws. Any infringement upon individual rights had made majority rule unpopular and undemocratic. The result was individual freedom circumventing social freedom. This was the clincher, resulting in a radical decline of law enforcement, social instability, distrust in religious and educational institutions, moral disgrace, and general chaos.

The totality of it had led to the civil revolt. It was sparked with the election of America's first black president and his subsequent assassination after one month in office. It had happened on Saturday, February 22, 2025.

It was a cold day in the nation's capital, a day which would quickly become one of America's blackest. At 2:00 P.M. Washington time, the president was assassinated.

Within thirty minutes of the assassination, twelve of America's larger cities were hit with hundreds of explosives of the time-bomb and remote control variety. The revolutionaries had targeted government buildings, churches, schools, utility facilities, and executive offices. Also, they had hit private homes of political, religious, and industrial leaders. Thirteen thousand innocent Americans were estimated to have perished and countless more were injured. Financial losses had extended well beyond thirty billion dollars. It was another American tragedy.

The surprise rebel attack was quick, well-conceived, and expertly executed. Most of all, it had served its purpose of spreading destruction, panic and confusion across the nation, rivaling the trauma generated by the Japanese attack at Pearl Harbor eighty-four years earlier or the terrorist attacks in 2001 that destroyed the World Trade Center in New York City and damaged the Pentagon in Washington D.C.

Except for the assassin, using a plastic grenade and simultaneously killing the president and himself, not a single rebel lost blood or played an active role during the brief attack. The rebels were underground, scattered throughout the country in cover-up schemes, acting as upstanding citizens. The nation's capital had alerted much of its security during the previous several months and was not a target.

That was a mere two months ago. Since then the damaged cities had begun their recovery, while the revolutionaries remained underground to evaluate and map new strategy. Their plan would be to narrow the scope of aggression. Hereafter they would strike at the heart of America's soul and the cornerstone of its constitution. They would go for the jugular and destroy America's religious institutions.

Because America's black president was killed by a white man, many

Americans assumed the revolt was between blacks and whites. This wasn't the case.

On the other hand, the oppressed Americans had a strong argument. The greedy American rich had grown fat at the expense of their country's natural resources or whoever crossed their path. Competition in the free enterprise system had become a gluttonous sport characterized by throat cutting, back-stabbing, and dog-eat-dog. Many of the wealthy had gained their power and riches illegally. Others had utilized tax loopholes and law discrepancies. The affluent had become smug and insensitive to the needs of the less fortunate.

The American poor were pitied but they didn't want pity. Raped of their initiative and dignity, they accepted their miserable fate. Even if they wanted, they couldn't have revolted. They had reason enough, but not the means or the stamina.

The revolt was organized and masterminded by a coalition of extremists and anti-establishment radicals, including communist sympathizers and Neo-Nazi leaders. It was financed by mobsters.

The large segment between the rich and the poor were decent, patriotic Americans who were sickened by the revolt. However due to the general corruption that had infested the country, many of these Americans had reverted to opportunists who were prepared to cheat, steal, or lie if it were to their advantage. The more radical of these were ready to kill with little provocation. Each community had degenerated into an isolated entity. Laws prohibiting firearms were ignored, especially since the revolt. Reverting to the ways of their pioneer ancestors, most Americans had found gun-toting to be a necessity if lives and property were to be preserved.

Not so with Peter Grant. He looked upon guns as a prelude to violence. Because of the tragedy which had befallen his parents, he also held an aversion for the automobile and he relied upon the taxi as his prime means of transportation.

Grant drew a parallel between his country's plight and that of his landlord, John Baxter. Both were victims of moral erosion, internal breakdown, and a potential for collapse. His last conversation with Baxter had been brief and as hectic as their previous conversation. It occurred a week ago, the morning after he had lunched with Press and learned of the crucifixion assignment. The conversation had ended with the arrival of Baxter's taxi, which was to again have taken him to Evanston for a second appointment with the alleged Doctor Wells. As before he had yet to return.

The following week, Grant had organized his studio and prepared his portfolio for the interview, but thoughts of his brash landlord had persisted. Now as the jet eased onto the runway at Kennedy International, he was reminded of his New York model, Tracy. But not for long, as his thoughts turned to Kay Allyson and the awful distance between them.

The artist checked into the New Yorker Hotel, which was only a fifteen minute drive to Nelson-Faust Agency. This offered him time to review his pieces before the ten o'clock interview. He showered, then spread his samples on the bed and against the walls. From his collection he had selected two dozen, all human form renditions. Included were several nudes reflecting his mastery of flesh tones, *The Vagabond* and *Pangs of Pugilism* illustrating human agony and despair, and sundry pieces exemplifying his versatility and imagination.

Also in the grouping was his preliminary sketch of the crucifixion of Christ. Grant had phoned Ambrose Thorne with his intent, then finished the sketch within twenty-four hours. It was sixteen by twenty-four inches, rendered in pastel, and depicting Christ on the cross in traditional front view. The dramatic impact of the portrait was the low eye-level and the intricate play of subdued hues against a dark contrasting background.

Although none of his pieces provided the satisfaction he wanted, he believed painting the crucifixion would be different. The thought of it caused his adrenaline and creative juices to flow. If selected for this assignment, the possibilities would be endless and commitment would be total. The challenge would equal his creative urges. Most of all, the assignment would provide relief from the emptiness Kay's sudden departure had caused. With portfolio under arm, Grant stepped from a taxi at Fifth Avenue and Seventy-first Street and entered the Renkert complex. Moments later, he was introduced to A. J. Thorne by an attractive secretary.

"Mr. Grant, pleased to meet you," greeted Thorne, with a gravel voice and a vice-like grip. "Miss Bates," he snapped, turning to his secretary, "no interruptions for an hour."

Grant noted more than a hint of impatience in the art director's words.

Thorne relieved the artist of his portfolio and withdrew a folder from a filing cabinet as Grant settled himself into a leather-cushioned chair. Except for Thorne's desk top, the office was neat and resplendent with redwood paneling and gold carpeting. But Grant was more taken by Thorne himself. The art director's face matched his tan shirt and pants, he was coatless with a loose tie at the neck, and his desk was cluttered with countless memoranda, some marked URGENT.

Clearing a spot with a forearm, the silver-haired Thorne placed the folder before him and looked up. His gray eyes were cold and his face was firm with deep lines. "I must say, Mr. Grant, you were hard to locate, but good to have you in the race," he said without enthusiasm.

"Glad to be in it. I know the competition is fast," said the artist as he loosened the middle button of his blue tweed jacket, "but I like fast company."

Thorne hung over his desk like a hungry bear. "Good," he said as he made a quick rummage of his desk top and found a package of cigarettes. He offered one to Grant and they lit up.

"Let me fill you in," Thorne began. "The original field of candidates for this assignment was cut to twelve some time ago. Even though we couldn't contact you, we considered your candidacy from the beginning and we assembled your dossier," he said, referring to the folder before him.

"I'm flattered," said Grant, taking the remark as a compliment while noting Thorne's smile was often but brief.

"Only this week," continued the art director, "our screening committee narrowed the list to six. So, Mr. Grant, I congratulate you on making the final cut."

Peter Grant was thinking about the competitors Press had revealed to him earlier. "Is there a selection deadline?" he asked.

"The selection committee, which I chair, will make its recommendation to the board within two weeks. We'll advise each finalist as to the results the following day," said Thorne, as he drew in deeply on his cigarette and watched the smoke dissolve into the air. "By the way, one of the finalists is a member of my staff, but I assure you our agency is interested only in securing the best qualified artist. It's a matter of integrity."

"Of course," said Grant, tipping his ashes and wondering to what extent he would go to get the assignment.

Thorne glanced at his watch. "Preston Thomas briefed you on the assignment, I presume?"

"Yes. A thumbnail sketch."

"Good." Thorne took a specification sheet from his desk drawer. "Here's the crux of it," he began. "Subject: portrait of the crucifixion of Christ in oil. Front view with the body still possessing life. Size: eight feet by twelve feet with larger-than-life figure of Christ. Frame: eight inch, gold with scroll, to be provided by Nelson-Faust Agency. Color scheme: to harmonize with the decor of Saint Michael's sanctuary interior, but with overriding discretion of the artist. Style: traditional realism. Deadline: April 18, 2027. That's it," Thorne concluded, looking up.

"That's it?" echoed Grant in disbelief.

Thorne nodded. "As you can see, the specifications are quite modest."

Thorne lit a second cigarette from the first and leaned back in his swivel chair. "The portrait, Mr. Grant, will be a gift to commemorate the founding of Saint Michael's Parish in D.C. one-hundred fifty years ago. The intriguing aspect of the gift is its purpose, which brings us to the Texan client-donor, Chester K. Hathaway." Thorne paused to find the right words. "Old Hathaway is ninety-two, rich in oil, and up to his neck in guilt. He admittedly has attributed his fortune to shady deals. Some were downright corrupt. Now his fear of death, hell, and condemnation has prompted this and similar philanthropic gestures."

"I feel sorry for the miserable millionaire," said the artist.

"The situation could be worse," suggested the art director. "Because Hathaway doesn't know good art from the piss-poor, he's leaving the details to the church. Our dealings are directly with Monsignor Kelly, and, as you have noted, his requests are most modest. However the monsignor had a second list of specifications aimed at the artist which we'll get to later."

Thorne's reference to a second list made Grant's cigarette taste bitter and he squelched it in the ashtray fastened to the chair arm.

Ambrose Thorne idly thumbed Grant's dossier then opened it. He scanned the first page then looked up, his cold eyes measuring Grant's, as he began to recount the highlights from memory. "B.F.A. degree, Chicago School of Art, 2019. Hired by Glick the same year, book and magazine illustrations, solid foundation, excellent rating." He dropped his head and again referred to the dossier. "At twenty-six, youngest recipient of the P.A.A. Award for figure interpretation. One-man shows in Chicago, Cleveland, Philadelphia, New York...freelance...." Thorne coughed several times and sat back. "These damn sanctioned cigarettes. Guaranteed to postpone emphysema by ten years," he muttered.

"I place little stock in guarantees," said the artist as he attempted to dig through Thorne's crusty exterior and determine what made him tick. Press had warned him that Ambrose Thorne was crafty and not to be taken at face value.

Thorne closed the folder and returned it to the filing cabinet. "Mr. Grant, as you might suspect, we have a bonafide listing and rating of your major works since you joined Glick six years ago, including those presently on exhibit." He turned his attention to Grant's portfolio. For fifteen silent minutes he studied the samples one by one, while Grant, in turn, studied Thorne's stone-like face, not envying the art director's assignment no matter how unctuous he might be.

"Your work, Mr. Grant, indicates a profound and exciting mixture of creative skill and imagination and is done in the true realistic tradition...a prerequisite for this assignment." His words filtered through a cool smile and Grant preferred not to respond.

Thorne sat back. "Care to comment on your work?"

Grant was expecting the question. "Not particularly," he said, picking at the crease of his gray flannel trousers. "In spite of what recognition I've received, my work has come up short of my expectations."

"Of course. The artist is his own severest critic," said Thorne.

"I prefer looking to the future," continued Grant. "I believe my best works lay ahead."

"Good," said the bulky Thorne as he lit another cigarette. He crossed to a corner cabinet with a false bookcase front. "Drink, Mr. Grant? Scotch? Gin?

"Scotch on the rocks will be fine," said the artist, sensing an apparent need for one.

"Saint Michael's is interested not only in the portrait, said Thorne, returning with the drinks, "but the artist as well...his habits, moral convictions, et cetera. You understand."

"Of course. It's not the typical Monday morning assignment."

Thorne withdrew another sheet from his desk drawer. "The parish has taken a hard line and came up with a second list of specifications in the form of objections. In essence, the artist must be free of vices and wrong doings." Thorne sipped his drink and drew deeply on his cigarette. "Tell me, Mr. Grant, what are your church affiliations?"

"I was baptized in a Presbyterian church as a child but rarely attend services."

"Consider yourself a Christian?"

Grant tasted his drink. "I do, but perhaps not a good one, if there is such a classification. I think I'm a decent person. I respect my fellowman. I'm no racist, if that helps. My best friend, Press Thomas, is black, as you know."

"As you might expect, Mr. Grant, atheism is the church's first and foremost objection."

Again Thorne glanced at his watch. "I'm obliged to confront you with the remainder of these 'sinful objections' the parish has conjured up. Criminal record, drug addition, sexual perversion...incest, sodomy, adultery."

The red button on Thorne's desk flickered and buzzed. He pressed it and leaned toward the intercom. "Miss Bates, I told you—"

"Mr. Thorne," his secretary interrupted, "pardon my intrusion, but the Hazeltine situation? It's heating up and needs your attention." Her voice was soft and melodious.

Thorne's eyes narrowed with irritation. "Come in," he snapped.

Miss Bates made an apologetic entry. The skirt of her powder blue suit hugged her hips and thighs as she crossed to Thorne and gave him a slip of paper. She withdrew with a smile to both of them.

Thorne stuffed the slip of paper into his shirt pocket. "She's a damn nuisance," he muttered, squelching his cigarette and lighting another. "Don't know why I tolerate her insubordination."

Grant was remembering her smile.

"Now then, Mr. Grant, where were we?"

"Adultery," Grant said.

The art director steered his attention back to the sheet of objections. "Yes, adultery." He pawed his chin, then went on. "Homosexuality. Now, that's a popular perversion. Hell, that objection alone would eliminate most of us!" Thorne sat back with hands folded as if mocking a judge. "Well, Mr. Grant, do I hear a plea?"

The artist judged Thorne to be making light of the issue. He finished his drink. "I plead innocent unless the charges include fornication."

Thorne chuckled. "Heaven forbid! That would put us all out of business."

Wesley's question about the auto accident came to mind, returning Grant's thoughts to the tragedy. If only he could have been helpful in some way. He considered the hopelessness felt by any survivor who is conscious and pinned under or inside the vehicle. He could empathize, knowing hopelessness is a dreaded state of mind. The artist had experienced the same emotion when Kay refused his marriage proposal eighteen months earlier. His thoughts dwelled upon this difficult period of time in his life. It was June, 2027.

Δ Δ Δ

When Grant awoke after two days of disappointment, he still felt the sting of hopelessness. Kay's action had dealt him the heaviest blow. To the artist, her response was the least expected and made the least amount of sense. Now he would fight back just as he always had. He would collect his wits, flex his muscle, and focus upon his portrait.

The setback made him feel less secure. With this in mind, and to lift his spirits, he would follow Press' advice and purchase a gun. It had been nine years since he had carried a firearm as an army volunteer, and although the idea to re-arm was contrary to his nature, Grant understood its necessity.

After breakfast he walked to a gun shop father north on Ashland Avenue.

"Nifty little tools," asserted the proprietor, referring to a case of small hand weapons. He pointed to a five-inch Colt revolver. "Six-chamber, guardless trigger, nub-handle, and it takes a thirty-eight. But the beauty is its concealment possibilities. Carry one myself."

"I'll take it, a couple boxes of shells, and a shoulder holster," said Grant.

With leisure time on hand, Grant hailed a taxi and was soon on the inner city belt. He would pick up his fountain pen at Kay's suite. The pen was only significant because of its sentimental value, having belonged to his father for many years.

The complex manager hesitated before honoring Grant's simple request. Yet while Grant found the pen where he had left it, he also found workmen gathering Kay's furnishings for storage. He felt it strange she had said nothing about moving. Nor could Reed & Lambert supply additional information, other than Miss Allyson had planned to relocate upon her return from her assignment.

Back in the taxi, Grant lit his pipe but it failed to satisfy. At his apartment he phoned Press, thinking his friend might shed light on Kay's plans. However Press was still unavailable.

He loaded the revolver, placed it in his dresser drawer, and turned to the easel.

For the next four weeks, Grant painted eight to ten hours daily. The routine was the same each day—review his pre-sketch, trip the spot lights, place the ladder, don his smock, mix his paints, and go to work.

The art director quickly turned sober. "One final objection, Mr. Grant. What are your drinking habits?"

"I'll have a drink on occasion," he responded without hesitation.

Thorne's penetrating eyes bore down on Grant's. "Ever miss a deadline due to excess use of alcohol?"

Thorne's query was expected, however, the manner in which it was delivered caused a tightness in Grant's gut. This raised questions of his own. Did Thorne know about his recent deadline failure? Was it a loaded question to test his honesty?

Peter Grant couldn't risk a lie. Too much was at stake. The crucifixion assignment was a once-in-a-lifetime opportunity and it was within his grasp. "Only once," he finally admitted. "It was my last assignment. There were extenuating circumstances upon which I will gladly elaborate if you wish," said the artist.

Thorne drew in deeply on his cigarette, then examined the burning end without actually seeing it. "Only once, you say. No, Mr. Grant, an account of it isn't necessary at this point. None of us are perfect."

Ambrose Thorne unexpectedly changed the subject.

"So, you're a bachelor. By circumstances or choice?" he probed.

"Circumstances," said Grant. "But the future looks bright. In fact, I may marry within the year. She's a field photographer for Reed & Lambert."

"Your glass is empty, Mr. Grant. Refill?"

"No thanks."

"Field photographer, you say. Could use a good one here. Our top man passed on recently. Heart attack. I contacted freelancer, Roger Toles, but the chap came down with a rare tropical disease last month. Poor devil. Took all the shots, but still may not make it."

The remark caused the artist to reflect upon Kay and her present tropical assignment.

"Reed & Lambert? Yes. We've had recent dealings with them," continued Thorne. "Actually, I've been somewhat out of touch. Vacation in Bermuda with the wife. Back two weeks and have yet to scratch this desk top."

Thorne ran a huge hand through his silver hair, then checked his watch. "Mr. Grant, let's talk money. Hathaway has insisted that each candidate specify a commission he would be comfortable with if selected. So, what's your price tag?"

"Seventy-five thousand," aid the artist without hesitation.

Thorne's brows lifted. "Only seventy-five? A modest figure, I must say." He leaned forward, pawing his clean shaven face. "Hathaway may feel offended or even insulted by such a figure. Remember, the man needs to pacify his guilt."

Grant wasn't impressed. "I think the amount I stated is fair and realistic. I'll stay with it."

"Seventy-five it is. If selected, your contract will be drawn up on that basis. Also, at that time you'll be supplied with color photographs of the parish sanctuary and arrangements will be made for your visit to Saint Michaels for further study of atmosphere, lighting, et cetera."

Grant nodded his approval.

"Should you wish to rework your preliminary sketch," continued Thorne, "it must be submitted for committee approval within thirty days of the dated contract."

"After a view of the sanctuary, I can do it in two weeks," volunteered the artist.

"Good. That should do it," said Thorne with a quick grin.

Both men stood. "Mr. Grant, under the circumstances and for everyone's safety and peace of mind, this assignment must be kept under wraps...even if you fail to be selected."

"I understand," replied the artist. At the door, he turned. "Thanks, Mr. Thorne, for considering my candidacy for such an important assignment."

Initially, Grant's reaction to the interview was one of optimism. He passed through the anteoffice and turned to Thorne's secretary. "Have a good day, Miss Bates."

The blonde secretary was sitting at her desk applying fresh lipstick. Her dark eyes measured him in depth and she smiled warmly. "You have a good one on me," she suggested with a wink.

Peter Grant sensed that she was telling him something.

Chapter 4
BonBon's Delight

As his taxi headed toward the New Yorker Hotel, Peter Grant sat back and loosened his tie with a finger. He would put the interview into perspective.

Press was right. Thorne was as deceiving and as phony as the false bookcase in his office, but Grant sensed there was more to the equation. Something was missing, but what? He reflected upon Thorne's demeanor and saw not only deception but also impatience, irritability, and preoccupation.

The artist sat up as the pieces suddenly fell into place, causing the picture to become crystal clear. Ambrose Thorne was having an affair with Miss Bates. Grant glanced at his watch. Almost eleven. A telephone booth came into view and he directed the cabby to drop him off. His mind was racing in overdrive as he realized the possibilities. Handled correctly, the opportunity could place him closer to the crucifixion assignment.

Once inside the booth, Grant paused. He knew risk was involved but he was willing to gamble on his gut instincts. He took a deep breath and dialed Thorne's number.

"Good morning. Nelson-Faust Advertising Agency," came the flowing voice.

"Miss Bates?"

She hesitated. "Mr. Grant?"

"I'm sorry, Mr. Grant, but Mr. Thorne is just leaving for lunch."

Again Grant breathed deeply. "Miss Bates, it's you I'm calling, not Mr. Thorne."

"Me? But...but I'm also about to leave," she said nervously, her voice losing its original spontaneity.

"Miss Bates, forgive my impulsiveness, but it is important that I talk with you," Grant persisted. "Over dinner, perhaps?"

"Gee, that would be nice. Why don't you phone me tonight...say about six?"

He had done it. He would cancel his afternoon flight and reschedule for tomorrow morning. After jotting her phone number, he headed for his hotel on foot. He needed to walk and think. If ever he needed a clear head, it was now.

With pipe and sunglasses in place, Grant fell in step with the busy crowd. The day was spring-like and the air tasted sweet as it filled his lungs, a far cry from the polluted environs of earlier years. Miss Bates had accepted his unconventional overture, and he felt a tinge of excitement mixed with uncertainty.

The streets gave every indication of a nation in revolt as armed military vehicles dotted the area, moving in various directions and receiving right-of-way privileges. After the National Guard had failed to squelch the initial looting, the new president had declared martial law and curfew in every city that had been bombed by the insurgents in the February uprisings.

Grant pondered the possible consequences of a Thorne-Miss Bates illicit affair. A boss-secretary relationship wasn't unusual, but this case could be significant. Gaining Miss Bates' confidence would be an advantage he hadn't anticipated. Having access to the office files, she might arm him with information which could pierce Thorne's armor and improve his chances of getting the assignment.

Grant's pace quickened as he considered the possibilities. If the art director was an adulterer, blackmail could be considered. The artist wondered to what lengths he would go to serve his cause. Most of all, he wondered if Miss Bates could be trusted.

That afternoon he phoned Tracy Duvall, his former model. During their last assignment she had posed with discipline. She had accepted his crudeness only to be pushed out at the end. She had deserved better, causing him to entertain the idea of inviting her to his room for early dinner.

The tone of Tracy's voice told Grant she was pleased he had phoned and seeing him again would be a pleasure, but he resisted. He was bushed. The evening ahead would require an alert mind and he needed sleep. So he lied, telling Tracy he had to catch the three-forty flight. As it turned out, he had neglected his dinner and failed to get much sleep.

That evening Peter Grant and Bonnie Bates met at the Hot Pepper—a small out of the way tavern in lower Manhattan. The place was her idea and it was obvious to Grant that she was a frequent patron. He also noted several changes in her appearance that made her even more provocative than earlier. Her blonde hair had been sculptured into an upsweep and her brown eyes had turned to an olive green that matched her knit dress. Even more noticeably, she was heavily scented with Spring Lilac, which assailed Grant's nostrils.

"This place isn't exactly the Ritz but the food is super," she said as Grant ushered her through the entrance.

"Good. I'm famished," he said.

She steered him toward a shadowed bar. "Buy me a drink, Mr. Grant?"

He obliged out of courtesy, although realizing a few drinks would also loosen her tongue.

At the bar she snuggled close to him and after her first vodka Collins, Bonnie Bates became talkative. After her second she became giddy and insisted he call her BonBon. Her closest friends called her that. Girls at the agency called her Bonnie. Mr. Thorne called her Miss Bates even when they were intimate. Only her mother called her Bonita.

When Grant asked if she knew Bonita meant "pretty" in Spanish, she giggled and called him a flirt.

She was thirty-five but felt much younger. Both her marriages had fizzled. She was childless, sterile, and supporting her ailing mother by the grace of her God-given goodies.

Grant exhaled deeply and braced himself.

She had lots of problems but money "sure as hell" wasn't one of them. For eighteen long months she had been working at Nelson-Faust as Thorny's "perrrrsonal prrrrivate" secretary. She giggled and placed a sanctioned cigarette between her full lips while trying to verbalize her next thought.

Although she had less seniority than other girls at the agency, her job paid more. She and Thorny had an agreement. She would give him sexual favors and he would pad her paycheck. Was she boring him with all this stuff?

"Oh no? On the contrary," Grant countered.

BonBon hesitated and tipped her cigarette ashes while the artist noted a shade of sadness clouding her eyes.

She confessed the arrangement with Thorny had evolved into nothing more than an "old-fashioned screw" twice a week. She insisted men were lousy lovers. Mostly they lacked tenderness.

Her knee began to nudge his leg in a gentle beckoning gesture.

Grant loosened his tie.

The nudging ended when the hostess interceded and escorted them to a prepared table in an adjoining room which was small, semi-private, and candle-lit. They ordered the pepper steak specials, after which BonBon picked up on her earlier thoughts.

Sex, she claimed, was designed for men with imagination, sensitivity, and...oh yes, staying power—the same qualities possessed by an artist. Right?

Grant grinned, shrugged his shoulders, and gestured that she continue.

She giggled again, then squelched her cigarette as a waitress delivered her salad.

Phoo. To be honest about it, her arrangement with Thorny was eroding. She had hoped a man of fifty would be more demanding of her assets.

At first they had sex three times a week. Now it was only twice. Thank God there were more fish in the pond. She suspected it would soon be only once a month because Thorny was wearing thin. Of course she would lose her padded paycheck. Damn.

Today was their day, she went on. The routine? She and Mr. Thorne would leave the agency separately about eleven, meet at Freefort, drive out Long Island to Blue Point, and shack up at Hazeltine Arms 'til four.

Damn Thorny's hide. Always ready to leave after a quick score. She giggled. Of course her reference to the "Hazeltine situation" during Mr. Grant's interview was her way of telling Thorny to move his ass.

Well, that's how her day had gone and it was a bust, but tonight...tonight would be different. Tonight the artist would satisfy her demands. Right?

Their dinners arrived saving Grant from a response.

Miss Bates continued her chatter. She admitted to having a good body. It was solid and full in the right places. Her goal in life? To marry again and make it stick. Her problem? She couldn't get enough male. Her hormones were screwed up. Besides, wasn't it a husband's duty to please his wife? Only God knew how she needed to be pleased. Less spirited women didn't begin to understand her problem. Most people didn't. Did he?

Grant nodded sympathetically. His only encounters with nymphomaniacs had been in books or locker room banter. He smiled faintly while wiping perspiration from his forehead with the heel of his hand.

Her onslaught continued as she flipped off a shoe and began to tease his leg with her foot.

Was it her fault if she needed a man to cool her craving? She likened herself to an addict hooked on hard stuff.

Grant's abdomen ached but he continued his probe. Miss Bates remembered reading about the deadline failure in his report. Thorne knew about it and had tested him after all.

As it had turned out, Grant's client had referred the unfinished painting to Henri Goosche, an artist on Thorne's staff and one of the finalists, as Grant already knew. However, BonBon was quick to add that Goosche did not rank at Grant's level of talent. His toughest competition? Pelty of San Francisco. She had overhead Thorny and other board members speak of Jon Pelty in flowing terms. So be it.

On that note their dinner ended. The preliminary was over and the main attraction was about to begin. Grant had milked Miss Bates dry of information. Now it was his turn to give and her turn to take. What would a nymphomaniac want? She would insist upon a damn good bed partner for the night. She would want it as badly as he wanted the crucifixion assignment.

The artist checked his watch. Almost ten. She suggested they engage her apartment, which was closer than his. Her invalid mother...bless her heart...would be sleeping soundly and without her hearing aid. He knew this tigress would bite, chew, and scratch...but for the crucifixion assignment, he would sleep with an over-sexed orangutan.

They arrived at her condominium in BonBon's dry-fueler25. Once inside, she quickly prepared a final drink and a toast to the "love of art and the art of love." She dimmed the lights and they undressed each other near an open window as a gentle breeze played upon their bodies. Grant pressed her hot torso against his as she maneuvered them toward the bed. She giggled and playfully pushed him onto it, eluding his grasp long enough to reinforce her lilac scent and add a touch of talcum.

Her tantalizing fingers began to scrutinize his body to determine if he had joined the vasectomy corps. No little scar. Good. He would flood her with millions of tiny, living creatures and, even though barren herself, her maternal instincts loved it that way.

The hot-blooded BonBon was giggly, breathless, and demanding. She made a game of it. Nine hours earlier her boss had scored twice and made her tingle. The artist must do better because he was younger and had better equipment. She made the rules and she was the judge. Bonita Bates was confident he would give her the screwing of her life, the kind all nymphos dream about but never realize.

She sat up unexpectedly and, as she did so, her torso was silhouetted by the window. Grant was taken more by her narrow waist and flat abdomen than her full breasts. Though she claimed to be thirty-five, the artist placed her closer to forty-five, making her figure all the more remarkable. She removed her rings, contacts, and hair pins, letting her hair fall to her shoulders. She laid back in complete nakedness. BonBon was hot, moist, and ready. Forget the foreplay.

During the next four hours, Peter Grant did what was expected of him, the prolonged effort attributed to his concentration and breath control. He had constantly fought off her aggressiveness and he remained in full command. As he had predicted, she bit, scratched, and sucked. She had also squealed, groaned, and went into momentary periods of semi-consciousness before finally passing out.

Grant glanced at the dresser clock. It was nearly 2:00 A.M. He oozed himself off her sweaty body, took a cold shower, and phoned a taxi. Before leaving, he went over and softly kissed Miss Bates's forehead.

At that moment, he felt a strange sense of guilt.

Chapter 5
Insight or Insanity

Peter Grant taxied to his hotel where a yawning desk clerk gave him his key and a message from Tracy. She had waited for him all afternoon at the airport and had asked him to telephone her before he checked out. Exhausted, Grant crumpled the note, removed his jacket, and dropped onto his bed.

Two hours later he was wakened by a nightmare. Tracy had drowned in the Amazon River before his very eyes. Unsettled and unable to relax, he decided to shower and catch the early bird flight out of Kennedy International. He forfeited some sleep time, but it had been a long twenty-four hours and he was anxious to return. Press would be awaiting news of the interview as would John Baxter, assuming he had returned from Evanston.

During their last conversation, Baxter had predicted a bad interview and Grant was eager to refute the prophecy. Yet the more he reflected on the matter, the more Baxter's prediction made sense.

As the Boeing lifted off, Grant loosened his tie and closed his eyes. Even before take-off, he concluded the interview had bombed. He knew the crucifixion assignment would revive his enthusiasm for painting and be the springboard to catapult him back on track. In a larger sense, the assignment could be the highlight of his career. Yet during the most important interview of his life, Ambrose Thorne had thrown him a curve.

The art director had forfeited the interview in favor of a sizzling piece of meat packaged in a powder blue skirt. He violated professional ethics and deserved to be blackmailed or worse.

The artist tossed the idea back and forth. Bonnie Bates had given him vital facts and he had access to Kay's Chicago apartment where photographic and recording equipment was available. He was confident the night desk clerk at Hazeltine Arms could be bribed. Yet time was short and the maneuver would be complex and risky. In addition, there was a chance he might get the assignment on his own merits in spite of Thorne's theatrics.

The jet lurched upward in a climb through heavy clouds, momentarily scrambling Grant's thoughts. Lightning flashes bounced off the windows and were followed by echoes of thunder, prompting a premature call for fastened seatbelts.

As the weather had turned quickly, Grant's thoughts did likewise, turning from blackmail to feelings of guilt. He had abused Bonnie Bates and Tracy, his model, had deserved better treatment. He had lied to her about his departure time and neglected her note. Then there was Kay. He wondered if the crucifixion assignment was worthy of his disloyalty to the woman he loved.

On the approach to O'Hare Airport the storm peaked with pelting rain and pounding wind. The landing was a mixture of bouncing, screeching, and silent prayers.

Whereas the storm had gathered momentum during the flight, Grant's frame of mind had turned inward to the point where he had accepted the nervous landing without concern. His earlier feelings of enthusiasm had turned to feelings of guilt, followed by melancholy and depression. His eagerness to return had dissipated.

His climb up the stairwell to his apartment was with heavy legs and an overpowering need for sleep. The weight of the past several weeks had struck him like a hammer. After fumbling with keys and gaining entrance, he dropped the portfolio on the kitchenette table and took refuge on his studio cot.

Grant awoke to a dark room and a headache. The dial of his watch read Monday, May 5, 11:00 A.M. He had slept only three hours.

He waggled the tweed jacket from his sweaty back and crossed to the bathroom where he doused his face and swallowed some aspirin. Soon afterward he heard footsteps at the stairwell followed by a knock at the kitchenette door. Grant reasoned it was John Baxter. The prospect of an encounter with his landlord at this moment was not to his liking so he ignored the knock. When the knocking became a persistent pound that sent shock waves through his brain, he relented.

"Painter! By God you're back!" Baxter chortled, stepping past the artist and sitting at the kitchenette table. "Heard you walking about. Am I intruding?"

Grant was caught up in Baxter's appearance and demeanor more than his remarks. Unlike earlier appearances, Baxter was clean and upbeat. Wearing gray flannel trousers, a black satin shirt, and the beginnings of a mustache and goatee, in no way did he reflect the seedy man Grant had encountered only a few days earlier.

"Painter, are you well?" Baxter queried, noting Grant's general lack of presence.

"Nothing more sleep wouldn't cure," he said casually.

"Rot! Sleep is a luxury no painter can afford. It's for babies, fat women, and old men," he blurted, as he peered into Grant's eyes. "By God, you look like the devil himself. New York can do that to a man...chew him up like a meat grinder. Bad luck with the interview, I take it?"

"It went well," Grant lied.

Baxter shrugged. "I was hoping otherwise for your sake."

Grant attributed Baxter's remark to sour grapes, resulting from the past accident that had caused his partial paralysis. Yet the artist was puzzled that Baxter indicated no sign of affliction when he had entered the kitchenette. His foot didn't drag and the paralyzed hand had pulled the chair from the table as he sat. It was obvious to Grant his landlord had faked his infirmities.

Grant proceeded to make coffee, thinking it might east his headache. "Cup of coffee, Mr. Baxter?" he asked.

"Never touch it," Baxter responded, with a shake of his head.

"You're looking well," Grant went on. "Is your Evanston doctor responsible for the turnabout?"

"No. I dumped Doc Wells and got me a better quack. He's an expert with electrodes.' Baxter leaned forward again, dropping his voice to a whisper. "This quack can fire up the brain tissues and cure any damn thing, man or beast."

"I'm impressed," Grant said absentmindedly, knowing the man was unhinged and with no credibility.

"Remember my paralysis?" Baxter continued. "Look!" He jumped to his feet, folded his arms across his chest, and briefly executed the Bear Dance, his shoes pounding the linoleum tile with rapid precision. The pounding resounded in Grant's aching brain, causing him to resent the man's deception even more.

"This brain-burner..." Baxter continued, returning to his chair and breathing hard, "...claims he can affect a cure for sin! Imagine that... cure for man's transgressions! Say...won't that make the Christians happy?"

Grant filled his cup with hot coffee and doctored it.

"Doc swears it's all in knowing where and how deep to probe," Baxter went on. "He contrived a machine which determines this. When the receptive areas of the brain are located, the little hot wires automatically penetrate the skull and...POOF! Amen!"

"Does it come with a guarantee?" Grant asked, after a sip of coffee.

"Full-life. Present, past, and future. Furthermore, painter, I strongly recommend that you avail yourself of my doc's expertise."

Grant's patience was wearing thin. "First, why not clean up your own act? Or are you picture perfect like a Rembrandt?"

Baxter sat back slowly. His eyes narrowed and his fingers drummed the table top. "I'm no sinner," he said with conviction. "Painter, we live in different worlds. There's no God in my world, so how can I sin?" Again, Baxter drummed the table top with his fingers. "Painter, I'll have that cup of coffee now—with pleasure," he said.

Grant complied,

"It was your God who created sin and labeled all mankind sinners...but that is in your world." Baxter stood and raised his cup in toast. "My world is of the devil and hell is my abode." He gulped down his hot coffee and sat again, gazing into space. "Your world, painter..." his voice growing more cynical, "your world is like the chromatic rainbow with its elusive pot of gold. Your world is worthless."

John Baxter sat back. Beads of sweat dotted his forehead and pulsating temples.

"Your God-created world is corrupt and stinks of decay. What good is your God?"

"All life is a gift of God," Grant said.

Baxter's cold eyes measured his counterpart. "But human life? Ha! Human life is sired by the lust of male pigs with bastards emerging from the womb of sick whores."

The artist got to his feet and rinsed his cup at the sink. "Mr. Baxter, your personal opinions are of no concern to me and I'm asking you to leave. I've just finished two busy days and I'm strung out."

Baxter's brows lifted. "Of course you are," he said. "You had a busy visit to New York. But was it all business? I mean, didn't you mix in some fun?"

Grant clenched his fists.

John Baxter smiled and stood. "By God, painter, you have spunk. But I only mean to be helpful. I remind you painting the crucifixion of Christ would be your undoing. It would ultimately destroy you."

His words fell heavily on Grant's conscience. Perhaps it was the way they were spoken.

"Why are you so interested in my welfare?" he asked.

"I'm not. I only state a simple fact. You don't honor your God. As for the crucifixion assignment, you don't fit the mold. In New York you chose to cavort with an acquaintance of mine—the devil. You did this to enhance your odds of getting the assignment. In some circles it's called cheating."

The unexpected disclosure caught the artist with a loss of words. He resented Baxter's prophetic view but also was astounded by the man's insight.

Baxter stepped to the door. "I must go. My brain is suffering from a chemical flare up and needs heat." He turned to the artist once more. 'By the way, painter, what did you think of Miss Bates? Oh, never mind," he quickly called back as he descended the stairs.

Chapter 6
The First Stroke

Despite his confrontation with John Baxter, Grant slept well and awoke the following afternoon with a clear head and a healthier view on the matter. He assumed his unpredictable landlord had phoned Nelson-Faust and talked with Miss Bates, pumping her for information. From the beginning, Grant had wondered about Baxter's curious interest in the assignment, yet considering the man's lack of accountability, it was nothing to dwell upon.

However marginal, Grant's concern was soon dispelled. Baxter had left the premises the next morning and had yet to return after two weeks.

On May 21, the day of Baxter's departure, Grant received a letter of approval from Ambrose Thorne. Later in the day, Thorne phoned to receive confirmation of the artist's acceptance. Officially the crucifixion assignment was Grant's.

The artist accepted the assignment with elation only to be tempered by Thorne's assertion that Bonnie Bates was dead. She had been raped and murdered only the day before. Her once hot body had been found in an alley near the Hot Pepper tavern. Later Grant would dig up the details in the Daily News. There were no leads. The crime would become another statistic in the cluttered files of the N.Y.P.D. headquarters.

Peter Grant felt a tug of sadness with Miss Bates's passing. Her thrill-seeking delights, while narrow and single-minded, had been fashioned with a spirit and zest which he admired. Even though more risky, her desire for sexual pleasure was not unlike his own craving for self-expression.

He would miss her. Despite piercing nails and pursuing tongue, despite a twisting torso that strained for deeper penetration, despite her unwavering demands on him, Grant would remember her with compassion. Perhaps he would remember her most as he had left her—a limpid, wet form, sleeping deeply, and bathed in a momentary peace and contentment which may have been her last.

That was history. Today the artist needed to regroup and focus upon the task at hand. Already the crucifixion deadline of less than two years lurked in the recesses of his mind. He realized his reputation as a gifted artist was on the line. He had to paint the crucifixion to his satisfaction and he had to beat the deadline. The challenge was there.

Kay would be pleased and excited to learn about the good news. It had been over a month since her departure to Brazil and not a day had passed that she hadn't entered his mind. Only hard work would ease the pain of her absence. When Grant related the good news to Press, they celebrated over a steak dinner, after which Press announced he planned to host an appropriate party for his friend in early June.

Grant withdrew the letter of approval from his desk drawer and reviewed the sanctuary interior color photographs which Thorne had enclosed. He phoned Saint Michael's Parish and made arrangements for his visit the following week.

This he did and was pleased with the results of the two-day Washington trip. The sanctuary alcove was ideally positioned to accommodate the portrait. It would be hung fifteen feet above the center altar and have ample overhead lighting. However Grant knew spotlights at floor level would enhance the portrait dramatically.

The sanctuary color scheme of light green, wine red, and mahogany was also ideal. Monsignor Kelly, a tall man with frosty hair and pale eyes, had been a genial host who expressed much enthusiasm and confidence in the portrait's potential to stimulate a rebirth to both parish and community.

On his return to Chicago, Grant finished the preliminary sketch and mailed it to Thorne with a brief explanation for his subtle changes. The sketch was returned three days later stamped APPROVED.

Revived and confident, the artist dug into preparations for the job. After purchasing the necessary supplies, he hammered the huge frame together and stretched canvas across it. He followed this with two applications of his own special mixture of glue for sizing and two coats of flake white priming, ending with a wash. Next, he arranged four spotlights to strike his canvas in precisely the manner in which the portrait would be illuminated at the parish.

Grant's approach was fostered by his earlier disappointments. The twelve years with his harsh uncle had taught him to be aggressive. He had to devise ways to gain privacy and draw his pictures. Though constantly forced into household chores, he had managed to earn spending money by mowing lawns, shoveling snow, and delivering newspapers.

His three years of military service had ended with his twenty-first birthday. This allowed him access to the trust fund provided by his parents and opened the door to art school. This also continued his need to strive for an objective. The pattern had been set. To fight and conquer with humility had become his lifestyle.

In preparation for the crucifixion assignment, Grant had elected to work from prints and resort to a model only if it became necessary. To this end, he gathered and studied countless reproductions, mostly of the earlier masters of religious art, including Raphael, Tintoretto, El Greco, and Rembrandt. He also studied individual works such as Gruenwald's *The Small Crucifixion* and Perugino's the *Crucifixion with the Virgin and Saints.* His objective was three-fold: to inculcate the humanization and spotlight luminescence of a Caravaggio; the serene ambiance of a Raphael; and the intense, gripping atmosphere of a Van Gogh.

Grant wanted his painting to remind the viewer of the purpose for which Christ had died, that being to save the souls of believers. To this end, he wanted the painting to evoke an emotion so overpowering it would cause the beholder to genuflect—to literally bend to his knees in reverence and reflect upon the immortality of the soul. With the world immersed in sin, repentance was a word to be scorned. Herein lay the challenge.

Early Monday morning on June 9, Grant was ready. He planned to paint for four days, then rest a day before the party at Press'. The party would be a welcome reprieve from the easel.

After a good breakfast, he stood before the huge canvas propped against a makeshift easel at the north wall of his studio. Made with two-by-fours, the easel was nailed atop back-to-back risers, allowing the canvas a foot clearance from the first step of the front riser. To one side was a stepladder.

Grant slipped into a smock. The pungency of paint and turp assailed his nostrils and anticipation surged through his veins. The beginning had come. His first concern was to capture the powerful underlying structure of the composition, beginning with the placement of the cross. Using a wide bristle brush, he stroked in the first line, the burnt sienna clinging to a canvas previously toned with a wash of umber and turpentine. For a portrait destined to create international fervor, the first stroke was made without ceremony but with a firm realization the deadline was a mere twenty-three months away.

He painted beyond midnight, stopping only twice for coffee and a sandwich. When he finally surrendered to sleep, he tossed for an hour thinking about Kay and wishing she had been there to share the beginning.

For three days Grant continued to lay in the general lines of his composition. His preliminary sketch, used only as a reference, rested upon an easel to his right. The composition would ultimately be an intricate play on foreshortening. Specifically, it would depict what one would see if kneeling near the front of the cross and looking up at the dying Christ.

On Friday morning Grant received a phone call from Press Thomas, who asked if he could invite an outsider to the party. "She's an old California friend flying through to D.C. She's a psychiatrist named Judith Gillespie," Press added.

"Fine," Grant responded with a yawn. "Too bad she can't squeeze in a session with my sick landlord and see what makes him tick."

"By the way, Pete, Tracy phoned me. She seemed upset. She asked for your address and I gave it to her. Hope you don't mind."

"No, I don't mind. In fact, I'm glad you did. I've been rough on her lately," Grant reflected.

Grant's door buzzer sounded.

"Press, I'm getting company. See you tomorrow night."

Wearing only pajama bottoms, Grant slipped into a cotton robe and opened the kitchenette door to a pair of wistful eyes.

"Tracy!"

"Hello...Peter," she said hesitantly, not knowing whether to smile or cry. Standing limp, she looked like anything but a model as her arms dangled at her sides and the strap of her overnight bag tugged at one shoulder. Her beige suit hung loosely and flaxen hair crossed her shoulders in a disheveled manner.

Grant smiled and hugged her in a fatherly fashion. "Tracy, come in," he said warmly, relieving her of her overnight bag.

"You're not angry that I came?"

"Angry? Tracy, I'm pleased that you came and I apologize for not seeing you in New York."

"I know you were very busy. In New York, I mean," she said with a faint smile. "Peter, I'm afraid to ask."

"Did I get the assignment? Let's take a look," he said, taking her hand and leading her into his studio.

Tracy panned the room and quickly spotted the covered canvas. "Peter, in heaven's name! Is that it?"

Grant nodded with a grin.

"But it's so big! How wonderful! I'm so happy for you," she said, reaching up and kissing him in a spontaneous gesture of joy.

He accepted her gesture in like spirit, then held her at arm's length. "Tracy, there's a restaurant around the corner and you look famished. Freshen up while I dress and shave."

Over a plate of ham and eggs, Grant brought Tracy up to date, beginning with her last sitting for him in New York, the night of Kay's ill-fated phone call. He was quick to exonerate her of any blame for his problem with Kay, but he was also quick to explain that Kay Allyson was still his woman. He felt Tracy was entitled to know the truth.

The young model understood and apologized for writing the message she had left for him at his New York hotel. Her work had fallen off, her roommate had moved out, and she had become lonely. She wrote the message because his phone call earlier in the day had encouraged her. It had taken her a month to muster the courage to contact him again.

She had thought of calling it quits and returning to her home in Reading but Grant promised to help her gain local employment and residency.

Tracy beamed when he briefly detailed his new assignment, and she was anxious to see his progress.

"In due time," he had responded.

His reference to "time" caused her to reflect upon the deadline date and how it would delay the opportunity for her to be his model again.

Grant interrupted her thoughts when he revealed the upcoming party. He invited her to attend as his guest but she politely refused. After all, she was an outsider and with no roof over her head.

"Nonsense! You would fit in perfectly."

"Peter, I do appreciate your asking me but I would rather not."

Grant didn't press the issue, thinking she would have a change of mind as the party approached. Before leaving the restaurant, he insisted she stay overnight at his apartment. Tomorrow morning he would help her search for suitable living quarters and investigate modeling agencies for hire.

In his studio, Grant pulled the draw-cord, exposing his efforts thus far. "It's slightly premature," he explained, "but your next viewing will reflect the unfinished product, hopefully."

Although seeing only the basic structure, Tracy was struck by its impact.

Her attention turned to his many paintings leaning casually against the studio north wall. Most of them were new to her and he briefly commented about those that had especially caught her eye. She was pleasantly surprised when he told her to accept one of her choice, for being a good model.

Later Grant drove to O'Hare to retrieve Tracy's luggage while she napped for an hour. At the airport, he took the opportunity to phone Press.

"Yes, Pete," Press was saying, "I told Tracy about the party but only in passing. Why do you ask?"

"I'm not sure. I invited her to attend but she refused, using a flimsy excuse."

"Perhaps it's just as well, Pete. As I told you earlier, she seemed upset. This may not be the time to pressure her."

So be it. Grant generally relied on his friend's judgment and he wasn't about to change now.

That evening Tracy and Grant dined at Peppi's, a fashionable Italian restaurant on the northside.

"*Il Pittore*! Good evening!" came the jolly greeting of Mondo, the fat proprietor. It was a northern Italian style dinner done with buttery sauces and Tracy glowed in the candlelight, presenting a picture far removed from the frightened girl who had pressed his door buzzer only hours earlier.

Later she found the peace and comfort of his studio apartment almost overwhelming. While she rested in his bedroom, Grant decided to paint until midnight. After an hour, however, his concentration wilted and he gracefully gave up. He showered quietly so as not to disturb Tracy, then stretched out on his studio cot.

After what seemed like hours to him, Grant crossed to his bedroom door and opened it carefully. Tracy was lying under a sheet with eyes closed. With arms stretched overhead, her twisted torso was turned toward Grant with her near leg free of the sheet. Her pillow was hidden by flaxen hair.

He eased to the bed and sat on its edge. As he leaned over her, a familiar aroma assailed his nostrils.

Her eyes opened slowly. "It's called Paradise," she said.

He lowered his head and kissed her lips lightly. "Goodnight, Tracy," he whispered.

Her arms encircled his neck, pulling him toward her.

As he went forward against her mouth, his right hand inadvertently braced against her bare thigh. It was a prolonged kiss that very gradually mellowed as her arms slowly relaxed. During the kiss, Grant was keenly aware of the warm, firm flesh under his hand.

"Peter...make love to me...please?" she pleaded.

He had never made love to Tracy during those months in New York, although he had always felt a special loyalty and fondness for her. Yet it would be so easy. The first move would be to stroke her thigh lightly with his fingertips. One stroke would set all her senses into action.

Tracy had laid back with closed eyes and arms overhead. She voluntarily contracted her thigh muscle, a signal urging his hand to massage and explore.

After a long pause, he leaned forward and softly kissed her lips once more. "Sorry, Tracy," he whispered and quickly left the room.

Shortly after Grant returned to his studio cot the phone rang. The man at the other end spoke distinctly and slowly. "You are under watchful eyes and listening ears."

His terse comment was followed by a dead connection.

Chapter 7
The Party

The taxi carrying Peter Grant, Tracy, and their son, Wesley, continued its slow progress toward Saint Michael's Parish and the special midnight mass.

The falling snow had eased but not the bitter cold. By now, the streets of Washington, D.C., had patches of ice and the crosswind continued to cause drifting and poor visibility. A sudden horn blast caused the cabby to jerk the taxi to avoid a fast passing late model Raven loaded with laughing teenagers.

"Damn fools!" yelled the cabby.

The black Raven made a swerving right turn at a fork in the road just ahead and disappeared from their view. Almost instantly a loud thud was heard.

"Wow! What was that?" asked Wesley.

"I think it was an accident, Wes," said his father.

"Damn fools!" barked the cabby as the taxi approached the fork and pulled over in full view of the wreckage. Just beyond lay the crippled car, resting on its left side at the base of an embankment, with wheels still spinning.

During the plunge, a teenage boy and girl had been thrown clear of the vehicle and lay motionless against the snow-covered bank. Porch lights went on as curious on-lookers began to emerge from nearby houses.

"How awful," whispered Tracy, putting a protective arm around her son's shoulder and turning her eyes away.

Grant glanced at the taxi dashboard clock. Five after eleven. Security had planned their arrival time at the parish to be eleven-thirty. "There are sure to be people trapped in that wreckage," he said. "They need help."

"Hold on! We're on a timetable," the cabby retorted.

Sirens were heard in the distance.

"I could be back in five minutes," Grant persisted.

"Darling, should you? I mean, you are on heart medication and help is on the way," Tracy reminded him, her eyes reflecting concern.

He recognized the look and he lightly squeezed her hand in appreciation as the taxi eased back onto the highway and left the scene.

For several minutes they reflected upon the accident. Grant, in particular, was caught up in the senseless tragedy, as it reminded him of the earlier accident which had befallen his parents. Only minutes ago those young people were laughing and carefree. Now they were injured or dead. Perhaps they were celebrating the approaching new year and their joy-ride climaxed the tail-end of a drinking party.

Grant sat back and closed his eyes as another party came to mind. It too, was a celebration party with an unexpected finale.

Δ Δ Δ

It was eight o'clock and most of the guests had arrived when Peter Grant crossed the patio and buzzed the rear door. Preston Thomas's condominium featured ample rear parking and a stretch of Lake Michigan shoreline. In addition to Dr. Judith Gillespie, Press had invited a half-dozen of Grant's former associates at Glick and their spouses. The affair would be informal, reflected by Grant's open collar shirt under a white knit sweater. The air was cool for mid-June and a light breeze tossed his hair.

"Hi, peaches!" he said, pinching the blushing cheek of Lotti, the Thomas' housemaid and cook of countless years.

"Pete!" Press had entered the vestibule from the dining hall. "Your colleagues await your pleasure."

In the dining hall Grant made the cordial round of renewing acquaintances dimmed by almost a year, accepting congratulations and meeting Dr. Judith Gillespie. The doctor was tall and husky with pepper bobbed hair and no makeup. Grant placed her in her fifties and was surprised at the ease with which she carried what he judged to be one hundred seventy pounds.

The room was cosmopolitan. Lounges and huge decorative pillows spattered the hardwood floor, while the walls featured brightly colored landscapes mostly from the impressionist period of the late nineteenth century.

A side table was covered with relishes, fresh vegetables, hot casseroles, and desserts with coffee and soft drinks at one end. Opposite a corner fireplace was a step-down entrance to an amusement room which featured an assortment of film, tapes, and exercise equipment. A forty-five foot pleasure boat was docked within walking distance for the benefit of Glick Publishing clients.

The guests soon gathered at a center table positioned under a cathedral ceiling and sparkling chandelier.

The dinner was spiced with high-spirited, one-on-one conversation, followed by a more restrained discussion involving the entire group. Later waitresses cleared the table of plates and provided them with glasses of white champagne. Press toasted Grant who, in turn, gave a brief update on the beginnings of his portrait.

Press stood again. "As you know, we are honored with a special guest. I had the privilege of meeting Doctor Gillespie twenty-three years ago under unpleasant circumstances in California. The doctor gave me a helping hand when I needed it most and we've been good friends ever since.

"At that time, Doctor Gillespie was chief of police in Sacramento, but not for long. She rapidly advanced in the ranks of law enforcement and is now considered an expert on criminal behavior, having authored numerous books and articles on the subject.

"As recently as last month, by presidential appointment, Doctor Gillespie was named director of the Council on Revolutionary Tactics. As such, she will organize and direct a massive workshop for special agents in D.C. even though her home base will remain in Chicago where she will plan and direct security undercover activities. Due to the secretive nature of her duties, I am mindful to divulge only what Doctor Gillespie has authorized.

"No one is more on top of the latest developments in our national crisis than Doctor Gillespie and she has agreed to respond to your concerns to the extent security is not violated."

After her introduction, Doctor Gillespie stood to a generous applause. "Thank you, Preston, for your kind words. My remarks will be brief as this evening belongs to Peter Grant."

The doctor removed her eyeglasses and placed them in her purse. Her cerulean dress was knee-length and smartly styled. More importantly, she was dressed for comfort. Yet her manner of dress was hardly noticed by her listeners.

"I'm honored to be here," she continued. "When Preston invited me to your party, I jumped at the opportunity to share in Mr. Grant's celebration."

Her low-toned words reflected a hint of masculinity, and her listeners were tuned in.

"As Preston told you, my comments will be guarded so as not to breach security as they relate to the present revolt. In this regard, I must be honest with you. Without your knowledge, I had each of you screened and cleared beforehand. No offense intended. Also, this dining hall and all adjoining rooms are bug free. This is standard procedure and Preston understands this."

Dr. Gillespie glanced at her wrist watch, took a sip of her brandy sling, and blotted her lips with a napkin. "Before I respond to questions, permit me to make an unexpected observation. Someone at this table is armed with a handgun."

Her remark caused the guests to stir uncomfortably.

"Don't be alarmed," she quickly added. "The gun isn't loaded." She scanned their faces. "Even though it is no longer illegal to possess a firearm without a permit, guns still make me itch. The gun to which I refer is presently concealed in a lady's clutch purse and is possibly a Derringer. Of course it isn't necessary the guntoter be revealed.

"I'm aware of the gun because I'm wearing a special wrist watch which reveals more than the time of day. My watch vibrates when a firearm is within forty feet. The hands will glow if a detected firearm is loaded. As you might suspect, the watch is one of several gadgets I wear for emergency purposes." She smiled. "Have you any questions?"

Howard Bojack, director of personnel at Glick, was quick to speak. "Dr. Gillespie, we're concerned about the risk Pete may face in painting such a celebrated religious theme while the revolutionaries are taking a strong anti-Christ posture. Are we justified in our concern?"

"Come now," cut in Grant. "I'm sure Dr. Gillespie is geared to more significant matters."

"Nonsense," replied the doctor. "The matter is by no means trivial. While Mr. Grant's life may not be in immediate danger, there is cause for concern. Let me elaborate," she continued. "The revolutionaries have just recently organized a fleet of young atheistic storm troopers called the Devil's Corps. The corps' sole mission is to destroy religious establishments—churches, synagogues, temples, parishes, but especially Christian institutions."

"Dr. Gillespie, is the Devil's Corps responsible for the recent church bombings in Philadelphia and Miami?" asked Ed Kissinger, Glick's top commercial artist.

"Yes, but more importantly, the corps is presently updating a list of religious leaders targeted for assassination."

Glick's executive vice president, Hatcher Boyle, cleared his throat. "Dr. Gillespie, what can you tell us about the so-called mysterious revolutionary leader we've been hearing and reading about in the media?"

"Most of what you hear or read is rumor. I will reveal their leader's name. It is Lady X."

Secretary Jean Juliet, fidgeted before breaking the silence. "Dr. Gillespie, how might the Devil's Corps react if they learn about Mr. Grant's portrait?"

The doctor considered her question at some length. "Of course the corps would follow orders from their leader. Since the portrait deadline is almost two years away, the corps would place Mr. Grant low on their priority list. With this in mind, Lady X would not likely order the corps to destroy the portrait and sever Mr. Grant's painting hand until early next year."

"How utterly uncivilized!" Miss Juliet responded with a gasp.

"It could be worse, my dear," said Dr. Gillespie. "The Devil's Corps would prefer to behead. Lady X, you see, is a staunch supporter of unusual and cruel punishment. Having said this and considering we are in mid-April, I would suggest Mr. Grant become familiar with a bodyguard by December at the latest."

Peter Grant had been listening intently. Also, he was thinking about the strange phone call he had received only the evening before. He was "under watchful eyes and listening ears," the man had said. Grant wondered if he had been overheard when he had talked earlier to Press or Tracy about his new assignment. He felt obliged to tell Dr. Gillespie about the phone call. "Dr. Gillespie," he finally asked, "can you tell us more about the Devil's Corps.?"

"Little else," she said. "The corps is one of three basic units making up their organization, with each unit designated to attack on a different front, namely military, government, and church. While the two main units are awaiting a single all-out effort, the Devil's Corps will continue its hit-and-run tactics. The corps is the least sophisticated of the three, but its members are diabolic and fearless with many having suicidal tendencies. It is highly active, most unpredictable, and deadly destructive. Need I say more?"

"Does the Devil's Corps consist of many blacks?" asked Marti Kaufman, a black lady herself and wife of Glick sales and distribution director, Karl Kaufman.

"An interesting question," said the doctor, thoughtfully. "About 20 percent. The corps is a mixture of races, creeds, and nationalities. The black revolutionary forces have combined with other minority groups in an effort to strengthen their hand and facilitate infiltration. Keep in mind, the government forces also consist of about 20 percent black. This is not a conflict between whites and blacks."

Hatcher Boyle again cleared his throat, a characteristic resulting from scarred tissues of a once cancerous larynx. "Can you tell us anything about the other two revolutionary units?"

"Only to say they are well organized and, unfortunately, biding their time for what they hope will be the death blow to our federal government."

Preston Thomas checked his watch and interrupted the discussion, informing his guests Doctor Gillespie had to be airborne in two hours.

"Let's have one more question," she suggested.

Karl Kaufmann responded. "Dr. Gillespie, can you summarize our basic strategy in this revolt?"

The psychiatrist patiently considered his question. "We feel it to our advantage to combat the revolutionaries with underground tactics similar to their own. This takes time but it will allow us to identify the greatest number of rebels for later prosecution. Unfortunately, time, numbers, and the element of surprise are in their favor. Also, the revolutionaries have had a head start, as they've been preparing for this revolt for many years.

"On the other hand, we have more sophisticated hardware, better communications and, I would like to believe, an edge in intelligence. With momentum on our side, we doubt they will make any significant strike before winter."

As the guests casually moved toward the amusement room, Dr. Gillespie took Grant aside. "I must have a word with you," she said.

Grant led her toward the vestibule. "Is this about my landlord?" he asked.

She nodded. "Preston filled me in. Of course Preston is concerned about your welfare," she added.

As they entered the vestibule, Dr. Gillespie replaced her eyeglasses and motioned toward a watercolor landscape on the wall. "Very good," she said. "I tried watercolor once but with horrible results. It wasn't fresh and spontaneous." As she spoke she casually fingered the sapphire brooch fastened at the neckline of her blue dress, activating its concealed recorder.

"Preston's concern is whether or not your landlord is a threat to you," she began. "Preston generalized about Mr. Baxter but what I need are specifics. The answers to four questions will do fine."

"I'll do my best," said the artist.

"Mr. Grant, how many encounters have you had with Mr. Baxter?"

"Three," he said without hesitation.

"Approximately when did these occur and how would you describe Mr. Baxter's demeanor on each occasion?"

Grant reflected as Dr. Gillespie turned to the watercolor landscape and lightly touched its ebony frame.

"We first met after my return from New York. It was the day prior to my moving into my apartment. It was April twentieth. Baxter's demeanor? He was very confused, skeptical, and consumed in self-pity."

"Good. Go on," urged the doctor.

"Our second meeting was about a week later, a day or two before my interview in New York. Mr. Baxter, as I recall, was obnoxious and smug. He ruled out any chance of my getting the crucifixion assignment.

"Our last encounter occurred just after I had returned from my interview. I was tired and somewhat confused at the time. Possibly it was the pressure of the interview. It was May fourth or fifth, I'm not sure. Anyway, I found Mr. Baxter to be overbearing and irate. He accused me of being sacrilegious and a sinner unworthy of painting Christ on the cross."

"Fine, Mr. Grant. Now tell me, have any of your acquaintances met your landlord?"

"No."

"Let's keep it that way. I can conclude Mr. Baxter has all the symptoms of a paranoid, but he's not dangerous."

"I didn't think so," said Grant with a sign.

"A final question, Mr. Grant. Aside from Mr. Baxter, have you told anyone else about your assignment?"

"Only one. My former model, Tracy Duvall."

"*Lapsus lingual.* An unconscious slip of the tongue!" the doctor explained. "Revolutionaries are everywhere, especially where liquor flows freely."

"Tracy Duvall is absolutely trustworthy," Grant assured her.

"Absolutely? Mr. Grant, none of us are exactly what we appear to be."

Grant revealed to Dr. Gillespie his strange telephone call the previous evening.

"And I'm sure your Caller I.D. was useless?" she surmised.

Grant nodded. "The caller's name was unavailable. No doubt he used a pay telephone."

"Have your telephone bugged, Mr. Grant, and report to Preston any further such calls. Preston will be my liaison."

Dr. Gillespie noticed an oil painting nearby. "I like this," she said.

"It was a gift to Press' late wife after she became ill several years ago. It's one of my better landscapes."

"It is?" May I photograph it?" she asked.

"It would be my pleasure," Grant assured her.

Dr. Gillespie removed a small camera from her purse and captured the painting. She checked her watch. As she did so she casually touched her brooch, deactivating its recorder. "By the way, Mr. Grant, you are perceptive with a keen sense of observation, yet I've deceived you. I'm wearing a hairpiece, my voice as you hear it is several pitches below my normal range, and under my garments are thirty-five pounds of padding. My point is, if I can deceive you, so can others."

"Dr. Gillespie, I bow to your deception," said the artist modestly.

She extended her hand. "It has been my pleasure, Mr. Grant, and I wish you well." At the door she turned to him. "Don't forget the bodyguard."

Shortly after Dr. Gillespie's departure, Press took Grant aside.

"Dr. Gillespie is a fantastic lady," said Grant.

Press nodded. "She's her own make-up artist, a throw-back to the days of movie actor, Lon Chaney. Pete, you would be pleasantly surprised to see her without her camouflage."

"Indeed, she is full of surprises," admitted Grant.

Press hesitated then cleared his throat. "My friend, speaking of surprises, someone is awaiting you in the vestibule."

Grant crossed to the vestibule and opened the door. Sitting on a chair and looking up at him was Kay.

Chapter 8
Homecoming

"Hello darling! May I crash your party?"

It was a joyful moment as Kay, her eyes magnified by tears, rushed into the arms of Peter Grant. Their lips met and the familiar mold of her body pressed hard against his. Grant's heart had quickened, forcing him to breathe deeply when their lips finally parted.

He held her at arm's length. "Kay…am I going mad? Is it really you?"

Kay Allyson was easy to observe. She was petite, coming barely above his shoulders, but every inch a woman. Wearing a green pullover sweater and flowing skirt, she looked fresh and exciting despite her tears and a tiring day.

"Kay, you're six weeks early! What happened in Brazil?"

"Wouldn't you know…tribal uprising. Our native guides ran scared and poof! The assignment aborted," she explained, flicking a stubborn curl from her forehead.

"The Munduracus Indians are at war?" he asked.

She nodded. "Luckily, we managed two weeks of shooting before the drums came, but I doubt it will cover expenses," she sighed.

Grant chuckled. 'Kay, only you would think about company expenses when Reed & Lambert constantly tosses you to the lions." Grant took a deep breath. "In the past three years, you've snapped anaconda, alligator, cape buffalo, gorilla, and now it's jaguar," he concluded.

"Darling, it's my job, it pays well, and I love my work. Besides, jaguar aren't all that menacing once you learn their habits."

Grant hugged her again. "All that matters is you are home, alive and well," he said proudly.

His last remark compelled her to hug him hard. "But Peter, I was worried about you," she said, facing him with a strained smile. "Yesterday, when I phoned your New York studio and learned you had gone, I was puzzled. So, I phoned Press."

"You phoned me from Kennedy airport?" he cut in.

"No, darling. From Mannos."

"Then you've just arrived?"

She nodded. "Press arranged to meet me at O'Hare. My return coincided with your party, so we decided to surprise you."

"Kay, you must be dead tired."

She saw the concern in his eyes. "I am, but mostly I'm excited. Seeing you again. Learning about your big assignment. It's overwhelming, Peter."

"Press gave you my assignment details?"

"Ooh no! Press said you should do that and I agree."

Grant nodded. "Tomorrow over dinner at Kahiki's?"

"Peter, I'd love that."

They embraced again, savoring the moment but mindful they had to join the others.

"Kay, we have catching up to do," Grant said, as they walked arm-in-arm toward the dining hall.

"Yes...and so little time to do it," she said faintly, as if not wanting him to hear her words.

He stopped and faced her. "So little time?"

She looked up with wistful eyes. "Peter, my assignment was only temporarily aborted. I must leave Monday, but only for a short while. Come, darling," she added quickly. "Our friends are waiting."

Even though Kay Allyson was more exhausted than Grant suspected, she joined in Grant's celebration until midnight. It wasn't until they had settled into a taxi and headed for her apartment that he pursued the gnawing prospect of her leaving in two days.

"Peter, may we talk about it over dinner tomorrow...your new assignment and mine? My day was very long."

"I'm sorry, Kay. Tomorrow will be fine."

The taxi edged into heavy traffic on Lake Shore Drive and continued south before Grant broke the silence. "Kay, I'm also sorry about our last telephone conversation. It must have hurt you deeply and I apologize."

"Peter, it isn't necessary," she said, resting her head against his shoulder. "That's behind us. Only the present is important."

After a pause, Kay changed the subject. "Where are you living, Peter?"

"At North Ashland at Summerdale," he said. "I paid a three-year lease on a nice duplex but it's messy right now." He knew under no circumstances could they stop there.

"I'd love to see your studio, Peter, but not tonight," she said.

"We'll stop after dinner tomorrow," Grant suggested.

She nodded and closed her eyes. She appeared relaxed against him as though sleeping. The artist had a way of making others feel at ease, and Kay especially had felt on easy terms with him from the beginning. Perhaps it was because they had suffered similar tragedies early on.

Her heartbreak had happened three years ago, during the quake of 2022. It was the year after she had come to Chicago, fresh out of photography school at Valencia, California. Her parents had perished in that disaster, leaving her in much the same dilemma Grant had faced much earlier.

Within a week of her arrival in Chicago, Kay Allyson had met Peter Grant.

It was a chance meeting during a Pierre Bonnard exhibit at the art institute. Grant had wandered into the photography wing and saw her standing alone, admiring a huge prize-winning shot of a charging elephant. She had been hired by Reed & Lambert Publishing Company that very morning and she was eager to share her excitement with the handsome stranger.

They had dated steadily thereafter without holding special claims. However after her parents had died a year later, they became closer. Now theirs was a special relationship.

The taxi entered the inner city belt and soon was climbing the spiral ramp at Glenn Towers. Her company had provided quarters for its employees within the same complex with Kay's suite on the twelfth floor.

She invited him in but he took a rain check, knowing she was tired. As Grant kissed her good night, his arms encircled her narrow waist, and he noticed she had lost weight.

"I'm only down to one hundred and ten, sir!" she said jokingly. "You know how women are vainly addicted to diets. Must I be different?" She grinned and flicked the stubborn curl from her forehead.

"You *are* different, Kay. Different from any woman I've ever known. Tomorrow I'll tell you how much."

In her apartment, Kay Allyson had slipped from her outer garments and was sprawled diagonally across her bed, wondering if she had the energy or the will to draw bath water. On her dresser top was a framed portrait she had taken of Grant shortly after they first met. It was a black and white shot with only natural lighting, but it had captured his sensitive eyes and casual smile and it was her favorite.

Grant returned to the party and it finally ended at two.

As the artist taxied to his apartment, he was consumed with a single thought. He would ask Kay to marry him. Tomorrow over dinner at Kahiki's would be the right time and place. Perhaps they could marry upon her return from the backup assignment. For Grant, the sooner the better.

Spirited by his decision to marry, the artist climbed the stairwell leading to his apartment with added gusto. He was aware of drawn blinds below, telling him John Baxter had still not returned from his mysterious travels. Once inside, Grant found Tracy sleeping soundly and he was careful not to disturb her.

He uncovered the huge canvas and studied his portrait only briefly before he decided to retire. His decision to propose marriage to Kay had disrupted his ability to concentrate.

He awoke to the shuffle of feet in the kitchenette and the mixed aroma of sizzling bacon and coffee. Dressed only in pajama bottoms, Grant softly stepped into the open kitchenette doorway.

Tracy was at the stove, facing away from him. She was wearing her exercise outfit of black huggers and halter, with a bandanna holding her blonde hair.

"Hmmm...smells good," Grant said.

She whirled. "Peter! You startled me!" she crossed to him. "Hi sleepyhead," she said, musing his already tousled hair. "Coffee's ready. Or would you prefer I wake you up?" she jested, pirouetting for him like a ballerina.

"It's a tough decision, coffee or *Swan Lake*," said Grant, dropping into a chair.

"How was your party?" she asked as she filled his cup.

Grant pawed his unshaved chin. "The party was fine," he said as he doctored his coffee and sipped it. "Delicious. Tracy, I didn't know the fridge was stocked with bacon."

"It wasn't. While you slept, I picked up a few items at the corner Quick Shop."

Grant jumped to his feet, almost spilling his coffee. "Tracy, don't you realize the streets are infested with madmen waiting to rape the likes of you? Don't ever leave this apartment alone and that, young lady, is an order."

She crossed to him, standing only inches away. "Peter, will you rape me?" she whispered.

Grant dropped back into his chair with a deep sigh. "Tracy, this is no good."

"Anyway, I'm glad you were concerned about me, Peter," she said, returning to the stove.

"Kay is back," Grant said levelly, studying her reaction.

She kept her back to him as she broke some eggs into the skillet and jabbed their yolks with a fork. "I hope you like your eggs scrambled and your bacon crisp," she said uneasily.

"I love scrambled eggs and crisp bacon," he responded, to ease the moment.

But Tracy wasn't listening. "I knew Kay had returned," she said finally. "Preston told me, Peter. He also told me Kay would be at your party. That's why I didn't go."

She returned with the skillet, filled his plate, and warmed his coffee. "Toast is coming right up," she said with little enthusiasm, returning to the stove. "I know Kay is your girl, Peter. But I won't be a problem. Tonight I'll pack my things."

"Tracy, we've decided that issue. You'll stay and I'll find you employment and an apartment.

She returned with the toast and sat. "So, you'll be dining with Kay tonight?'

"Yes," he replied.

"That's okay. I was planning a nice dinner for you but the truth is I'm a lousy cook. Most models are, you know."

This time it was Grant who wasn't listening.

"Tracy...tonight I plan to ask Kay to marry me."

She stood and reached for a napkin, but no matter how hard she tried, the tears came.

Grant moved to comfort her but she turned away.

"I knew it would happen one day, Peter, but not this soon. Not this sudden," she said, dabbing her eyes. She blew her nose with the napkin and sat. "Peter, eat your breakfast before it gets cold. Cold scrambled eggs taste awful."

Grant faced her eye-to-eye. "Tracy, you are very special to me," he said, emphasizing each word. "I admire you more than you know. Perhaps more than you'll ever know."

"But you don't love me," she said with a weak smile. 'Why must there always be a but to spoil everything! Peter, I do understand. I really do. I mean second place can't be all that bad, can it?" she asked without expecting an answer.

She dabbed the corner of her eyes. "Peter...I feel homesick. Isn't that odd? I visited my parents only six weeks ago. It was after I missed seeing you in New York and I was feeling low. Now I suddenly miss my parents very much," she said.

Grant reached across the table and placed his hand on hers. "Tracy, don't your parents live in Reading?"

She looked up. "Yes, they have lived in the same house since I was six years old," she reflected.

"But I've never met your parents, have I?" he asked.

"So?"

"Don't you think it's time?"

Tracy looked puzzled. "Peter, what are you telling me?"

"Let's visit your parents next weekend for a couple days," he replied.

Tracy dropped a spoon. "Peter! That would be wonderful! But—" She stopped short. "But Kay is here. Shouldn't you be with her?"

"Kay is leaving again," he said soberly. "She's leaving tomorrow at noon on a back-up assignment."

"I'm sorry she's leaving again," Tracy said with sincerity.

"It won't be a long assignment," Grant assured her. "Possibly a couple months somewhere in Central America. I'll know tonight."

The kitchenette telephone rang as Grant was thanking Tracy for a good breakfast. As he lifted the receiver, the thought that it might be the mysterious phone caller crossed his mind. However it was only Press checking in.

Later while shaving, Grant's thoughts returned to the mysterious phone call he had received two days earlier. *You are under watchful eyes and listening ears*, the phone caller had said.

Grant had difficulty taking the phone call seriously and now he would see if he was tailed to Reading. Of course he wouldn't be, he surmised. The possibility that someone would tail him from Illinois to Pennsylvania was ridiculous. Only the Devil's Corps would have reason to be interested in him, and the corps didn't warn their victims with telephone calls or follow them across the country. It wasn't their style.

To be on the safe side, however, Grant decided he would hire a security guard to occupy his apartment during his absence. He wanted his painting to be intact upon his return.

Chapter 9
A Magnificent Moment

Grant and Kay stepped from a taxi at Chicago's inner belt and entered the Kahiki restaurant by way of its famous step-down spiral escalator.

The restaurant had an air-cooled atmosphere of soft flowing palms and enchanting vibrations of steel guitar mixed with whistling birds emanating from hidden speakers. The interior was a refreshing contrast to the stark hardness of skyscrapers just beyond its walls and had long been a favorite eating spot of theirs.

Chan, the soft-spoken headwaiter, recognized them and approached smilingly. After a cordial greeting, he led them to a reserved table graced with two lit candles and a decorated cake. Adjacent to the table was an aquarium stocked with a variety of slithering goldfish.

"Peter, I'm overwhelmed!"

"Welcome home, Kay," Grant said, echoing the cake's inscription as he adjusted her chair and softly kissed her cheek.

She responded by squeezing his hand, then blew him a thank you kiss after they were seated.

Kay Allyson scanned the room. It featured rows of tables separated by low partitions, each supporting huge planters of live tropical plants. Her eyes finally came to rest upon her escort, noting his broad-shouldered frame packed into a blue, British-cut suit, his easy smile, his sensitive eyes.

As a professional photographer, she knew she was good, but in him she saw a singular talent—a unique blend of determination and creativity which she believed had unlimited potential. Certainly he represented a level she and her camera were not likely to attain.

Of no less importance to her was his thoughtfulness. His earlier gesture to Chan indicated they would forgo cocktails. Because she didn't drink, he always abstained in her presence. It was a gesture she considered unnecessary but becoming. The same was true about smoking. She didn't so he wouldn't. Ordering the cake was his touch. Later he would have Chan box the leftovers for her.

Finally their reserved table near the aquarium of goldfish was for her benefit, the goldfish episode being a private one between them. As a child, she had sadly overfed her pet goldfish, causing them to die. However the fondness for them remained. An elaborate aquarium in her apartment and a smaller facsimile in her office was testimony of this. Yet tonight Kay hoped he would not offer her more than she could accept or ask of her more than she could give.

Grant sipped his water while trying to read her thoughts. "You're preoccupied," he concluded with a grin.

"Thinking of you," she confessed.

"Dreadful thought," he replied as he observed the shadows frolic about her face. He was about to ask if her taffeta dress was new when Chan noiselessly intervened with a tray of egg drop soup, vegetables, and Polynesian pork.

"Looks delicious," Kay said, adjusting her napkin. She leaned toward him, her eyes wide with anticipation. "Peter, I can't wait another minute. Tell me about your assignment, please?"

Grant was still peering into her green-tinged eyes that were accented by her flowing auburn hair. "Ladies first," he said. "I'm just as anxious to know about the urgency for your reassignment."

"Okay, you win," she conceded. She drew a deep breath as she flicked her salad with a fork. "Peter, since my assignment is only a back-up, it shouldn't exceed a month. Reed & Lambert had anticipated possible trouble with the Mundurucas, so preliminary preparations had already been made in Nicaragua."

"Hmmm...Nicaragua is it? At least it's closer and the country isn't at war."

"Actually, darling, Nicaragua is still having border skirmishes with Honduras, but that's been going on for generations."

"I suppose the assignment translates into more jaguar?" he mused.

She nodded.

"Rainy season there, too, I suspect?" he asked.

"Yes, but the Mestizo are a friendly people and the Kurinwas River is sweet and gentle compared to the Amazon."

"You make it read like a tourist guide," he said, sipping his coffee. "By the way, Kay, where's your gear?"

"Already shipped ahead," she replied.

"And your itinerary?"

She rolled her expressive eyes in thought. "Leaving tomorrow noon by United. A flight change in Dallas. Meet my party in Managua tomorrow night and pick up my gear. From Managua we'll rail to Metagalpa and take on additional guides. Fly copter to the mouth of the Kurinwas where our barge awaits us."

Kay sipped her coffee and continued.

"We'll navigate only the first fifty or so kilometers, going ashore perhaps a dozen times but never over night. When my film is exhausted, we'll return by the same route." She sat back and smiled at him. "Now, sir, it's your turn," she said, pushing the curl from her forehead.

Grant revealed the details of his assignment and touched briefly on his progress to date.

"Peter, it's marvelous! So perfect!" she said, after he had finished. "The crucifixion of Jesus. The ultimate of man's sin and God's sacrificial love. Tragic, yet beautiful." Her green eyes clouded with concern. "And dangerous for you, Peter. Christianity is so rejected today and you could be hurt badly."

"Perhaps even shot at," he said casually.

"Please don't joke about it," she pleaded.

A callous remark, he thought, *even if only meant to prepare her for any eventuality.* "Sorry, I didn't mean to sound cavalier." He smiled at her. "Kay, my assignment is the opportunity of a hundred lifetimes. I would never let it be jeopardized by intruders. Sure, I may be harassed or intimidated, but I promise you everything will go well."

She sighed with relief. "Peter, your assurance means very much to me," she said, lifting her water glass as if in toast.

Grant sensed her seriousness and gestured toward her with his own glass. "Water is sweeter than wine and more sustaining," he quipped.

"To your success, Peter," she began. "May your portrait of Jesus reflect the great gift you possess. May it be your answer to a nation torn apart and to a world of ugliness and disbelievers." She paused and grinned. "And with the help of the good Lord, may your assignment beat the deadline!"

Grant tipped her glass with his and they laughed together.

Chan had waited for the moment to subside before intervening to warm their coffee and whisk away used tableware.

During her toast, Grant's eyes had followed Kay's lips—full, wet, and red, sliding over white teeth and a flicking tongue. But his mind had recorded her thoughtful, sincere words, some of which he hoped would not return to haunt him.

"Darling, your mastery of figure painting makes the assignment so right for you and I predict total success," she beamed.

"My landlord, John Baxter, thinks otherwise."

"Your landlord?" she asked with inquisitive eyes.

"Kay, Baxter is a long and boring story. In short, he thinks I'm spiritually unsuited for the assignment...morally inept. He predicted my lack of Christian virtues would betray and eventually destroy me. It would be my *coupe de grace*," Grant stated flatly, as he pinched one of the candle wicks, momentarily smothering its flame.

"Peter, who cares what he thinks? The man doesn't really know you."

The artist grinned. "As a prophet, I'll choose you over Baxter. You've predicted my success and you're much prettier," he said in a light vein.

"You chose me because I do know you, Peter," she countered. "I know you as well or better than anyone," Kay added emphatically.

Do you know me well enough to suspect I'm about to propose marriage to you? he thought.

"Your landlord sounds like a prophet of doom," Kay said.

"Amen to that," he said. "Baxter wrote the book on doomsday. However in fairness to the man, he is sick and not to be taken seriously." Grant paused and sipped his coffee. "On the other hand, you are Baxter's antithesis. You never see shadows on the horizon."

"I don't?" she asked, looking up from her plate. "Darling, I'm no pessimist, but we all must perish...eventually," she said, her eyes turning toward the aquarium.

Grant assumed she was reminded of her goldfish that had perished years ago. "Yes, one day all of us will be gone," he said almost absentmindedly, as he began to admire her face in profile. His eyes glided down her curved forehead to a straight angled nose. However when they traced her rounded recessed lips, they were distracted. Something in the background had caught his attention and held it fast. It was the back view of blonde hair, piled high, and worn by an unescorted woman seated three tables removed. As the woman slid from her chair and prepared to leave, Grant's mind reeled. *That powder blue skirt! My God, it is Bonnie Bates! But she can't be here*, he thought.

Kay was speaking but Grant was missing her words. "Darling, are you all right?" she asked, noting his sudden detachment.

"Sorry," he said, turning to her. "It's nothing, Kay. I thought I saw a New York acquaintance, but I was mistaken. You were saying?"

"I was suggesting we talk about something pleasant. This is a happy occasion."

"Good. Let's talk about life instead of death," Grant said, pushing his main course aside. "By the way, Kay, did I tell you Hathaway, the donor-client, stipulated that my assignment must depict Christ as still possessing life?"

"Yes. Why would he require that?" Kay asked.

"Ambrose Thorne didn't say and I didn't ask. My guess is Hathaway's monumental guilt couldn't permit his being responsible for a dead Christ, even on canvas."

"If that's true," she said with a sigh, "I feel sorry for Mr. Hathaway."

Grant was reminded of his own guilty feelings about Tracy. "Kay, you remember Tracy Duvall?"

"Your New York model, wasn't she?"

Grant nodded. "Tracy is presently unemployed and having a tough go. She arrived from New York two days ago and got my address from Press. So, I'm putting her up until she finds work."

"Peter, that's thoughtful of you. I do wish her well because I'm sure she's a good person."

Kay's words of understanding and goodwill made the artist feel small.

"Peter, would I be prying if I ask how you plan to meet that specification? Jesus still possessing life in your painting, that is."

"Glad you asked. It's the crux of my composition." He leaned toward her, his eyes narrowing with concentration. "My portrait will capture that moment when Christ spoke to the thief hanging on the cross to His right. More specifically, it's when Christ forgave the thief of his sins and promised him a place in God's kingdom."

Kay sat back and slowly nodded her approval. "I love that, Peter. What a magnificent moment! In an instant of time, Jesus grants everlasting life."

"As to the pictorial aspects," Grant continued, "with Christ so near death and His physical strength almost spent, His head will be slumped forward with His chin pressed against His right clavicle. In this awkward position, Christ's eyelids will be raised slightly in a painful effort to see the thief. His mouth will be ajar and contorted. The index finger of His right hand will be partially extended, pointing toward the thief. Basically, that's it," he concluded, sipping his coffee.

"Peter, I can clearly visualize your interpretation and I can feel its impact."

Kay did the honors and cut them a slice of cake.

Shortly afterward, she broke a brief period of silence. "Peter, do you believe in the hereafter?"

"Life after death? I do. There must be some form of life beyond the grave, otherwise life on earth would have little meaning."

Kay smiled. "*Your* life has meaning, Peter. Your life is full."

That was it! That was the opening he had awaited. "Kay, did I hear you say my life is full? Well, now...shall we say half-full?" he suggested, twirling his half-empty glass of water with his fingers.

"Kay, I've changed since returning to Chicago five weeks ago. Oh, my rough spots are still there and with the new assignment in hand, it's true much of my life is coming together. However, I've come to realize something vital is missing. My life needs to be shared."

Kay felt a tightness in her throat and her vision blurred. She sipped her water.

"Last night," Grant continued with even softer words, "you equated yourself to other women. The fact is, there's no comparison." He took her hand in his without noting the coldness of her touch. "Kay, I've always admired your courage. Any woman who will stalk jaguar armed with only a camera is courageous. But just as significant...in graciousness, goodness, and beauty, you begin where other women leave off. You're the only woman who can make my life full." He lifted her hand and kissed it. "Kay, I'm saying—"

"Peter...." Kay interrupted.

Grant raised a hand. "I'm sorry, Kay, but I must finish."

He sat back and gazed into her green moist eyes. "I'm saying I love you and I'm asking you to marry me."

"Peter...." Kay touched a napkin to her eyes and tried to smile. "Peter...you do know how to catch a girl off guard," she barely whispered.

In her eyes Grant saw only pain. "Kay, I realize this is sudden. Perhaps too sudden, all things considered."

Yes, all things considered, she thought. *Too much is happening too quickly and too late.* "I'm sorry, Peter, but I can't give you an answer now. I just can't. Tomorrow I will. Tomorrow, when you take me to the airport."

"Fine. I can't expect more than that," he said, forcing a smile and pushing back his chair.

As the cashier was ringing up Grant's bill, his thoughts lingered on the packaged engagement ring in his jacket pocket, while another ring across town was alerting Preston Thomas. It was a long distance phone call from Washington, D.C.

"Preston, Judith Gillespie here."

"Judith! Thank you for returning my call so soon. How's your workshop shaping up?"

"Sufficiently well. I work my staff unmercifully."

"With good results, I'm sure," said Press.

"We're making progress, which leads me to our last conversation. A member of my staff, Roger Davis, is looking into the situation. Of course my presence at the party was very helpful. Unfortunately, what I observed tends to substantiate your theory."

"I was afraid of that," Press said.

"Preston, the immediate future looks glum. How quickly can you gather Mr. Grant's dossier for me?"

"Two days?"

"Humor me and make that twenty-four hours?"

"I'll have it ready, Judith. Shall I deliver it?"

"No thanks. I'll drop by at seven tomorrow evening. By the way, Preston, include everything that relates to Mr. Grant's medial history."

Chapter 10
Retrogression

Kay Allyson took another raincheck on a visit to Grant's studio apartment. He understood because she had to be up early. He would pick her up at eight and they would eat breakfast at O'Hare prior to her noon departure.

It was ten o'clock before Grant said goodnight to Kay and stepped from the Glenn Towers elevator into the cool air. He hailed a taxi and instructed the cabby to take a long route to his destination. He wanted to relax and think about the turn of events.

The artist had difficulty keeping his hand off the small packaged box in his jacket pocket. He had purchased the ring earlier in the day at the Block. Banner's Block was a quarter billion dollar enterprise featuring the world's largest twenty-four-hour shopping and recreation complex and was noted for its jewelry line.

As the taxi turned off Central and onto North Ashland Avenue, the moon appeared from behind black clouds. Noting it, the cabby began to gab about the newly developed sol-lunar powered engines being tested in Detroit.

Grant wasn't listening. Earlier at dinner, his proposal of marriage to Kay had been tabled. Yet despite the temporary setback, he was optimistic. He was confident she would have a favorable response after much-needed sleep. In hindsight, he realized it was too important a decision to expect from her without some thought.

During his brief stay at her apartment, they had engaged in only light conversation but the air had remained tense. This changed during their parting embrace as Kay had permitted her body to mesh with his. She had covered his face with kisses in a breathtaking moment of passion and, although they had never made love, he felt this would have been the moment had she accepted his ring. In his heart he believed Kay loved him.

A car ran a traffic light just ahead, causing the cabby to swerve the taxi and vent his frustration with profanity.

Grant sat back and withdrew his planner booklet to review notes he had taken on Kay's assignment itinerary. However he was quick to discover the attached pen was missing. Reflecting, he had written the notes at Kay's dining table. He had left it there. No matter. He would get it when he picked her up in the morning.

Again he tried to relax and his mind focused upon his portrait. He envisioned it completed and hanging in the sanctuary alcove at Saint Michael's Parish. He could see the delicate detail of extended veins, wood grain, nails, and blood, as well as the caressing interplay of lights and shadow that gave shape and substance to his composition.

His mind returned to the packaged diamond ring still in his possession. From this his thoughts turned to the large gold ring with the encased anchor that fit snugly in the inside breast pocket of his jacket. It was the ring that symbolized faith and was his graduation gift from the director of the Chicago School of Art. As if by instinct, Grant withdrew the large ring and looked at it.

At that very moment, the taxi crested a hill, bringing into view a tavern sign to their left. The tavern's neon sign spelled the name THE ANCHOR. Fastened to the bottom of the sign hung a huge iron anchor with flashing blue lights continuously tracing its shape.

Grant's eyes were riveted to the sign as he clutched the large ring. He instructed the cabby to pull over. The area looked ominous and he still was unarmed, but he was curious about the coincidence and a nightcap might help to lift his spirits.

The cabby pulled into the near-empty parking area behind the tavern and Grant paid him an additional ten minutes of waiting time.

"But only ten minutes, then I'm gone. This ain't a friendly neighborhood," the cabby yelled after Grant.

The artist went through the rear entrance door and found a large, dimly lit room with blue-shaded lights throughout. His eyes strained to make the adjustment as only the bar directly ahead was clearly visible. Booths lined either side of the room while small tables were scattered about the floor. The booths blended against gray walls, which were livened by cheap paintings of naked lovers. The interior decor in no way reflected the nautical facade, as Grant had expected to see reproductions of seascapes and replicas of ships hanging about.

He could see only a handful of patrons. Two men sat at the right end of the bar, while four people of undetermined sex occupied the corner booth to the left of the bar. An oversized bartender completed the picture.

The artist had long developed the practice of keeping alert to strange circumstances. He sat at the left end of the bar and continued to survey his surroundings while ordering a beer. High against the wall behind the bar was a television set presently not in use. Almost directly to his front were swinging doors leading to what Grant concluded to be a kitchen.

His attention was drawn to loud conversation from his rear. Two men had just entered the tavern and took the booth next to the foursome. In a glance, Grant noted one of the men to be a shabbily dressed Negro. It was the man's companion who demanded a closer look. Grant recognized the black beard and the black satin shirt. It was John Baxter, his landlord. But how? How could Baxter be here at this moment?

Grant replaced his beer glass and leaned on the bar counter with his elbows, his left hand shielding his face. He had the feeling it would be to his advantage not to be detected. Knowing their eyes would not have yet adjusted to the dark room, he quickly departed the premises.

As his taxi turned onto North Ashland, Grant sat back and closed his eyes. Earlier he thought he had seen Bonnie Bates. That was obviously a mistake. This, however, was no illusion. The man he had just seen was John Baxter. Grant's eyes remained closed until the taxi reached his apartment.

He was surprised to find the entire duplex in darkness. He took the side steps two at a time and entered an empty apartment. Tracy was gone.

There was no sign of a struggle. On the contrary, she had tidied the apartment before leaving. He found no note, nothing...except the subtle aroma of her perfume in his bedroom.

Grant stripped off his jacket, loosened his shirt collar, and poured himself a drink before dropping onto his studio cot. He knew Tracy's luck couldn't hold forever and the thought she may die in the Bonnie Bates tradition made him nauseous. First it was Kay and now Tracy pulled the rug from under him after she had agreed to stay. He turned his head toward the huge covered canvas but the hour was too late.

When his phone rang at seven the following morning, Grant had already showered, dressed, and was having a cup of coffee. *Who the devil?* He thought, crossing to the bedroom. Knowing he often painted into the late hour, perhaps Kay was checking that he hadn't overslept.

"Mr. Peter Grant?" came an impersonal tone of a woman's voice.

"Speaking," Grant responded.

"This is the switchboard operator at Reed & Lambert Publishers. One moment, please."

Grant felt uneasy. He knew when a local operator handled a local call and put you on hold, the result was usually a recorded message. He felt his call was being transferred to Kay's hotel suite.

He was right. He heard a phone ring, followed by a short buzz which triggered a recorder. Kay's voice was clear but unsteady:

"Peter, forgive me for not facing up to you as I had promised, and forgive me for leaving you in this manner. I'm neither as strong nor as courageous as you think.

"I do love you, Peter, this is why I dare not let you think of marriage at this time. Darling, you are on the brink of a glorious creation. I feel this deeply.

"Peter, if you wish to make me happy, give your portrait total commitment. Your energies and talents must be allowed their full reign and marriage would not permit this. Let me hope and dream and pray for both of us. Permit me the luxury of crying now and then, as I find tears have a way of cleansing and lifting my spirits. Faith will be my source of strength and I pray it will be yours.

"Tonight at our lovely dinner, you assured me 'everything will go well.' Peter, I know you will keep your promise because I have faith in you.

"As you hear my voice, I will be somewhere in flight over Texas. With me will be your photograph. It will remain with me and you will remain forever in my heart.

"I love you, Peter Grant. God bless you and please keep the faith."

The telephone buzzer sounded, ending the message. Sweat had beaded Grant's forehead and his throat felt dry and tight.

Immediately following the buzzer, a series of short beeps alerted the artist to the opportunity for replay and a chance to tape the message. This he did with the use of a televox. Even though he made the recording and listened to the message a second time, the realization of its meaning was only beginning to take hold. He played the two-minute farewell message over and over. In the end, he had memorized the words but it was her final words of "*love*" and "*faith*" that had hit him the hardest.

These were words he had difficulty understanding. How could she leave in this manner, yet ask him to give his assignment total commitment? Leaving as she did would trigger a response from him she prayed would not happen. It would kill his drive, his inspiration, or even his instinct to paint.

Grant tried to understand Kay's reasoning. She implied an engagement at this time would infringe upon his portrait, that her presence would stymie his talents and energies. On the contrary, the artist felt her presence would give him support, stability, and peace of mind. He concluded his new assignment may be part of her thinking, but not the total picture.

Today Grant was a two-time loser. Kay had left without his ring and Tracy walked out without a word. He felt the need to talk with someone, however Press' answering service stated he would be out of town for two days.

Grant had another drink and dropped onto his bed.

It was nightfall when he awoke and rolled to his feet. He made a ham sandwich and turned to the canvas, this time ignoring his smock. He would paint in spite of everything. He would reflect his ugly mood by laying in the foreboding sky. It would contain dark, low clouds that were charged with energy and about to explode. The ominous sky would contrast with the serene and submissive figure of Christ, magnifying His hopelessness and foretelling His doom.

Grant prepared his palette with haste, mixing and dulling his colors and loading several three-inch flat brushes. He would paint broadly, working from dark to light and using little turp and linseed oil. For the session, he would use ultramarine and cerulean blues, veridian, titanium white, and touches of burnt umber and raw sienna.

He worked in what appeared to be a careless manner, yet his brush strokes were firmly controlled by a driving unconscious instinct. After six hours of intense painting and with pain surging in his tired legs, the artist retired to his cot.

Sometime later in the recesses of his mind, Grant heard pounding and clamor at his kitchenette door. The pounding slowly faded and diminished into silence.

Chapter 11
A Model Confesses

As their taxi continued its pilgrimage toward Saint Michael's Parish, Peter Grant, his wife, Tracy, and their son, Wesley, were still thinking about the auto accident that had occurred ten minutes earlier.

"Dad, do you think anyone died in that accident?" Wesley asked, breaking a period of silence.

"We can only hope no one did," Grant replied.

"Help was coming, Wesley, and the paramedics do a good job," his mother cut in quickly.

"They're trained to handle serious accidents," Grant added.

"When I learn to drive, I won't ever speed," Wesley assured them, his remark filling his parents with pride.

Grant checked his watch. "Eleven-fifteen," he said to Tracy. "We should be there in fifteen minutes."

"We'll make it, darling," she said, again resting her head on his shoulder.

Grant knew they would be cutting it close. He closed his eyes and visualized Monsignor Kelly wringing his bony hands with anxiety. The monsignor would be expecting them soon and they would occupy assigned seats in the front row. Grant recalled the sequence of planned events. The proceedings would open with a prayer by Monsignor Kelly, after which he would introduce Grant. The artist would briefly introduce his portrait prior to unveiling it. The Special Mass would follow.

For the aging monsignor, Grant knew the pressure of the historical occasion would be staggering.

Using a toned-down burnt sienna he gave substance to the head of Christ.

Christ's head would hang limply with chin resting on the right clavicle. The face would be somewhat contorted with the inner edges of the brows raised, the forehead furrowed, and subtle drop at the corners of a slightly ajar mouth. The eyes of Christ would be half open and peering in the direction of the thief hanging to His right.

The remainder of Christ's body was also given more substance. From research, Grant had learned how Christ must have tried to relieve His ever-growing agony. With nails holding His wrists against the crossbeam and a nail holding His feet together, Christ had to alternately raise and lower his torso to relieve the pain.

To ease the pain at His feet, Christ would have had to relax His legs and let His nailed wrists support the weight of His body. In this position, His arms would sag. But when the suffering had become intense, He would have pressed down on His nailed feet, raising His torso and bringing temporary relief to His chest and arms.

In this position, Christ's arms would be horizontal and the thigh muscles would be contracted, strained, and ultimately cramped as the pain would traverse the legs, abdomen, and finally the diaphragm, where paralysis would eventually stop His breathing. In this position, with arms horizontal and relatively relaxed, Christ would be more able to point His finger as He spoke to the thief. For his portrait, Grant would capture Christ in this position.

As he gave substance to Christ's body, Grant was mindful of other evidence of life. Blood would be trickling from the temples, caused by the thorned crown, and from the feet and both wrists where nails had been driven. Also, veins would be distended and the wound at Christ's rib carriage would be absent. It was *after* Christ had died that a make sure guard threw a lance, piercing Christ's right thoracic area.

The four weeks of painting had passed quickly and for the first time in seemingly ages, Grant's painting gave him a sense of accomplishment. It was in this refreshing frame of mind, on July eleven, that he responded to the door buzzer and greeted Tracy Duvall.

"Hello, Peter," she said uneasily, but with more composure than when she had visited him a month earlier.

Despite the nature of her earlier departure, Grant was pleased to see her. She was safe, thank God. He held her at arm's length, viewing her fitted blue dress and blond hair that hugged her head with a bow at the nape, then fell loosely down her back.

"No luggage?" he asked quizzically.

She smiled. "At a motel around the corner. I couldn't be sure."

"We'll correct that," he said, putting an arm around her waist and leading her into the studio.

She stopped and faced him. "Peter , I'm sorry for running out on you."

"Forget it," he said with an easy smile as they continued. "You're back. That's all that matters."

They sat on the sofa facing the cold fireplace.

"Visit your parents?" Grant asked.

"Oh yes. Aside from dad's arthritis, they are fine. And you, Peter?" she asked, gesturing toward the huge covered canvas.

"Good. In fact, lately I've been doing my best painting since I did *the Maiden* three years ago.

"Wonderful! And Kay?"

"I'm not sure."

Before Tracy could respond, the artist changed the subject. "Look Tracy," he said, glancing at his watch. "It's almost four. Let's freshen up and visit Peppi's.

Tracy was reintroduced to the restaurant's quaint Florentine tapestries and delectable food. Over braised meatballs, Grant learned that she had flown to Minneapolis and, for a week, visited her former New York roommate, Vickey Valentine. The remainder of the month was spent with her parents in Reading.

"Kay rejected my marriage proposal last month," Grant said, after a moment of silence.

"Peter, I'm sorry. It must have been dreadful for you."

"I'll survive," he said confidently. He would take each day one at a time. Already he was wondering what the evening would hold.

A month ago, she had begged him to make love to her and he had refused. Tonight a different scenario may unfold. Had Kay accepted his ring the situation would be different.

Later she would give a more detailed accounting of her visits during the past month, after which they caught the six o'clock TV daily report on the civil revolt.

Grant was especially concerned about the news highlight. Two outspoken religious leaders had been abducted in St. Louis, the second such episode of hostage taking within the week. The first involved the disappearance of a high ecclesiastical dignitary and his wife in New York City. The Devil's Corps has claimed responsibility for both abductions but no demands have been made.

That evening, Tracy and Grant slipped into lounging clothes and decided to relax on the studio sofa. The artist was wearing maroon pajamas under a bed jacket, while his former model was dressed in a belted satin robe over a black negligee. Grant offered to mix her a drink but she politely refused.

Tracy looked inviting and Grant would have sat closer to her, except he still had the TV news report on his mind. The abductions recalled the mysterious phone call he had received over a month ago. Even though he doubted it would reoccur, he was glad he had purchased the gun and he would wear it beginning tomorrow.

Tracy leaned toward him and rested her head against his shoulder. Her tapered hands were clasped together on her lap and her body was turned slightly toward him. He watched her abdomen rise and fall to the sound of her heavy breathing.

Grant touched her flaxen hair and gently kneaded her ear lobe. After several minutes, he gently massaged her shoulder. However when his hand slid under the negligee covering her breast, Tracy stirred uneasily.

Withdrawing gracefully, he mixed himself a drink.

"I'm sorry," she said tearfully.

"It's okay, Tracy. Something's on your mind. Care to talk about it?"

"Peter, I could use that drink now."

"One Manhattan coming up."

Tracy's eyes were troubled.

She rested her head back onto a pillow and looked away. "Yes," she said finally, "something has been on my mind for some time." She sipped her drink. "Peter, if I've been distant tonight, it's because I have a problem and I can't handle it alone." She signed deeply, still avoiding his eyes. 'Peter, I came back today because there's something I must tell you. I must confess something to you."

Noting the gravity of her words and demeanor, Grant moved to comfort her, but she stood and stepped to the fireplace. After a moment, she placed her drink on the mantel and turned his way. Her face was lined with pain. "Peter...I have a child! A son!"

She began to sob and Grant assisted her return to the sofa.

"Tracy, lots of women have children. Babies are born every minute of every day."

"But his name is Wesley and he's five years old," she said, as though her son's name and age held some kind of significance.

"I don't understand. Why wouldn't you have told me this sooner?"

"I couldn't. I was afraid to tell you."

Grant offered her several tissues and she dabbed her eyes.

"Is your child ill?" he asked.

"Oh no! He's handsome and bright and good and everything a mother would want her child to be. But, Peter...he's also yours!"

A strange silence filled the air as her eyes glistened with tears. "Peter, I said my child is our son...yours and mine! You're his father!"

Again, there was silence.

"Tracy, did you say *my* son?" he asked, disbelievingly.

"Yes. Yours and mine."

Grant got to his feet and Tracy followed his lead. He placed his hands on her shoulders. "Now, wait one little minute, Tracy," he said, shaking his head.

"Peter, let me explain," she pleaded between sobs.

"Sure. I'll listen," he said as they sat again.

Tracy hesitated in an effort to reflect upon a speech she had memorized years ago. "Okay," she began, clearing her throat. "When I applied to be your model, you may recall my resume stated I had graduated from the Chicago Modeling School. Also, I was immediately employed by Avalon Advertising Agency in Chicago.

"But...what you didn't know, Peter," she continued, while dabbing her eyes again, "while living in Chicago, I had become familiar with you. I mean...I followed your artistic accomplishments while you were an art student. I admired you from afar.

"After your graduation from art school, I followed your progress at Glick through newspapers, periodicals, and even seminars. Your work enthralled me and I wanted to model for you."

"Unbelievable!" Grant said.

"But true, Peter," she went on while trying to restrain her tears. "When you moved to New York City, I quit my job and followed you."

"When you graduated at the Chicago School of Art, I was there. I wanted to meet you, so I went to the lobby and waited after the program had ended.

"You and a gentleman friend came through the door and stopped within earshot of me. I heard your friend suggest having a drink to celebrate and I heard the name—Terry's Tavern."

Grant was no longer looking at Tracy. He was sitting back on the sofa with his eyes on the ceiling overhead, but not seeing it. He could hear words that were gradually making sense as they penetrated his foggy memory of six years ago.

"I had difficulty finding the tavern," Tracy went on, "and I had to muster courage to sit next to you at the bar. You may recall, I was a brunette that evening. I was wearing a wig."

"My Lord," he murmured. "So, that was you," he said, turning her way.

"Yes," she said with a nod. "Later we shared the night at a hotel. Remember?"

"Tracy, there's no need to go on. We shared a motel one night six years ago and our son was the result." He shook his head slowly. "I can't believe I'm a father," Grant said, barely above a whisper.

Tracy placed her hand on his. "Peter, I was only twenty-one and very naive. Also, I want you to know it was my very first sexual encounter and also my last."

"I believe you, Tracy."

"I'm glad you believe me, Peter," she said, smiling faintly while wiping tears from her cheeks with her hand.

"Our son's name?" he asked.

"Wesley. I gave him your middle name. It's Wesley Peter and he has all your features."

"And you've been living this secret for six years," Grant mused.

"I was afraid to tell you, Peter. I thought doing so would drive you away. Yet the longer I delayed, the more guilt I felt. I wanted to be close to you but, as it turned out, being closer and knowing you loved Kay made matters worse.

"When I visited you last month, I thought making love with you would help me confess. I only knew I had to tell you before you married Kay."

Grant reinforced his drink and retrieved Tracy's drink from the fireplace mantel. "May I freshen yours?" he asked.

"Please do."

He returned to the sofa and reflected briefly as he watched the cubes swirl in his drink. "Tracy, I'm glad you told me," he said finally, "and I realize how difficult it was for you. Most of all, I'm glad you didn't abort. If you had, I doubt I could forgive you."

He looked at her. "Yes, I'm very glad you had our baby. Also, I'm sorry I wasn't sober on that special occasion, but knowing a son resulted from it is helpful and makes our relationship more binding."

"Peter, I'm so glad you feel that way. Also, I want you to know I would never have aborted our child. Never!"

Grant took Tracy into his arms and kissed her. "I'm sure you've kissed our son many times for me," he said.

"Many times, Peter."

"And what have you told our son about his father?"

"The truth," she said, without hesitation. "Only yesterday I told him and this gave me the courage to tell you. Wesley has been living with my parents all these years and I couldn't let you visit my parents without knowing about our son."

"Mother and Dad adore him and they respect his father. However, Wesley wants to see you and I promised him I would tell you about him."

"He'll see and get his father, Tracy. That's a promise."

The telephone rang.

Grant answered it and found an anxious Press Thomas at the other end.

"Pete, I've got bad news! I must see you tonight!"

"Is it about the Devil's Corps?" Grant asked.

"No. It's worse."

Chapter 12
A Photographer's Farewell

Thirty minutes later, Press was at Grant's apartment door. Together with Tracy, they took chairs at the kitchenette table.

Preston Thomas looked at his friend with strained eyes and his face was sweaty. "I'll come to the point," he said, leaning forward on both elbows. "Peter, I've got the worst kind of news about someone most dear to you."

"That would be Kay," Grant said without hesitation.

Press nodded.

Grant hunched forward. "An accident?"

Tracy's anxious eyes followed theirs in turn.

Press took a deep breath as his eyes measured his friend in a gentle way. "No accident, Pete. Kay is very ill. She has a terminal disease. She was stricken nine months ago by the T-cell leukemia virus."

Grant's eyes closed momentarily, then he slowly got to his feet and turned away.

Tracy quickly moved to his side. "Oh Peter. I'm...I'm so sorry...so very sorry," she stammered and started to sob.

The three of them came together as one, arm in arm.

"Press, are you sure? I mean...there's no mistake?" Grant asked.

"No mistake, Pete. Kay has the best physicians using the best drugs and procedures, but to no avail. It's a damn shame."

They returned to their chairs.

"But...her assignments?" Grant asked with a dry throat.

"Pete, Kay never made the second trip to Brazil. Nor did she go to Nicaragua. She was at Mercy Clinic in Minneapolis."

"My Lord," uttered Grant, sitting back and rolling his eyes toward the ceiling."

"Kay swore me to secrecy," Press continued. "She didn't want you to know."

The artist touched the corner of his eye with a finger, catching a tear. "Do you know Kay is only twenty-six?" he asked, not expecting an answer. "So talented...so beautiful...so full of life...and only twenty-six." He gazed blankly at the table top as his mind whirled through their last moments together.

Tracy continued to sob with a tissue at her eyes, while Press studied his friend closely.

"I never suspected," Grant continued. "Not for a moment. Press, how many months did you say...when Kay was stricken?"

"Nine months ago, Pete."

"Hmm...that would be last October, shortly after I decided to free-lance."

Grant suddenly looked up. "Press, you said Kay swore you to secrecy, yet you're telling me now. How much time does she have?" he asked, his eyes reflecting pain.

Press wet his lips. "I just returned from the clinic where Kay has been comatose for three weeks. Today, she rallied briefly and asked for you, Pete. Then she slipped away again. The end could come any day...any hour."

Grant took his friend's hand and squeezed it hard. "Would you make flight reservations for me?"

"I already have," said Preston Thomas, removing a packet from his coat pocket and giving it to Grant. "American Airlines, flight four-forty. Departs in one hour. It's all there," he confirmed, glancing at his watch.

"We'll see you off," said Tracy, still dabbing her tears.

After farewells at the terminal, Grant stepped to the gate and turned to them. "Press, I just discovered I'm a father. I have a son, Tracy will give you the details. Thanks to both of you for everything," he said with a wave, and departed.

It was shortly after 1:00 A.M. when Grant entered the lobby at Mercy Clinic. He was given permission for a brief visit and directions to the south wing intensive care unit. Stepping from the elevator at the sixth floor, he was met by Doctor Brookes, director of the wing.

The doctor, a thin man, spectacled, and in his late sixties, extended a hand. "Mr. Grant...sorry to meet you on such a solemn occasion. I've followed Miss Allyson's case closely and, through Mr. Thomas, I've been made aware of your relationship with her." The doctor talked quickly, as if to be conserving time. "Yesterday afternoon she spoke your name but she has since relapsed. At this stage, her chances of regaining consciousness are remote. Please enter." He gestured toward a room to Grant's immediate front. "By the way, Mr. Grant," the doctor said in afterthought, "Miss Allyson spoke another word in addition to your name. She said the word: ring."

Grant felt a numbness.

"At the time, the nurse was bathing her," the doctor continued. "When Miss Allyson's hand was touched, she moved it and spoke. Does the word hold any significance?"

"Yes, it does," Grant said.

Peter Grant opened the door and gently closed it behind him. Kay's bed was to his left. She was lying straight and still under a white sheet which was folded neatly at her waist. Her head was slightly raised and resting on a firm pillow. She was wearing a gray clinic gown with elbow length sleeves. Her arms were at her sides, with an IV tube extending from her left wrist, coiling upward to a plastic bag suspended from a hooked rod. An oxygen tube protruded from her nose and various colored wires connected her body to a machine which recorded her vital signs onto a nearby monitor. Grant's eyes shifted to a low stand at her bedside. On it was a photograph of himself which Kay had snapped shortly after they had met two years earlier.

His eyes turned to her placid face. *How is it possible*, he thought, *that she can look so beautiful, yet be so terribly ill?* Without taking his eyes from her, he pulled a chair to her bedside, and sat. Now he was beginning to understand how she had coped with her predicament without arousing his suspicions. Now he realized how she had steered their conversations toward issues that had deep, personal meaning to her—his work, faith, life, and death. She had also resorted to fun, gaiety, and live-for-the moment chatter.

Finally she had done a good deal of reminiscing. Along with emotional anguish, she must have endured great physical pain throughout the pretense, he concluded.

He thought it ironic that man can be so blind to what's in front of him, only to recognize it after it has passed. It is sad that man will see the true worth in another only after that person is no longer available to be seen. It is even more tragic when man is reluctant to perform those menial acts of kindness and appreciation to those who deserve them but are no longer present. *I loved Kay for years, yet I only told her so when I proposed marriage.*

Grant failed to hear the gentle tap at the door as Doctor Brookes quietly entered to inform the artist he had unrestricted visitation privileges. The remainder of that night until sunrise of the following morning, Grant maintained a vigil at Key's bedside.

Noting the daylight at the window, he stepped to it and pulled the drapery slightly to one side. It was a bright morning, this thirteenth day of July. The sunlight reflected upon his face, highlighting a stubble of beard and strained lines. He turned and viewed the room in panorama. It was small with a working TV monitor in one corner, recording all vital activity onto a set in the nurses' station down the corridor. The room temperature was mild, but Grant had long since removed his jacket and loosened his collar.

He returned to Kay's side. Leaning over her, he placed his hand on hers, finding it limp and cold. He watched her breasts slowly rise and fall while his fingers searched for a weak pulse at her wrist. Her auburn hair hugged her head in a myriad of curls with the usual stubborn one resting at the corner of her forehead. He watched her eyes feeling they would open at any moment and recognize him. He watched her lips, hoping they would part and speak his name. He leaned over and kissed her. "Kay, I love you," he whispered. "I love you so much."

He squeezed her hand ever so lightly, after which he removed the engagement ring from his pocket, kissed it, and slipped it onto her finger. As he stepped back to view the ring in its total perspective, the unexpected happened.

The fingers of Kay's left hand began to move. Almost simultaneously her arms slowly lifted and her eyes opened partially. Her head rolled in his direction. Her arms extended sideways and Grant momentarily thought she was reaching toward him and might possibly speak. However just as quickly, her arms dropped, her head slumped, and she was still.

The screen which had been monitoring her vital signs was blank and a beeper was sounding. Although Grant's intellect and instincts rebelled against it, he knew Kay had expired.

He was vaguely aware that a doctor and nurse had entered the room and had begun their final routine examination. After finding no heartbeat or blood pressure, the doctor closed her eyes with his tumbtips, removed the oxygen tube from her nose, and covered her head with the bed sheet. They extended brief words of condolence to Grant before they departed. There was no attempt to apply emergency life support measures in compliance with Kay's living will.

For sometime the artist was transfixed and without conscious thought. The vision of a lifeless Kay, the weight of hopelessness and futility pressing on his heart, the terrifying stillness and silence of the room—all of this was overpowering. It wasn't until a faint ambulance siren was heard, growing louder as it approached the clinic, that he began to recover.

However his recovery was brief. As he carefully lowered the bed sheet, exposing Kay's face and arms, Grant reeled backward.

Kay's arms were extended horizontally on the bed. The fingers of her left hand were clutched while those of her right hand were relaxed. The exception was the index finger which was slightly extended and pointing toward his photograph on the nearby stand. Her head was lowered with the chin resting near her right clavicle. Her eyes were partially open. In her dying moment, Kay had assumed the pose of Christ on the artist's canvas.

Grant could only gaze upon her lifeless form, his weary mind being unable to comprehend or analyze the parallels her pose presented. Finally he leaned over her. With thumb and forefinger he carefully eased the stubborn curl from her forehead and kissed her goodbye.

Chapter 13
In Hector's Way

As Kay's executor, Preston Thomas had handled her funeral arrangements and legal matters. This included her internment near her parents at Doveland Gardens in Valencia, California, and the stipulation Peter Grant was to receive her camera equipment and all her photographic works.

Kay's cancer had been a type which attacks the spine and ultimately spreads to the brain, where it paralyzes the vital processes. Fortunately the disease had hit her upper thoracic region, causing her survival period of pain and deterioration to be lessened. Still, she had to be sedated with periodic injections of morphine.

The first month following Kay's death, Grant did nothing but grieve. Although the crucifixion deadline was fast approaching, he wasn't ready to paint. Nor was he ready to talk about Kay's death scene. Yet he knew positive steps had to be taken if he was to maintain control.

He had to stay physically and mentally active. He had to learn to accept his grief and talk about it. He had to care for himself, especially as it pertained to diet and exercise. He knew that faith in God was a powerful aid in coping with bereavement and he considered affiliating himself with a local church in spite of a recent successful church bombing within the county.

In the midst of it all, Kay's death scene continued to haunt him, especially at night. Also, his heart ached for a chance to meet and hug his son. He felt this would ease the grief process as much as anything. To this end, he formed a plan for the immediate future. He needed to get away from Chicago and be alone for a brief period. On November tenth, he would revisit Kay's grave site in California, while Tracy would visit her family in

Reading. After a week or two, he would join them and finally meet his son and Tracy's parents.

After visiting Kay's grave, Grant took a bus to Sequoia National Park where he breathed fresh air and strolled among the majestic redwoods. The experience was uplifting but Kay's death image still lurked in his thoughts. Most of all, he couldn't forget Kay's eyes when he uncovered her head. They were slightly open and he was sure the doctor closed them during his final examination. Upon his return, he would share the death scene with others in the hope it would ease his mind.

Grant traveled to Reading a week later and was accepted by Tracy's parents unconditionally. Her parents were of the Christian fundamentalist faith and deeply rooted in forgiveness. Meeting Wesley was a tearful experience for all and it drew the artist even more closely to Tracy.

Grant found his son to be a typical five-year-old, shy at first but quickly warming to his father's affectionate nature. Tracy had prepared the boy well to meet a father he had never seen and it was also obvious to Grant his son had his facial features.

That evening Press Thomas telephoned. An urgent security development had occurred and Press suggested that his friend return to Chicago immediately. Tracy and Wesley could remain with her parents until Grant notified them.

Δ Δ Δ

"Sorry we rushed you back," Press began over a cup of coffee. It was the following morning and they were sitting in Press's private study. "Pete, yesterday Security intercepted a rebel message and broke its code."

Press sipped his coffee and slowed his pace. "The message began with a listing of dates for upcoming church bombings but with no locations. It was the latter part of the message that was startling and prompted my call."

Grant was listening closely but he was also studying Press's eyes. They were expressive and revealing eyes. Mostly they reflected concern for his friend, and recently Grant was seeing that expression more and more.

"Pete, the message made reference to you and your portrait. In short they're on to you!"

Grant sat back with a deep sigh. "I can't believe what I'm doing is that important. It's only a portrait."

"The rebels think it's important," Press said. "Fortunately, they don't know your whereabouts. Security has reason to believe they are combing New York City."

The artist folded his hands behind his head and contemplated. "The Devil's Corps will trace either me or Tracy back here. It's only a matter of time. My guess is the leak about my painting came from Ambrose Thorne's office. Bonnie Bates could have disclosed it with ease."

Press withdrew a note from his pocket. "The message contained another point of interest," he continued. "The Devil's Corps has assigned one of their cutthroat leaders to you. His name is Hector and he referred to your painting as '*a sneaky but futile attempt to perpetuate the Christian folly.*'"

Grant's heavy brows lifted as he bit at his lower lip. "So what's next, my friend?" he asked.

Press sipped his coffee and leaned forward. "Pete, you have a son. For his safety as well as your own, Security is recommending you have a change of identity.

Grant's eyes rolled toward the ceiling. "So it has come to that. You mean looks, name, occupation, the works?"

Press nodded. "But only until you finish the portrait."

"How would I explain this to my landlord?" Grant asked.

Press reached for the coffee pot and warmed their drinks. "I've been assured by Doctor Gillespie that Mr. Baxter will pose no problem. All we need is your permission."

"I don't know, Press. It all seems so complicated and unnecessary," Grant said.

"They're closing in on you, Pete, and you have a great deal at stake. If I get your okay before noon today, I'll make a phone call and the ball will start rolling. We have an hour."

"My identity change is Doctor Gillespie's idea?"

"No. The doctor has put Special Agent Roger Davis on your case. His assignment is to protect you, your family, and your portrait. It was Agent Davis' idea with Doctor Gillespie's approval," Press said.

"When would the change be made?"

"One week from today. November twenty-fifth," Press said.

"So, what's the plan?" the artist asked.

Press leaned forward and cleared his throat. "There will be a fire in Queens the day following your identity change. A broken-down structure in a remote area will be targeted and reported in the newspaper as an art studio. A lone fire victim will be burned beyond recognition, except for identification by dental examination. Of course the victim will be you, Pete."

"So, now I'm dead."

"No. Peter Grant is dead," corrected Press. "You will have been Allan Gray for twenty hours. Peter Grant's obituary will be in the *Daily News* the following day," Press continued. "A mock service and burial has been scheduled two days later, November twenty-eighth. That's only ten days from today. You can see how quickly plans may materialize."

Grant shook his head. "Unbelievable! Security has gone great lengths on my behalf and I appreciate it."

"Your residence won't change," continued Press, "and you appearance will only be slightly altered. You'll look ten years older and you'll be employed by the Rainbow Realty Agency as an agent who specializes in lake-front properties. Also, you'll be a member of the Starving Artist Society. As such, you can continue your painting."

"Press, I've heard enough. Make the phone call."

That evening Grant phoned Tracy over a safe line and gave her the latest developments. As he expected, she offered him wholehearted support and her blessings.

The following week—November 25—Grant and Press met Special Agent Davis at the Rainbow Realty Agency on Chicago's west side. Earlier in the day Grant had been instructed to bring a change of clothing in a suitcase. Agent Davis was a tall man in his forties, dressed for business and carrying a suitcase of his own. The three men came together in a small basement room with hardly more than a table and three chairs.

Agent Davis turned to Press. "Mr. Thomas, you'll find coffee on the corner tray and restrooms across the hall." He handed Press a notebook. Its cover contained in large print the name "Allan Gray." "Most of this was compiled well before the Queens fire," he said, referring to the notebook. "It should be interesting reading. Mr. Grant and I will be—"

A knock at the door interrupted the agent.

"Agent Davis, a phone call for you in the red room," came a voice through the partially opened door.

The agent excused himself and returned ten minutes later with a blank facial expression. "Gentlemen, the planned identity change has been aborted," he said.

It was a big disappointment.

That evening Press invited Grant to his house for dinner, after which they had a lengthy discussion to clear the air.

Later that evening Grant phoned Tracy from his apartment.

"But why did they abort?" she asked.

"The rebels got wind of it. That's all I know. I swear they have spies in the woodwork.

"Peter, I'm very worried about you!"

"Tracy, I also have some good news but not over the phone. It must wait until I see you."

"When will that be, Peter?"

"When? Let me put it this way. I've done some serious thinking since today's misfire and it adds up to one thing. I'll be with you tomorrow."

"Wonderful! Peter, we'll be happy to see you!"

The following morning Press drove Grant to O'Hare and saw him off.

During the flight, Grant had time to reflect long and hard about many things—his parents, his career, his friend Press, Kay's untimely death, Tracy and Wes, his own predicament. Press had reminded him the Devil's Corps was closing in on him and that he had much at stake.

During their dinner conversation the previous evening, Press had told him about an earlier dialogue he had with Doctor Gillespie. The doctor had told Peter his friend needed a strong positive experience to counter Kay's death.

When told about this, Grant's first thought was to marry Tracy. When he had expressed the idea to Press, his friend not only favored the idea but encouraged it. Actually, Grant had been thinking about it from the moment he learned Tracy had given birth to their child.

The artist realized it had been only four months since Kay had died, but his circumstances were unusual and time was pressing. If it is true the rebels have his number and were only marking time, then he had some unfinished business to do. He had to continue painting and he had to get his house in order. His son had been without his father much too long and needed him. Most of all, Tracy, Wes, and he needed to be a family.

While he would always love the memory of Kay, Tracy Duvall was a woman he admired and respected. She could never replace Kay, but she was the mother of his son and, in time, he could learn to love her deeply.

During their dinner conversation, Press had phoned Special Agent Roger Davis regarding Grant's consideration of marriage. Their conversation was brief.

Later, after consultation with superiors, Agent Davis phoned Press with Security's blessings. It was recommended they reside at Grant's present address, although the apartment would be under constant surveillance, and Wesley would be immediately enrolled in a private school where supervision would be close.

Grant knew the final decision to marry must come from Tracy because the road ahead could be bumpy or worse. He wondered if he was asking too much of her. There could be no guarantee of safety or happiness or even peace of mind. Grant could only be sure his wife and son would be financially secure.

Upon Grant's arrival in Reading, he took Tracy aside at his first opportunity and made his proposal.

Tracy was stunned. Even before she could wipe away happy tears, the telephone rang.

It was Doctor Gillespie and she asked to speak to Tracy.

Despite the doctor's positive reasons for the marriage, she felt obligated to remind Tracy of the dangers that may lie ahead. Not only did she ask Tracy to consider Grant's external problems but those that may arise from within as well. The doctor also felt obligated to stop short of revealing the artist's most serious problem.

One week later, on December third, in the presence of her parents and Wesley, Peter Grant and Tracy Duvall were married in a private ceremony at Press's house.

They were a family at last.

Chapter 14
Death Image

The snow finally stopped and the taxi driver turned off the windshield wipers. It was eleven-twenty and Grant estimated they were within a half-mile of Saint Michael's Parish. The Special Midnight Mass would climax the beginning of the year 2028 and the unveiling of his portrait would highlight the services.

Thank God the cat and mouse game is almost over, thought Grant. The last two years had been a long pull. There had been disappointments, tears, pain, even death.

Grant's thoughts turned to Kay and the emptiness he felt, knowing how much she would have enjoyed the unveiling. He was reminded of her final words in her recorded message to him: "*God bless you and please keep the faith.*" He marveled that she was able to think about the welfare of another, knowing her own life was soon to end.

He placed his hand into his inside jacket pocket and touched the gold ring that symbolized faith. On more than one occasion, the ring had given him strength.

The taxi approached a hill and began its slow climb. As it reached its crest, Grant felt a sudden pain in his chest, causing him to straighten and take a deep breath.

"Peter, are you all right?" Tracy asked anxiously.

Grant smiled at her and sat back again. "Just nerves and excitement," he assured her, breathing more evenly as the pain subsided.

Impressed by the steepness of the downgrade, Wesley's eyes were at the window and he missed the incident.

The artist's heart condition was common and not considered serious. A leaky mitral value was detected during his high school swimming competition and it was controlled by the drug Inderal. On rare occasions, during physical exertion, he would feel a slight squeezing sensation of the heart, but he had never experienced pain until tonight.

Breathing slowly and deeply, he began to relax and his thoughts turned to Saint Michael's Parish and his covered portrait presently hanging in the sanctuary alcove.

With a deadline of April 18, the unveiling was originally scheduled for June 2 to commemorate the parish's sesquicentennial. However, that date had been changed to accommodate certain features of the portrait which were unexpected and strange. After a careful study of the portrait by a committee, it was decided the unveiling would occur at a Special Midnight Mass the last day of this year, 2027. That hour was only minutes away.

Two obstacles in particular had plagued Grant while painting his portrait. The first of these came to light one week after his marriage to Tracy.

They had decided to wait and honeymoon in Hawaii during the Christmas break. This would allow Wesley to accompany them and not miss school. It would also permit Grant to resume his painting with no further delay. He hadn't touched a brush since Kay's death in mid-July and the portrait deadline was a mere sixteen months away.

Kay's death image still caused him to suffer moments of apprehension and doubt. He wondered if he would be able to stand before the portrait with brush in hand and not flinch. As he painted, he wondered if he would picture Kay in his mind instead of Christ. He decided not to share the unpleasant death image experience if it didn't impede his ability to paint.

He also decided to paint one of the most difficult features first—the right hand of Christ. It would be a limp, expressive hand with the index finger pointed toward the thief. The gesture would be a signal of recognition which would ultimately lead to the thief's repentance and his acceptance into God's kingdom.

Yet when Grant started to paint, it quickly became apparent something was amiss. Each time he concentrated on the outline of Christ's hand, it would change before his eyes and become Kay's hand as he remembered it at her deathbed. One week later, he was still attempting to paint the hand.

Knowing his problem was psychological, the artist had attempted to fight through it, yet the more intensely he painted, the more pronounced Kay's image had become.

He kept the struggle within, but Tracy sensed he was having difficulty. Still she said nothing, knowing he would eventually confide in her. Not wanting to upset her, Grant decided to share the death image experience with Press and go from there.

On December 17, after a week of futile painting, Grant met Press at Glick's coffee shop. It was the noon rush hour but they occupied Press' private booth, which had a degree of seclusion tucked away in one corner of the triangular room.

A waitress approached and they ordered a light lunch.

"Pete, what's the painting problem?" Press asked.

"Peter, darling!" interjected a strange voice.

They stood and looked into inquisitive eyes. The woman was fortyish, blonde, and trimly dressed in a gray business suit.

"Peter Grant?" she questioned, looking at the artist. "You *are* Peter Grant?"

Grant nodded. "I'm sorry but I don't seem—"

"Oh Phoo! You don't remember me," she interrupted with a pout. "Peter, darling, I'm Jennifer! You know, the birthmark?" she persisted.

Grant began to appreciate the humor in the scene and he wanted to grin but he resisted. With a shrug of his shoulders he turned to his friend. "Press, do you know a Jennifer with a birthmark?" he asked.

"Years ago, I knew a Jennifer who had a missing front tooth," Press said with a straight face.

"Peter, I'm Jennifer Springer!" the woman continued impatiently. "Senior prom? Euclid High School?"

Grant's brows suddenly lifted and he dropped back into his seat with a hearty laugh, while Press broke into a broad grin.

The woman, not to be outdone, joined him in laughter as she nudged him over with an elbow and joined him in the booth.

"Doctor, you had me going for awhile," Grant confessed after catching his breath.

"Blame Preston," Doctor Gillespie said with a smile. "When Preston phoned and asked that I join your meeting, I decided to come in disguise. It's a new one and it was a chance to test it."

"Hmmm...a conspiracy. Anyway, Doctor, you were great," Grant admitted.

Their waitress arrived with their lunches while Doctor Gillespie had only coffee.

"Apparently not great enough. How did you know?" she asked.

"Your eyes," the artist responded without hesitation. "By the time you got to the prom and high school, your eyes told me who you were."

"Preston, our friend has good powers of observation. He would make a good undercover agent. Also, Mr. Grant," she continued, turning to the artist, "I like your humor. Humor makes a man more approachable but, more importantly, it's very therapeutic."

Doctor Gillespie sipped her coffee. "Do you find marriage to your liking?" she asked Grant.

"Indeed. Of course, our son is a big plus."

"Good. I had a prior conversation with your wife-to-be. Perhaps she told you?"

"Yes. Of course Tracy appreciated your concern. We both do."

Doctor Gillespie glanced at her watch. "Preston tells me you're experiencing painting difficulties that relate to Kay's death? Perhaps I can help."

"Yes," Grant said tersely.

The doctor moved to Press' side of the booth to better observe the artist.

In response to their questioning eyes, Grant gave an emotionally detailed account of the crucified Christ-like pose Kay had assumed the moment she died. "Simply put, with each painting effort I make, my mind's eye sees Kay on the cross instead of Christ," he concluded.

Doctor Gillespie sipped her coffee. "Two questions come to mind," she said, touching her lips with a napkin. "What, if anything, does Kay's death pose signify? Why is there an image transfer? If these are your prime concerns, Mr. Grant, we'll use these as a starting point."

Grant nodded.

"To arrive at a plausible answer," she continued, "let's put the situation into perspective."

Both men were ignoring their lunches.

"From what you've told us, I would weigh these important factors. First and foremost, Mr. Grant, you were the lone witness to the death of a loved one. You were almost totally unprepared, having only hours to come to grips with Kay Allyson's predicament. Her death was caused by an insidious disease. Your situation was hopeless. You were powerless to help or even to communicate with her. Finally your trauma could have been compounded by feelings of guilt."

Guilt! The word hit Grant hard, striking a nerve and provoking a response. "I can assure you I'm a likely candidate for the guilt farm," he admitted, as his thoughts retreated six months to his depressing return flight from the New York interview. He remembered his guilt for maneuvering and manipulating others, even at the expense of his loyalty to Kay, to satisfy his painting ego. This to be followed by his encounter with John Baxter and his landlord's prophesy: "...your guilt will devour you."

"...that we all must accept our—" the doctor was saying before she abruptly stopped. "Mr. Grant, are you with me?" she asked.

Grant straightened. "I'm sorry, doctor. My thoughts were drifting."

"That's quite all right. In response to your remark about guilt, I was saying...the feelings of guilt are normal, that we all must accept our fallibility."

She sipped her coffee. "Gentlemen, eat before your lunches get cold."

After their dishes were whisked away, the psychiatrist resumed her leadership role.

"In response to the first question dealing with Kay's death pose," she began, "I think her coma had resurfaced enough to make her conscious of the ring being placed on her finger. I would even suggest the closing of her hand signified her acceptance of your ring, Mr. Grant. Her outstretched arm could have been her way of drawing attention to your photograph, thus indicating her awareness of your presence. In other words, she communicated with you in one last moment of life. As to her pose reflecting the Christ in your portrait? In my opinion, it was purely coincidental."

"Those are beautiful words to hear," Grant said solemnly. "Doctor, your interpretation is what I was hoping for."

"Good. Preston, have you anything to add?"

"Not really. My contribution is primarily one of listening," he said.

"In that case, let's move to the second question dealing with image transfer. As a psychiatrist, I can more fully appreciate and understand this strange behavior."

"Again, those are welcome words to hear," said Grant.

She smiled faintly. "As an artist, you have well-trained powers of observation. This you proved earlier with my little ploy. Also, as an artist, your degree of sensitivity is highly developed. Unfortunately these two qualities tend to intensify an emotionally charged death scene and this could create a deep-seated image of the descendent in your mind. Kay's death image most likely will remain with you for some time only to eventually fade away. The fact that her image is similar to the Christ in your portrait, it logically follows it will be reinforced each time you paint, slowing the fading process in your mind."

Grant sat back and ran a hand through his hair. "I hope the fading process won't be too slow. I have only sixteen months before the deadline," he said.

The doctor looked pensive. "I would say after two months or three at the outside, the death image won't be a factor as you paint."

"You'll fight through it, Pete," Press assured him.

Doctor Gillespie glanced at her watch. "By the way, Mr. Grant, Christmas is a week from tomorrow and the Devil's Corps may double their efforts for the occasion. Have you any plans?" she asked in a lowered voice.

Grant softened his voice also. "Yes. Wesley's sixth birthday is this Monday, the twenty-second, and we'll have the traditional party for him at home. The following day, Tracy, Wes, and I will fly to Hawaii for our delayed honeymoon. We'll return December twenty-eighth."

"Because the corps may have special plans for Christmas Day, knowing your whereabouts will help Special Agent 340," she explained. "Perhaps Preston has told you, Mr. Grant, I've taken the liberty to assign Special Agent 340 as your bodyguard. He already has your apartment under twenty-four-hour surveillance and he'll report any irregularities to me."

"Doctor Gillespie, Press told me my bodyguard was Special Agent Davis," Grant questioned.

"He is," said the doctor. "Special Agent Davis and Agent 340 are one and the same."

Doctor Gillespie's wrist watch buzzed. "Sorry, gentlemen, but I must run." She stood and turned to Grant. "Mr. Grant, I assume you've received no further mysterious phone calls?"

"None, doctor."

That evening Doctor Gillespie telephoned Preston Thomas.

"Yes, doctor. What's your analysis?" Press asked anxiously.

"Let's call if psychoanalysis."

She paused. "Mr. Grant is articulate and perceptive on the surface, but there are complications in the recesses of his mind."

"A mental illness?"

"One of the worst kind, Preston."

"But...isn't there something that can be done for him?"

"Very little. Preston, his problem goes deeper than the death of Kay Allyson. Many years deeper. If Mr. Grant finishes the portrait at all, it will be a minor miracle. In this regard, if significant progress with his painting isn't made within the next few months, I would suggest you contact Mr. Thorne so that he may arrange for a back-up artist. The truth is, our friend is hanging by a mental thread."

"My God!"

"I'm sorry to be telling you this over the telephone, Preston, but the sooner you know, the better. Meanwhile, keep this to yourself and try to respond to our friend in a normal way."

"But Kay's death scene," Press persisted, "Pete remembered it in such vivid detail."

"That's the point. Unfortunately Mr. Grant saw none of it! It never happened. Kay never moved. I checked with the doctor and nurse involved. Kay's arms were at her sides, her head was to the front. She simply had not moved."

"Then your response at luncheon today was for Pete's benefit?"

"Yes. Preston, let me tell you what actually happened at Kay's death bed.

"You will recall, Mr. Grant is painting a Christ who still possesses life. In a hopeless situation and with a desperate unconscious effort to save Kay's life, Mr. Grant had mentally positioned her body as Christ is positioned on the cross in his painting. He saw her opened eyes because he wanted her to be alive. That's it."

As Preston Thomas replaced the telephone receiver, Grant was lifting his in response to the ring. It was Ambrose Thorne at the other end.

"Just checking in, Mr. Grant. It has been seven months and I assume your progress is significant?"

"The assignment is coming fine," he lied.

"Good. By the way, I was sorry to hear you recently lost a loved one."

"Yes. She was the photographer I had made reference to during my interview."

"It's good to know your personal loss hasn't affected your painting and, if it's any consolation, I guess all of us will eventually be a terminal case."

The artist considered Thorne's philosophical remark to be asinine and not worthy of a response.

"With the deadline on the horizon, I had to be sure your painting is on schedule, you understand."

"I understand, Mr. Thorne. Call me anytime," said Grant.

As Grant replaced the telephone, he was reminded of Doctor Gillespie's earlier question regarding further mysterious telephone calls. He hadn't bugged his telephone as she had suggested and he had no intentions of doing so. The phone call came over six months ago. Only Hector of the Devil's Corps was interested in him and he wouldn't play games over the telephone.

Chapter 15
A Constructive Idea

"Darling, I hope that wasn't more bad news," Tracy said as she entered the studio. She had just showered and was wearing a lilac dressing gown with her blonde hair piled high and held with a bandanna. "But before you tell me, let me give you good news. I purchased our honeymoon tickets today while you were at your meeting with Press," she said, excitedly.

"Good, but I still worry when you venture out," Grant said as he lit the gas burning fireplace and returned to the sofa. He was in his pajamas and robe and he fluffed a pillow for Tracy as she joined him. "The phone call wasn't bad news unless you consider Ambrose Thorne bad news," he finally answered.

Until their marriage, Grant had found little need for the fireplace. Now, however, it would take the December chill from the air but mostly it was for Tracy's comfort and pleasure. After her nightly bath, they would often share the sofa as they watched the flames and listen to tapes of Mozart. Wesley would be asleep on the cot at the far end of the studio.

"What did Mr. Thorne have to say?"

"He inquired about my progress with the assignment. So I lied and told him I was on schedule."

Tracy stirred. "Peter, that's no lie!" she said emphatically. "You're doing beautifully."

He looked into her blue caring eyes and saw only uneasiness. He realized now was the time to tell her his problem. "Tracy, my progress is too slow. I haven't painted for almost six months and I have no idea when I'll paint effectively again," he said soberly.

She straightened and faced him. "Peter, I don't understand. Is something wrong?"

Grant took Tracy in his arms and kissed her. "I'm sorry for having caused you so much worry, Tracy, but everything will end well. My ability to paint, the assignment, the deadline—everything will be fine."

Grant gave Tracy a shallow account of Kay's death scene but he elaborated on the image transfer and how it has affected his ability to paint.

"I could have told you sooner," he went on, "but I wanted time to work through it, only to discover I couldn't. At my meeting with Press today, we were joined by Doctor Gillespie. My painting problem is psychological, so I told them about it, thinking the doctor might be helpful."

"Was she, Peter?"

"She was encouraging and she laid the groundwork which enabled me to come up with an idea to solve my problem."

Tracy leaned toward him and kissed his cheek. "Darling, you always find a way."

"Oddly enough, Tracy, the idea came to me tonight, while you were bathing," he said, returning her kiss.

She nestled closer to him.

"My idea is to weaken Kay's image in my mind by strengthening the image of Christ. The question is, how can I best do it? Any ideas?"

"Reading the Bible may help, especially the crucifixion scriptures," Tracy suggested.

"While preparing for my preliminary sketch, I read those scriptures. Of course I could read them again but I need to do something more profound. Something more intense," he said, pawing his chin.

"Like praying?" she asked.

"Another good thought, Tracy. I do pray often and, lately, more than ever. I believe in the power of prayer but I also believe each of us should attempt to solve our problems and not expect miracles from God each time we pray."

"Peter, I have a hard time disagreeing with you," she said with a smile.

"Tracy, an idea is lurking in my mind and I need to think on it," he said.

He sat back and rested his head against the soft pillow. Looking at the flames with half-closed eyes, he began to think about something John Baxter had said during their last encounter seven months ago. In the flames he saw Baxter's face emerge. He saw the sly grin as Baxter fingered his patch of goatee and let the words flow from his lips: "Painter, do you honestly expect to identify with your Christ as you dabble with His image?"

Baxter's face faded from the flames but his words lingered until Grant had reduced them to one—"identify."

"Tracy," he said, turning her way, "in order to strengthen the image of Christ in my mind, I must more closely identify with Christ. I must find a way to experience something of what Christ had experienced when he was crucified."

Like Kay before her, Tracy had an undying faith in Grant's ability to conquer all odds. "Darling, you'll find a way," she assured him. "You'll create a way."

Grant had gotten to his feet and was pacing slowly between sofa and fireplace as Tracy was speaking. He was thinking along lines of hypnosis and her remarks had fallen upon passive ears.

He returned to the sofa, leaned back, and closed his eyes. "Tracy," he finally said with eyes still closed, "what did you say a moment ago?"

She looked puzzled.

"It was the last thing you said when I was pacing," Grant went on. "You said something important."

"Peter, I think I said you'll find a way to identify with Jesus."

"Okay, Tracy. But you said something after that, remember?"

"After that?" She reflected for a moment. "I said if you can't find a way to identify with Jesus, you'll create a way."

Grant's eyes opened. "Yes! Create is the word I had heard. That's it, Tracy! Except rather than create, I'll recreate!"

He took Tracy in his arms and kissed her. "Thanks for coming to my rescue," he said.

"Peter, if I was helpful, I'm glad. So, you have a plan to identify?"

"Yes. It's in the rough but I know it will require sacrifice by you and Wes and it will need to be executed quickly." He hesitated. "It has one drawback, Tracy. It would delay our honeymoon again. Would you mind very much?"

She leaned her head against his shoulder. "Peter, no sacrifice will be too much," she assured him. "Before Wesley and I shop tomorrow, we'll swing over to O'Hare and refund the tickets. There will be a penalty fee but we'll handle that," she said.

Grant admired her willingness to relent. "There's one consolation, Tracy. My plan should enable you and Wes to visit your parents between Christmas and the New Year, but I'll think it through and give you the details tomorrow evening.

The following afternoon, after Tracy and Wesley taxied to a nearby mall known for its Thursday specials, Grant invited Press over for a briefing of his plan.

"I'll need your help for this one," Grant said as he hung up Press's overcoat and hat.

They found chairs at the kitchenette table and in arm's reach of the coffee pot.

"Pete, you say the key is for you to identify more closely with Christ?"

Grant nodded. "The stronger I identify, the better."

Press sipped his black coffee. "What's your plan?" he asked.

"I construct a cross in my studio and hang from it for three days," said Grant matter-of-factly.

Thomas gulped. "Did you say hang for three days?"

"Words to that effect," said the artist. "Of course I'll be tied in place with rope."

"But, Pete, that kind of physical punishment...that type of self-imposed torture could do more than sap your energy. My God...it could break your spirit!" Press said with quivering lips.

"Break my spirit or renew it," said Grant.

Press was remembering Doctor Gillespie's earlier observation that his friend was already mentally ill. He sat back and shook his head. "I can appreciate your logic behind the plan, Pete, but hang for seventy-two hours? That would be an eternity!" he said in protest.

Grant sipped his coffee and smiled faintly. "I seriously considered two days but the whole idea is to suffer. It's a one-shot deal, so I decided to go full throttle." He sat back. "Press, I'm not deluding myself. I know three days will be hell, that's why I'm soliciting your help."

Grant added more sweetener to his coffee. "There's another reason for my hanging," he said, as he watched the saccharin dissolve. "Kay's death was cruel and senseless. It caused me to lose faith in God and in myself. Hanging may help restore my faith in addition to solving my problem at the easel."

Preston Thomas was still thinking about the three-day hang. "Pete, I have a suggestion. Would you reconsider and settle for two days? The results would be essentially the same—the identity and your restoration of faith. It doesn't make sense to extend the ordeal when it isn't necessary," he concluded.

Grant shook his head and chuckled. "Press, I swear you are the world's greatest salesman. I'm convinced about three days of hanging and you change my mind in a minute. Okay. Two days it will be."

"Good. A shrewd decision, my friend."

Grant's willingness to compromise convinced Press any further attempt to reduce the hang time would be unwise, so he changed the subject.

"Pete, what kind of rope will you use?" he asked offhand.

"Soft nylon, one-inch. I'm told it is least likely to cut the flesh."

Press warmed their coffee. "When will the hang begin?" he asked.

Grant thought for a moment. "Reducing the hang time by a day won't change the starting time. That will be the morning of December the twenty-eighth at eight o'clock. That's one week from tomorrow."

Press had taken a pad from his jacket pocket and was taking notes.

"My plan," continued Grant, "will allow me about five days to make an attempt to prepare myself physically, mentally, and spiritually. More importantly, it will enable my family and me to spend our first Christmas together," he said.

"Pete, I'm sorry your plan interferes with your honeymoon plans."

"Yes, it does. It's the only part of the plan I dislike. Press, will you inform Doctor Gillespie of my new plan? She should know."

"I'll tell her today. Have you told Tracy your plan?" Press asked.

"Not about the hang. I'll tell her tonight after Wes is asleep. Wes won't know about the hang. He's too young."

"I agree, Pete."

"Tracy and Wes won't be here during the hang. They'll be with her parents in Reading."

Press nodded his approval.

"As for the honeymoon conflict," continued Grant, "I've already told Tracy and she has accepted it in stride."

"Well, it appears you've touched all the bases, Pete. I only need the specific times of those occasions when you'll need my help."

After Grant complied, Press assured his friend he would be available and willing.

As Press was preparing to leave, Grant received a telephone call from Tracy.

He asked Press to mark time, as Tracy was in a predicament and needed their help. She was phoning from the local shopping mall where she had lost her purse to a mugger.

Press drove Grant to the mall, arriving within minutes, and they heard the story from Tracy's quivering lips. After shopping and as she and Wesley were walking toward their taxi in the parking lot, a man snatched the purse from her shoulder. When she tried to resist, she fell. Wesley had tugged at the assailant's coat, but to no avail. The man had quickly escaped in a waiting car.

She was not hurt, only shaken up. She had reported the theft to the mall security office, noting the only lost items of significance were their apartment keys, the reservations to Hawaii, and $100.00.

Grant was quick to discount the purse and its contents. He realized how easily his wife and son could have been killed by the thug, prompting him to give each of them a thankful hug and kiss.

After returning to their apartment, Tracy invited Press to join them for dinner at Peppi's, but he had a previous commitment.

"Press," Grant said, extending his hand, "thanks for your help today."

"We are grateful," added Tracy.

That evening, Grant decided to delay telling Tracy his plan. She had a bad scare and needed to wind down and relax.

The following evening, December 19, Tracy was smiling again and Grant decided the time was right, as a family, to share the delightful experience of decorating their first Christmas tree.

Later, as Wesley slept, Grant told Tracy his plan. She signed deeply when hearing about the two-day hang, however, she understood.

She and Wesley would look forward to their return to Reading. Her parents would be delighted to have them, especially during the holiday season, and Wesley would understand if it were not for the painting, his dad would be with them.

Tracy and Wesley would leave for Reading on December 26 and return after the first week of the new year. Press would advise her as to the exact time.

Grant assured his wife he would be ready and fit for the hang. Tomorrow he would begin a conditioning program of jogging and exercises to strengthen specific muscles. He would resort to concentrated foods high in nutritional value. He would read selected Bible scriptures daily in an effort to prepare himself spiritually and emotionally.

Press would be with him at the beginning and conclusion of the hang and make periodic visits. In addition, Press would phone her daily and, in turn, she could phone Press at any time, day or night.

Grant was pleased by Tracy's willingness to accept his plan. She assured him she and Wesley would do their part. It was something which had to be done and they would do it together, as a family.

After they made love and Tracy slept, Grant thought about the hang. His door locks would be changed and he had a bodyguard. Also, he would be isolated and helpless on the cross.

For a brief moment, he questioned the logic of his plan.

Chapter 16
The Hang

Wesley's sixth birthday came three days later.

Grant was mindful of his own sixth birthday when an auto accident had claimed his parents. Consequently he took special pains to make Wesley's birthday a happy occasion.

Christmas day followed closely and, despite the revolt, it arrived in typical fashion in their household. Wesley was up at daybreak and eagerly opened his presents as Tracy and Grant proudly looked on.

Press Thomas had been invited to join them for the day and he arrived only minutes after ten o'clock. However even before he could remove his overcoat, they were shaken by a series of thundering explosions coming only seconds apart.

Grant hurried to the south window and scanned the horizon as the others followed his lead. In the direction of downtown Chicago, they saw a white billow of smoke beginning to roll skyward. To their far left, they saw two more.

"What does it mean, Peter?" Tracy asked, taking his hand.

Before Grant could respond the telephone rang and he quickly answered it.

Security was at the other end.

"Tracy, will you turn on the television?" Grant asked.

He talked with Security briefly then joined the others.

The television networks had interrupted all regular programs and a commentator was reporting a special news bulletin:

"At eleven o'clock this Christmas morning, Eastern Standard Time, bombs are reported to have exploded simultaneously in New York City, Philadelphia, Miami, Boston, Cleveland, and Cincinnati.

"Even as I speak, bombings are reported to have just occurred in Chicago, New Orleans, Kansas City, St. Louis, Dallas, and Houston. Early reports indicate the number of bombings within each city have ranged from three to five, with only religious structures being the targets.

"The National Security Council in Washington, D.C. has reported the Devil's Corps—the radical wing of the revolutionary forces—has claimed responsibility for today's bombings. The N.S.C. has also announced the bombs used were of the remote-control and time-devise variety, identical to those used in the initial uprising ten months ago.

"A late bulletin was just received. It is reported and confirmed by the N.S.C. that all bombings have stopped.

"Between 10:00 A.M and 10:05 A.M., Central Standard Time, fifty bombs exploded in twelve different American cities.

"Only churches and parishes that had scheduled special Christmas services were bombed, an obvious intent by the revolutionaries to kill as many Christians as possible. Fortunately, almost half of the targeted churches and parishes had postponed the services due to the threat posed by the revolutionaries.

"It is too early for federal and local authorities to estimate the number of casualties or of property damage.

"The president will address the nation on the bombing disaster at 1:00 P.M. today, Central Standard Time."

While the president's reaction would come later, Grant's reaction to the bombings was one of utter contempt and it firmed his determination to carry out his plan.

The following evening found Tracy and Wesley safe in Reading, while Grant was in his studio measuring and sawing wood. The revolutionaries had gone underground once again to evaluate the results of their previous day's handiwork.

On the morning of December 27, Grant began to build the cross. He removed the makeshift easel from the riser and placed it upon the floor between the riser and the back wall. This would allow his huge canvas to rest one foot above the floor. Next, he separated the two risers, allowing ten inches between them. The risers would ultimately be used to brace the cross.

In constructing the cross, Grant used boards ten inches wide and two inches thick. The upright consisted of two nine-foot boards nailed back-to-back. The crossbeam consisted of two six-foot boards nailed back-to-back and bolted against the upright two feet from its top.

Next he made a foot brace, using a two-by-ten, ten inches long, and braced it horizontally to the upright one foot up from its base.

Grant drilled two one-inch holes near each end of the crossbeam, one just above the other, where his wrists would be while hanging. In like fashion, a single hole was drilled in the center of the upright at a position that would approximate his ankles while standing on the foot brace.

Four boards were used to brace the cross, nailed diagonally and horizontally to the two heavy risers positioned six feet to the rear of the cross. Completed and in its upright position, the cross had a slight backward tilt and was placed where the noonday sun would infiltrate the skylight and strike it.

Finally Grant rigged a chest harness using the one-inch rope. While he hung the harness would fit loosely and provide no support. Rope fastened to each shoulder strap of the harness would pass over the cross beam and be secured to a riser handle grip below. The harness would enable Press to slowly lower Grant to the floor once the ordeal was over.

As Grant worked on the mechanics of his plan, his thoughts had constantly replayed the senseless bombings of two days earlier. The president's speech to the nation, in Grant's view, had done little to inspire the patriots or to prevent their fears of future such bombings.

The artist stepped back, viewed his ominous creation, and decided it would suffice. He needed only to tie up loose ends.

He placed a 35-millimeter camera on the end table near the doorway leading to the kitchenette. Press would use it to capture several shots of Grant during the later stages of his hang, providing the artist additional material with which to identify as he painted the crucified Christ.

Purely for the psychological boost it provided, Grant crossed to his bedroom and returned with the revolver, which he placed in the drawer of the end table.

He was ready.

During the past seven days, he had exercised strenuously and had reduced his intake by eating concentrated foods. He also did some nightly reading of light poetry for relaxation and Bible reading to focus in on mood. Press was scheduled to arrive at seven-thirty in the morning. The hang would begin at eight o'clock, Sunday, December 28.

After a sleepless night, Peter Grant was still in his pajama bottoms when his telephone rang at seven-fifteen. Because Press was soon to arrive, Grant assumed his friend was merely checking in.

His assumption was wrong.

"You are under watchful eyes and listening ears," came the familiar message before the line went dead.

When Press arrived, Grant related the disturbing phone call and his friend promised to relay the incident to bodyguard Agent 340 upon his return to his office later in the morning.

They reviewed the hang schedule a last time.

Grant would mount the cross at 8:00 A.M. and Press would stay for an hour to assure a good beginning, after which he would return at 8:00 P.M. On Monday, Press would return at 8:00 A.M. and again at 8:00 P.M., at which time he would take photographs. At 8 A.M. Tuesday, December 30, the hang would end.

Grant glanced at the wall clock. "It's time for make-up," he said, getting to his feet and crossing to the bedroom.

Facing the dresser mirror, he examined his face briefly, then removed a bottle of liquid adhesive from the medicine cabinet and applied touches of its contents to his cheeks, jaws, chin and under his nose.

He removed a fake beard with attached mustache from the drawer and placed it to his face where it held fast. This done, he placed a brown hairpiece on his head and observed his reflection in the mirror. He had to admit he saw a resemblance of what most artists had depicted as the general features of Christ. From the beginning, he felt looking the part would help him feel the part.

They entered the studio where Grant removed his pajama bottoms and replaced it with a prepared strip of sheeting, wrapping it around his hips and pinning it securely on one side. He stepped onto the foot brace with his back against the upright and extended his arms sideways against the crossbeam.

Working from the stepladder behind the cross, Press pushed rope through both holes at one end of the crossbeam, catching Grant's wrist and tying the rope. He did likewise with Grant's other wrist. Finally, he secured Grant's ankles in like fashion, however, unlike one foot upon the other as Christ's feet had been placed, Grant's feet would rest side by side on the foot brace to provide more comfort and better support.

The hang had begun.

Grant tested the rope at his wrists and ankles by alternately hanging limply with knees flexed, then straightening the legs to transfer the weight of his body from his wrists to his feet. He knew the longer he hung, the more often he would need to alternate the two positions to seek relief, just as Christ must have done.

He began to concentrate on deep, even breathing and relaxation.

At eight-thirty, Grant felt reasonably comfortable and, even though Press had planned to stay the first hour, he suggested that Press leave early. Press obliged after assuring Grant he would return promptly at eight that evening.

Before departing, Press made a security check of windows, then switched on a table lamp near the studio window directly to Grant's front. He also removed the lamp shade so Grant could see the wall clock above the table at nightfall. The artist wanted to be reminded of the drudging hours that would lay ahead. His intent was to suffer but he wasn't sure how much he could endure.

Six hours later, Grant was alternating his torso position every thirty minutes. During the afternoon, his thoughts mostly were about Kay, her life, her death, and her recorded words: "...you are on the brink of a glorious creation...give your portrait total commitment...I love you...keep the faith."

When Press returned at 8:00 P.M., the artist was sweating and the muscles of his neck, shoulders, and thighs ached. His breathing, however, was even and unhurried. Press climbed the stepladder and sponged his friend's face, shoulders, and chest with cool water. With effort, Grant lifted his head and drank. He also assured Press all was well.

From Grant's view, Press' hour-long visit had come and gone much too quickly and he felt a growing sense of loneliness as the night wore on. It was as if his ties with the real world were being severed slowly and inevitably, one by one. He even forgot to ask Press if he had phoned his bodyguard about the distasteful phone call. Thank God for the light across the room. Already it was serving as a beacon of hope for him.

By ten o'clock, Grant was trying hard to keep his mind on positive thoughts. He recalled the day Tracy walked into his studio in New York City with resume in hand. He remembered his first meeting with Wesley and how they quickly shared a loving dad-son relationship.

He dozed only for brief periods and each unconscious movement of his body alerted him to pain. He searched for relief and found it easier, but no less painful, to flex his knees and hang limply, with his weight supported only by his wrists. Only in this position was it possible for him to doze.

The artist was conscious of daylight and the presence of Press. He also had a vague notion he had been hanging for twenty-four hours. He was halfway through the hang and at this point he questioned whether he would make it. His tongue moved over dry lips without wetting them. He would restrict conversation with Press to conserve strength and make breathing easier.

Again Press sponged his body and his thirst was quenched. Press squeezed a concentration of liquid food into his mouth from a plastic tube. Despite Press's smile and words of encouragement, Grant was alert enough to see the worried look in his friend's eyes.

Press offered him the use of a urinal, however, he refused. He would let nature take its course.

Shortly afterward, or so it appeared to Grant, his friend was gone. God, how the time would escape him when Press would visit. He was irked that he had neglected to ask Press to bring a sleeping drug on his next visit. More than anything, he wanted to sleep.

After several hours of hanging with intermittent dozing, Grant's shoulder joints throbbed and his hands had become numb. He transferred his weight to his legs but his thighs began to spasm, forcing a return to the loose hang. He decided he would not stand erect again unless it became necessary to assist his breathing. At this point, Grant was very conscious his breathing was becoming more and more difficult.

He became aware of a scraping noise coming from above. He knew a tree branch at the northeast corner of the building would often brush the roof during a heavy wind. When he heard the noise a second time, he was convinced it was the tree branch.

The noise made Grant thankful he had a bodyguard even though he had never met or seen Agent 340. Knowing the bodyguard was aware of his hang was comforting. Surely Press or Doctor Gillespie would have kept the agent abreast of his hanging plan.

Grant thought he might have dozed because he was surprised to hear a voice. Press was on the stepladder talking about the photographs he had just taken.

Using a kit, Press checked his friend's pulse, respiration rate, blood pressure, and temperature. He had taken the same readings prior to the hang and noted the pulse and respiration rates had increased, while the others remained constant.

Again he sponged Grant's face, shoulders, and chest. Again Grant's thirst was quenched, this time by using a plastic straw. The artist also took a small amount of liquid food.

Twelve hours of hanging remained.

Press suggested the hang should end now, that his friend had suffered more than enough.

Speaking slowly and with effort, Grant said he only wanted something to make him sleep.

Press slipped into his overcoat and assured Grant he would return within minutes with a sedative.

After Press had gone, the artist realized how difficult it was for him to speak. Also, his awareness of his labored breathing began to overshadow the pain that racked his body. Each time he exhaled, his chest cavity seemed to squeeze inward, making each breath shorter than the previous one. It was frightening, for he knew it would eventually lead to gasping, then finally to no air at all.

Panic began to sweep over him. He was alone, he was helpless, he was a target, and he was barely breathing.

Grant tried to lift his head to see the clock across the room but his neck muscles began to cramp, so he let his bearded chin fall back to his chest. Press had assured him he would return very soon. Upon his return, Grant would have Press lower him to the floor. The artist decided to end the hang.

Again, Grant heard a noise from above. This time it was a different sound and it was closer. A breeze crossed his body. After a moment, the breeze came again, this time accompanied by faint wrestling sounds.

An overpowering sense of danger forced Grant's chin to lift and his stomach churned as he saw the end of a thick rope dangling in the air directly in front of him. He knew someone was coming down the rope from the direction of the overhead skylight.

Instinct would have had Grant tug at the ropes holding his wrists and ankles, but even that innate drive was gone. He didn't move. He was trapped. His gun was fifteen feet away in the drawer of the end table. His only hope was for his bodyguard to arrive or for Press to return. He closed his eyes and silently prayed.

A thumping noise caused Grants eyes to open. He was confronted by a man standing tall and looking up at him. The man's all-black apparel included a cap and half-mask. Without speaking, he crossed to the kitchenette where he unlocked the outside door and returned with a partner, also dressed in black, but much shorter.

The taller man stepped to Grant's front. "How do you do, Mr. Jesus?" he remarked, using a slow sarcastic tone as he bowed deeply with a sweep of his cap.

"Judas, where's your damn manners?" the leader asked his shorter partner. "Tip your cap to Mr. Jesus," he sneered without taking his eyes off Grant's.

The shorter man grinned and quickly tipped his cap.

Physically, Grant was a beaten man but his mind was still working. It had to. He was confronted by diabolical killers and his only thought was to survive.

"Mr. Jesus, sir, forgive my partner, Judas," the taller man continued. "You see, Judas is stupid as hell. Ain't you stupid as hell, Judas?"

The shorter man nodded vigorously and grinned as he tipped his cap.

Grant was without expression as he kept his eyes unfocused and gazed straight ahead.

The leader stepped closer to Grant and scanned him from toe to head. "By God, you do look like Jesus. Here you are, hanging on the cross and looking like a man about to die. Of course Judas and me, we'll take care of that," he said, jabbing his forefinger toward Grant's helpless frame.

Grant's body was numb and the pain had subsided considerably. His breathing was in small, quick gasps. One question dominated his thinking: Where was Press? His only chance for survival was for help to come in time.

"Of course, if by chance you ain't the Mr. Jesus I think you are," the leader was saying, "Judas and me will sure as hell git our heads busted in when we make our report. Won't we, Judas?"

This time the short man skipped his obedient routine as he grabbed his leader's arm and pointed to the covered portrait resting on the huge easel to Grant's rear.

"All in due time, Judas. My friend is getting restless," said the leader, his cold eyes still riveted on Grant's face. "Judas thinks Rome was built in a day. Of course, you know all about Romans, don't you, Mr. Jesus? Those gentle Roman soldiers. Judas," he yelled over his shoulder, "I think it's time me and you show Mr. Jesus how nice we can be."

The little man responded with sheer delight—grinning, clapping, then tipping his cap repeatedly as he did a little jig.

With that, the two men went to work. First they uncovered the portrait and placed it on the floor to Grant's front, face up.

Grant closed his eyes. *Oh merciful God...protect me from evil...that I may see my wife and son again*, he prayed silently.

The clock above the lamp indicated Press had been gone for an hour.

While the short man searched the shelves against the north wall and found turpentine, his leader was about to make a torch. He grabbed the sheeting pinned to Grant's hips and tore it free from his body. Next, he found a length of two-by-four, wrapped the sheeting around one end, and soaked the sheeting with turpentine.

The short man emptied a quart of turpentine on the portrait, while the leader poured a like amount at the foot of the cross and upon Grant's feet and legs. Using his cigarette lighter, he ignited his torch and turned to Grant. "Fire is the tool of our trade," he boasted, holding the torch near Grant's glistening face.

Grant's eyes remained closed and he continued to pray.

The men stepped back as the leader threw the torch onto the portrait.

The flames sprang upward, causing Grant to give one final agonizing cry.

Chapter 17
Resurrection

Earlier the snow had stopped, and now the gusty wind began to ease as the taxi carrying Peter, Tracy, and Wesley turned onto Wabash Avenue. Ahead they were pleased to see the towering, brightly lit steeple of Saint Michael's Parish—their destination.

The cabby reactivated the liquid fuel intake as the taxi moved slowly over the chemically de-iced pavement.

The dashboard clock reading was 11:25. With their arrival scheduled for 11:30, security guards and presiding religious dignitaries would be edgy.

Grant envisioned Monsignor Kelly nervously pacing his study. The massive news coverage, the element of danger in spite of high-level security, an anticipated sign from God—these were reason enough for the monsignor to furrow his brow and pray for strength.

A fire siren broke the silence, causing Wesley and his mother to lean forward, their eyes searching for the orange flashing light. Grant noted the expressions on their faces. A speeding fire engine will excite the imagination of any eight-year-old boy, but his mother's tense face stemmed mostly from fear. She knew arsonists were rumored to strike the parish.

Although Grant had faith in Security, he realized risk could only be minimized and not entirely eliminated. With the Devil's Corps prowling the city, he and his portrait would remain at risk. Risk invites fear, especially high risk.

Δ Δ Δ

Grant's decision to hang was a high risk gamble. When he faced the prospect of death, he experienced an overwhelming fear, a kind of fear that would distort the senses of any rational man. Yes, Peter Grant was sick even before he mounted the cross—the same cross that was set ablaze, causing flames to burn his feet and move upward over his already tortured body.

Amid the certainty of death emerged a sense of mild contentment. It was a glimpse of comfort that teased his beaten body into believing a breath or two remained. His labored breathing, the spastic thigh muscles, the intense heat and pain—all began to wane. It was as if his cross had uprooted and began to drift aimlessly into the winds of endless space and time.

As the fluid motion eased to a stop, sedate music soothed his ears. Firmness was felt under his back. The fire that had mirrored in his eyes had diminished, only to return again, first to one eye then the other. It faded, leaving a vision of milky gray. The flames that had stung his feet had turned to tender touches of human hands.

Grant's eyes blinked and gradually focused upon a sky-blue ceiling. Hovering near his head was a man in white who had just examined his pupil dilation with a small light. A second man in white stood at the end of his bed, gently massaging his feet.

The examiner rose with a sigh. "Good morning, Mr. Grant. You are a patient at Edgewater Memorial Hospital, and I'm Doctor Mason." He gestured toward the younger man whose deft hands continued their light kneading. "Your masseur is Doctor Adler." Grant's throat was parched and he made no attempt to speak. He was also confused, his head ached, and his vision was blurry. However, *he was alive.*

"Glad to have you back," said Doctor Mason, referring to Grant's return to consciousness. "You've had a rough go with your wrists taking a physical beating, but a couple weeks will show a big improvement.

Grant's arms were under the bed sheet but he knew his wrists were heavily bandaged. He eyed the glass of water on his bedside tray and Doctor Mason obliged by holding the glass while Grant sipped through a straw.

"Your friend, Mr. Thomas, brought you in three days ago," said Doctor Mason. As he recorded Grant's vital statistics on a monitor, Doctor Adler applied the finishing touches to the foot massage. At the door Doctor Mason turned to Grant. "You should be sleeping soon and I'll drop in later today. By the way, today is January first. Happy New Year," he said with a smile.

Grant's eyelids soon became heavy and he slept until late the following morning. When he awoke, his eyes gradually focused upon a familiar pair. Doctor Gillespie and Preston Thomas were sitting at his bedside.

"Hi," Grant said lazily. "You two make a pretty picture."

"Welcome back, Pete," said Press, while the doctor leaned over and kissed his cheek. "Preston and I are just as pleased to see you, Mr. Grant," she said warmly. She was wearing the same pin-striped suit and short bob she wore sixteen days earlier at Glick's coffee shop.

"Press, does Tracy know I'm here?"

"Yes, she does, Pete. I phone her every day and I can assure you she and Wesley are fine."

"Good. Give them my love. Tell Tracy I'll phone at my first opportunity."

"Dare I ask how you're feeling?" Press ventured.

"Like I've been crucified," Grant jested. "Actually, I ache all over but mostly I'm confused," said the artist.

"You have every right to be confused, Mr. Grant. Would you care to elaborate?" Doctor Gillespie asked, nudging closer.

Grant gazed at the sky-blue ceiling. "My memory is fuzzy, especially the events that led up to the hang. It's a strange, out-of-touch feeling, one I've never had before," he said.

"Anything else?" she probed.

"Yes, my eyes occasionally lose their focus and this leads to a headache. In fact, I have one now. Maybe I need glasses."

"Fortunately, your symptoms are temporary and will disappear in a few days. Meanwhile, Doctor Mason will give you medication to relieve your headaches." She paused and reflected upon Grant's responses. "You referred to a fuzzy memory. How much of the hang do you remember?"

"Every last detail," he said with emphasis.

With clarity, Grant gave an account of the painful experience, ending with the two intruders, their taunting behavior, and his fiery demise. "It was hell. It was as if they actually set me afire and I died on that cross. It was horrible," he said grimly.

"Indeed you did die, Mr. Grant, and now you are resurrected," said Doctor Gillespie, as she placed an assuring hand on his shoulder. "You had a bad hallucinogenic experience and even though you had only imagined it, that doesn't make it any less painful. I must say, if your purpose for hanging was to suffer, you did a top-flight job."

"Any chance my injured wrist will effect my ability to paint?" Grant asked.

"Not likely," she responded.

"Good. I'm anxious to paint again. Press, did you get some good shots?"

"Exactly what you wanted," Press said.

"Then I need only to get on with it. Doctor, how soon can I be discharged?"

She considered his question thoughtfully. "You seem to have strong powers of recovery. I would say two weeks, three at the most."

Doctor Gillespie checked her watch and stood.

Press followed her lead and helped her with her coat.

"Tell me, Mr. Grant, was the hang worth it?" she asked.

"I'll know when I paint again."

"You'll do fine," she said.

"Pete, we'll be in touch," added Press.

At the door, she turned to the artist. "By the way, Mr. Grant, one of my agents is stationed outside your door. It's an around-the-clock precautionary measure."

Shortly afterward, Press and Doctor Gillespie stepped from the elevator into the lobby.

"Preston, our friend is not alone in his confusion. I'm probably more confused about his state of mind than he."

In the parking lot they donned sunglasses to dull the brightness of the snow and it wasn't until they had entered Press' Dodge Delta that he responded to her last remark.

"Judith, I thought Pete struck a positive note."

"That's the point, Preston. Any measure of logic told us our friend would emerge from his coma suffering from disorientation and a mixed bag of neurotic symptoms. Instead he was calm, coherent, and in control of his faculties. Doctors Mason and Adler are as puzzled as I," she said.

Press pulled into the heavy traffic.

"Judith, are you implying Pete isn't as ill as you had indicated earlier?" Press finally asked.

"Sorry, but no. Mr. Grant's illness is a fact. It is also serious and complicated."

Neither spoke a word until Press pulled into the rainbow Realty parking area.

Doctor Gillespie turned his way. "Preston, you have been very patient and I'm grateful. After Mr. Grant's party last June, I told you our friend had a serious mental illness but I withheld the details and I apologize for that."

Press was beginning to feel uncomfortable, sensing she was leading to bad news.

"Because Mr. Grant had symptoms of a rare disease," she continued, "I wanted to make sure my findings were on track. I solicited doctors more qualified than I and, unfortunately, they verified my diagnosis. Under the present circumstances, Preston, I think it's time you are told the particulars of Mr. Grant's illness."

Press's stomach felt tight and his breathing had lost its easy rhythm. For over six months he had waited, knowing she would tell him in her own time. Now, he wasn't sure he was emotionally prepared.

Doctor Gillespie glanced at her watch. "Are you available for an hour at seven tonight?" she asked.

That evening, Doctor Gillespie and Preston Thomas set at the large oval table in Press' dining room. Press had poured two glasses of water for them.

"I'll begin with background," she said, taking a pad of notes from her purse and slipping on her reading glasses.

"In 1931 an Italian named Anthony Cerroni was diagnosed as having a mental disease which proved to be a first in medical science. Mr. Cerroni was a tenor virtuoso from Milan."

She continued her reference to notes. "Twelve years later, John Cabot Riley, a syndicated journalist from Sidney, Australia, was discovered to have the same disorder. Fortunately, Mr. Riley had kept a thorough accounting of his medical history, including detailed symptoms of this particular disease. This provided the medical profession its first well-documented case.

"Twenty-three years later in 1966, a London concert pianist of substantial repute, Howard Goode, became the third victim of this disease.

"The cases had interesting similarities. Each victim was creatively oriented. Each had experienced a series of emotional crises during their formative years and beyond. Each had a deep-seated guilt complex."

"Each victim experienced hallucinations which had become progressively more severe. In addition, and this is the oddity of the disease, their hallucinations were focused upon an antagonist who had a physical likeness of their own."

The doctor slowed the tempo to emphasize her words. "Now fifty-nine years after Mr. Good's affliction, Mr. Grant became the fourth victim. This dreaded disease has become known as the Flip-Flop Syndrome."

Doctor Gillespie put her note pad aside and sat back.

Preston Thomas was sweating. He sipped his water and loosened his tie.

"Up to this point, Preston, Mr. Grant fits the pattern straight down the line. I say up to this point because each of his predecessors had committed suicide within two years of the disease's onset. Their self-imposed demise was due to the hellish torment attributed to their antagonist, or nemesis, if you will, who had dominated their hallucinations."

Press Thomas stirred in his chair and dabbed perspiration from his forehead with a handkerchief. "Judith, if I understand you correctly, you're saying John Baxter is Pete's antagonist."

"Yes, Preston."

"But...that means...John Baxter is a product of Pete's imagination," Press said hesitatingly.

Doctor Gillespie nodded. "Mr. Baxter doesn't exist except in Mr. Grant's mind. Nor did his mysterious phone call occur. These are facts, I'm sorry to say."

"My Lord," Press muttered, lifting his head with closed eyes.

Before he could further respond, Doctor Gillespie continued, "I told you, Preston, the three victims prior to Mr. Grant had committed suicide within two years of the disorder's onset. We believe Mr. Grant's mental breakdown occurred upon his return to Chicago eight months ago.

"The breakdown coincides with his break up with Kay Allyson. It was then that he returned to Chicago and had his first imaginary meeting with John Baxter.

"Mr. Grant' s portrait deadline is scheduled for April eighteen of next year. The onset of his disease and his deadline is a two-year span. If Mr. Grant follows the pattern, he will be cutting it close. However, we believe Mr. Grant won't commit suicide as soon as the others, if at all. By comparison, he is more strong-willed and resolute."

"Judith...this disease...this Flip-Flop Syndrome...what exactly happened to Pete's mind?" he asked.

Chapter 18
The Flip-Flop Syndrome

"Preston, I'm sorry to be putting you through this ordeal."

"No, no, Judith, please go on," he urged painfully.

"Preston, I told you the syndrome is complex so bear with me. As you know, my training in psychiatry is focused upon the criminal mind, consequently, most of my consultations were with Doctor Harriet King, an expert on mental disorders of the kind in question.

"In addition, I had assigned Special Agent Roger Davis to research Mr. Grant's early experiences as they relate to the present. Agent Davis' findings provide the basis to the answer of your question, Preston.

"Mr. Grant had suffered three major traumatic experiences. The first occurred when, at age six, he lost his parents in a sudden tragic accident. Worse yet, it happened on his birthday, as you know. To a child of this age, such an experience can have cruel psychological consequences.

"This misfortune was followed by his placement in the custody of his maternal uncle who was harsh and demanding. This was the boy's second crisis and the living arrangement had lasted for twelve years.

"By now, Mr. Grant was responding forcefully against the model his uncle presented. Fortunately, Mr. Grant had loving parents and his energies were channeled in positive ways. Early parental praise of his artistic talents propelled him to strive for success with a drive and determination which became his trademark.

"At this point, agent Davis was assisted by Doctor King to determine an accurate interpretation of the psychological and psychiatric aspects of the case.

"While Mr. Grant's talent and determination led to impressive artistic achievements, he had never considered himself successful. This was because of a basic feeling of inadequacy which prevailed the moment his parents were lost. His grief heightened by a deep-seated guilt because he felt responsible for his parents' death.

"Finally, Mr. Grant was confronted with a third crisis—the sudden break up with Kay Allyson, a talented, beautiful, courageous woman he had come to love. The break up hastened the onset of the syndrome.

"I became suspicious of a mental problem when I questioned Mr. Grant at his party. I recorded our conversation, beginning with his detailed account of three encounters he had with John Baxter. It was only later that I learned each encounter had followed a depressing experience.

"As Mr. Grant and I walked into the vestibule, I saw a portrait of you, Preston, hanging on the wall. Mr. Grant told me it was a gift to your wife and he gave me permission to photograph it. Preston, he referred to your portrait as a landscape. He told me the painting was one of his better landscapes!"

Press shook his head.

"When I returned to D.C. that evening," she continued, "I phoned Doctor Davis and played the recording of my conversation with Mr. Grant. Doctor Davis asked me to phone Mr. Grant the following day and ask him one final question: Would he recount the circumstances that led up to his first encounter with Mr. Baxter, beginning with his arrival at O'Hare Airport?"

Again Doctor Gillespie referred to her notebook. "Preston, the following is an account of Mr. Grant's answer to the question Doctor Davis had requested:

'When I returned to O'Hare Airport, I stored my luggage in an overnight locker. I was despondent and decided to walk until I located a hotel or motel, thinking there would be ample lodging nearby. The light rain intensified and I became drenched.

'I lost my sense of direction until I found myself in the North Ashland area where I came upon an apartment. It had a vacant sign, a skylight, and lights burning. As I approached the apartment a speeding car turned onto Ashland Avenue.

'Its headlights spotted me and its occupants began firing automatic firearms sporadically. I ran the back streets for some time before escaping the thugs. Again, I lost my sense of direction and my chest was burning but I continued to search until I found Ashland Avenue and finally the apartment with the skylight. I knocked at the door and Mr. Baxter answered.'"

Doctor Gillespie closed her notebook and dropped it into her purse.

"Preston," she began, "Dr. King and I believe Mr. Grant gave an accurate account of his activities from the time he arrived at O'Hare until he met John Baxter. We also believe the breaking point occurred when Mr. Grant encountered the thugs in the car. Such a traumatic experience very likely was the final blow. This being the case, when Mr. Grant knocked at the door at 5210 North Ashland, he had already stepped across the thin line separating sanity and insanity.

"John Baxter doesn't exist. It was Mark Richards who opened the door because Mr. Richards is the owner of the apartment. It was Mr. Richards with whom Mr. Grant had negotiated the lease deal. The owner has since moved to Miami after placing the responsibility of his leasing properties into the lap of Base Realtors, a local realtor."

Doctor Gillespie took a sip of water. "More specifically, this is how the Flip-Flop Syndrome works. The series of crises Mr. Grant had endured since early years had resulted in a multitude of imagined inadequacies combined with a deep-seated guilt complex.

"This combination can be deadly, causing a chemical imbalance in the brain. This leads to severe hallucinations and a gradual diminishing sense of self-worth. Later, his dislike turns to hate.

"Finally, the condition will manifest itself in the creation of a new personality. The victim, in a frantic effort to absolve himself of his predicament, conjures up in his mind a scapegoat. His new creation will be the recipient of the victim's inadequacies, shame, and guilt.

"When Mr. Grant opened the door at 5210 North Ashland, rather than seeing Mr. Richards, he saw himself as a weak, inept man. This represents the Flip in the syndrome.

"Follow me, Preston?" she asked.

"I'm trying to," he said with a slight nod.

The doctor continued. "Mr. Grant named his new creation John Baxter not by chance but rather by unconscious design. To him, the name represented strength of character. The name was easy to trace. It was his father's given name, while Mr. Grant's mother's maiden name was Baxter."

The doctor hesitated momentarily, then continued. "Now, Preston, we come to the Flop in the scenario. The irony of this phenomenal malady is this: John Baxter, the new creation, immediately sets about to refute his maker much like the fictitious Frankenstein monster. He will ridicule, antagonize, and hate his creator until he becomes unbearable, causing the victim to commit suicide.

"That's it, Preston. I'm sorry for painting such a gloomy picture."

Press Thomas sighed deeply and leaned toward her. "Is there any possible cure?" he asked.

"There's very little hope. Understandably, the disease is rare and has a low profile. Brain chemical dysfunction and environmental factors are believed to be the cause, but no cure looms on the horizon."

"Where do we go from here, Judith?" Press asked wistfully.

"Of course Mr. Grant must be told. Would you prefer I tell him, Preston?"

"Yes, but I would like to be present. When will you do it?" he asked.

"When Mr. Grant sufficiently recovers from his present setback. In two or three weeks, I would think."

"But wouldn't such shocking news worsen Pete's condition?"

"That's the chance we must take, Preston," said the doctor, getting to her feet. "I think Mr. Grant has the inner toughness to survive longer than the victims who preceded him. For how long, who knows? Meanwhile, my friend, will you inform Mrs. Grant her husband is progressing, but slowly? For the benefit of all concerned, encourage her to stay in Reading until notified."

Chapter 19
A Hopeful Sign

Two weeks later, Press Thomas arrived home from his office only to hear the door buzzer sound even before he had removed his coat.

He was greeted by a woman who presented him with a letter of introduction written by Doctor Gillespie. The woman was Doctor Harriet King, head psychiatrist at Edgewater Memorial and presently assisting Doctor Gillespie in Grant's case.

Press tended to her wraps and they settled into comfortable chairs in the living room. The doctor was tall by women's standards, in her mid-forties, and wearing a light brown suit that matched her hair. She crossed her legs at the knees while hand-brushing hair from a shoulder in one fluid motion.

"Mr. Thomas, I have positive news about Mr. Grant. Do you have thirty minutes?" she asked, glancing at her watch.

"My Lord, yes!" Press gasped. "Doctor, my time is yours," he said moving to the edge of his chair.

"You must understand, it's not a breakthrough," she was quick to add. "That may come later. Presently, I have only a theory. Please let me explain.

"When Mr. Grant was admitted at Edgewater, and once he regained consciousness, I was prepared to test his mental capacities in such areas as tolerance, will, determination, et cetera. Meanwhile, a routine E.K.G. told us he had suffered a slight heart attack within the past several months. This was followed by a C.A.T. scan that indicated a possible brain tumor.

"We know Mr. Grant complained about headaches when he arrived from New York. Also, we know when Mr. Grant hallucinated."

Press Thomas was devouring every word.

"Under the circumstances," she continued, "I encouraged Edgewater's board of directors to permit neurological surgeon, Doctor Mason, to use exploratory procedures in Mr. Grant's case.

"A week ago, Doctor Mason performed what is called a cerebral puncture. The process consisted of withdrawing a small plug of brain tissue through a trephine opening. This is a common procedure, having been used for many years as an aid in diagnosing puzzling mental cases.

"When the puncture was made, however, no tumor was found. What was thought to be a tumor proved to be a severe concentration of chemicals reacting within the brain tissue. This was the plug the cerebral puncture had withdrawn.

"From the beginning, I believed chemical reaction was the primary cause for the hallucinations that characterize the Flip-Flop Syndrome. Now I was in a position to study a severe concentration of these chemicals for the first time.

"After a careful examination of these brain chemicals, I'm convinced the only cure for this disease is to stop the victim's hallucinations. To do this, I believe Mr. Grant's antagonist must be eliminated. This is to say Mr. Grant must hallucinate that he kills John Baxter one way or another. I believe I can bring this about by means of hypnosis." She sat back with a sigh. "That, Mr. Thomas, is my theory."

"It sounds fantastic!" said an elated Press Thomas.

Doctor King smiled for the first time.

"As a result of this development, Doctor Gillespie has decided to postpone telling Mr. Grant about his misfortune," said Doctor King. "She wants to see how well he paints after his hang experience. Meanwhile, she and I will decide the best time for resorting to hypnosis."

"I'm glad for the postponement," said Press.

"Before I leave, Mr. Thomas, I must tell you Doctor Mason performed a second procedure on Mr. Grant in conjunction with the cerebral puncture."

"In this instance we violated Mr. Grant's privacy and, eventually, I will apologize to your friend. This procedure was made for Mr. Grant's safety and for the security of his portrait. Too many people know about Mr. Grant's painting and, for some time now, Doctor Gillespie has had his apartment bugged, including the installation of microcameras.

"In spite of this, Doctor Gillespie felt it was necessary to go deeper," continued Doctor King. "In the second procedure, Doctor Mason performed a single implant by inserting a microelectronic detector into Mr. Grant's cranium." She gestured by touching a finger to the back of her head.

"Actually, the detector is one-half a centimeter in length and inserted into a drilling two millimeters in diameter. The detector fits flush with the exterior and interior surfaces of the skull and the procedure was completed in fifteen minutes, including a stitch.

"Doctor Gillespie had informed me about the significance of a detector," she continued.

"It not only will provide Doctor Gillespie's headquarters with a constant and exact reading as to Mr. Grant's whereabouts within an eight-kilometer radius of Chicago, but it will also provide a monitored E.E.G. These visual tracings of the electrical activity of his brain will indicate to what extent Mr. Grant is physically, mentally, and emotionally active. From this they will have a good idea as to when he is eating, painting, sleeping, et cetera."

Doctor King stood and extended her hand. "That's my news," she said.

Three days later, Grant was discharged from Edgewater Memorial. When Press dropped him off at his studio apartment, the only physical evidence of his recent ordeal was bandaged wrists. Press wanted to see his friend inside but an appointment prevented this.

The artist was apprehensive as he ascended the staircase, but once inside, he gradually adjusted to a scene which had so recently held a horrible experience for him.

The cross was gone. There was no lumber laying about. Even the sawdust on the linoleum floor had been vacuumed. He assumed Press had restored his studio to normalcy to shut out his bad memories. His heart quickened as he crossed to the portrait and pulled the draw cord. Thank God. His painting was whole and undamaged as Doctor Gillespie had assured him it would be.

First, he would phone Tracy and let her know all was well. He was out of the hospital and feeling good. He was under the watchful eye of a bodyguard. The suffering he had experienced from the hang had drawn him closer to his subject and he was ready to resume painting.

"Darling, I'm so happy you phoned," Tracy said, after hearing his good news. "Tonight, I was planning to phone you, except my news isn't so good, I'm afraid.

"Tracy's father had received word that his mother unexpectedly passed away. She was seventy-five, lived in London, and services were planned in three days. Tracy had never met her paternal grandparents and when her father handed her the telephone, her grandfather had made a passionate plea that she and her family accompany her parents to the services.

"I told my grandfather Wesley and I would come, but you were committed to your portrait assignment. Did I make the right decision?"

"Yes, Tracy, you did," Grant replied. "It was very proper. As the years go by, it will mean even more to you and Wes for having gone. I'm sorry I can't join you but you'll be in safe hands and in my prayers."

As it turned out, Tracy's visit became prolonged. Her parents decided to lease their house in Reading and live with Tracy's grandfather until he recovered from his loss and made a positive adjustment to a different lifestyle.

Grant wired her money as needed and she acquired a tutor for Wesley. It was at this point Tracy decided to stay until her husband would send for her and Wesley. At month's end, Tracy's father returned home only long enough to contact a real estate agency to handle all the details. He cleaned up business matters, shipped their personal belongings to London, and rented his Reading house furnished.

Grant was painting daily and discovered he could handle his brushes with ease. After he studied the portrait, he had plunged into correcting flaws that appeared to be jumping out at him. *He could identify. There was no death image of Kay.* His first major painting setback had been solved and he was elated. He could finally relate to the agony of the crucified Christ.

The mouth of Christ was corrected first. It had needed a more downward thrust on the right side. Both brows were raised. The chest expansion was made more pronounced as was the muscle tension of the thighs and abdomen. Conversely, muscle tension in the arms, neck, and cheeks was lessened. He still had to rework the flesh tones and make them more shallow.

During all of this, he hadn't forgotten Tracy's birthday in mid-March, sending her a personalized card and wiring her yellow roses.

The month of April found Grant immersed in his painting but still feeling the loneliness a separated family can bring.

He would see Press for lunch occasionally and phone Tracy every evening. Doctor Gillespie would phone him several times a month to check on his progress. She was pleased to hear the pieces were coming together and she notified Press of her intention to continue the postponement of telling Grant about his illness for the present.

Doctor Gillespie had also given Grant a brief update on the Christmas church bombings. The bottom line had the bombings traced to a Corey Thompson, confessed leader of the Devil's Corps, who was arrested only hours ago in Charlotte, North Carolina. Doctor Gillespie was adamant in her conviction that a much tighter lock be placed upon church security, especially with Christian religious holidays looming on the horizon.

Grant told her he was getting headaches during his prolonged painting sessions and she suggested he limit the sessions to only three or four hours. He did this and it seemed to be helpful.

Palm Sunday, Good Friday, and Easter passed quietly but not without tension. The Devil's Corps leader was convicted of murder and put to death by lethal injection to close out the month.

The days quickly turned to weeks and Grant's conscious painting moved to the next level as his brush strokes became automatic. He responded intuitively to the previous stroke as if a force beyond him had taken control and his brushes merely responded. The results of each session continued to be gratifying as his feelings were ably expressed and the tonal quality was effectively controlled.

Satisfied with the flesh tones, Grant again returned to the muscles of the body.

He reworked the reduction of tension in the arms and neck by making the tones and highlights softer. Reducing tension in one area would, by contrast, tend to increase it elsewhere, thus the changes had to be subtle. In the midst of it, Grant remembered to wire Tracy roses on Mother's Day.

He reworked the chest area once again, increasing the tension and expansion. The change was dramatic as it denoted an increased agonizing pain and a gasping for air in Christ's last moments of life.

Since his release from the hospital, Grant had painted five months with good results.

He phoned Ambrose Thorne to reassure the art director of his progress. In the same high spirit, he phoned Tracy and suggested she and Wes might be home sooner than expected if his progress continued at the present pace. Although it wasn't necessary, he reminded her the portrait deadline was a mere ten months away.

Tracy assured him Wesley was doing fine and liked his gentleman tutor. Her grandfather was still grieving deeply and she wondered if he would have survived his loss had her parents not been able to come.

Her parents decided to remain in London until August, at which time the six-month lease on their house in Reading would expire. Although she and Wesley missed him dearly, she now felt obligated to stay and return with her parents. Even so, she and Wesley would grab the first flight to Chicago if her husband said the word.

Time appeared to accelerate as the summer months faded to fall. His deadline was slightly over five months removed and he visualized completing the portrait well in advance of this. With this in mind, he considered the idea of holding off sending for his family until the portrait was finished. Upon their return to Reading in August, he would suggest that Tracy enroll Wesley in the second grade at the same public school Tracy had attended as a child twenty-one years earlier.

Grant was ready to paint the Latin letters *I.N.R.I.* on a plate on the upright beam above Christ's head. Upon the conclusion of this, the artist had only to paint the gently oozing blood of the dying Savior.

Chapter 20
The Anchor

In September, Tracy and Wesley had returned to Reading with her parents and, as Grant had suggested, Wesley was enrolled in the same elementary school Tracy had attended many years before.

Because his painting had been progressing so nicely, it was also agreed that Tracy and Wesley would join Grant the moment his portrait was finished. At this point, Grant expected to beat the April 18, 2027, deadline by as much as three or four months.

It was also in September when Doctor Gillespie notified Press the completion date of the portrait would serve as an appropriate time to tell Grant about his illness. The artist was making good headway with his painting and they would not interfere.

By the end of the month, Grant had painted the plate and the Latin letters, I.N.R.I., signifying *King of the Jews.* Only the blood remained to be painted.

He stepped from the ladder and viewed the portrait from several paces. He saw an exquisite array of color, form, and feeling. He knew it was his best work thus far and he was reminded of Kay's prediction in her recorded message: "...you are on the brink of a glorious creation which will exceed even your own expectations."

But the portrait wasn't finished. Even so, Grant decided to take a break of several weeks just to relax, enjoy some solid meals, and catch up on sleep.

On November 1, he mixed his red pigments and dulled them. The areas of blood would include the temples and across the forehead where the crown of thorns had pierced Christ's skin; the wrists, each having been pierced by a nail; the left foot, which overlapped the right, with a huge nail driven through both; other sporadic areas where the blood had dripped or had flowed to a standstill.

He climbed the step ladder and gingerly touched his loaded brush to the left temple of Christ.

He painted for a week and, for the first time in many months, the results didn't please him.

The artist took a two-day break and painted again but the results were the same. He puzzled over it, wondering if his oils were contaminated.

The following day, Grant took his reds, greens, and whites to a local chemical outlet. Three days later he received a lab analysis indicating his oils were of excellent quality. He closely examined the surface of his canvas in the blood areas but found nothing amiss. The odor of his turp and linseed oil told him they were not defective.

It wasn't as if painting blood was a new venture for the artist. Grant had painted human blood on many occasions, most noteworthy being his prize-winning *Pangs of Pugilism*, which was a commentary on blood.

A week later, Grant had lunch with Press at Glick's coffee shop and revealed the problem.

"It's only a temporary snag," said Grant, minimizing the situation.

That evening Tracy phoned him.

"Have you any Thanksgiving plans?" she asked.

"Not really. Press and I will no doubt have dinner at Kihiki's."

"Why don't you fly over and have dinner with Wesley and me?" Tracy asked coyly.

Grant liked the idea. He needed a change of pace and, more importantly, he missed his family.

After his visit with Tracy and Wes, he returned to the easel.

He decided it had to be a technical oversight. He was using the same greens he had always used when dulling his reds, yet he was painting a blood that reflected too much life. The blood was too rich for a man on the edge of death.

Three weeks later, Grant's efforts were cut short because he wanted to be in Reading for Wes's birthday on December 22. This time, he would stay for Christmas and return the second of January.

The new year—2027—arrived and Grant had ten weeks to complete his assignment. Only Press knew about the sudden turnabout he was having with the blood and the artist decided it would end there. It was his problem to solve.

After another month of dissatisfaction, Grant began to question his ability. He was physically fit. The wrist of his painting hand never felt better. He was emotionally primed for the task. He felt a compassion for the dying Christ. What was wrong?

He remembered John Baxter's prediction, and Grant began to question his worthiness to paint the blood of Christ.

When Press questioned him about his progress, Grant admitted he was worried.

Press notified Doctor Gillespie about his friend's dilemma and she, in turn, conferred with Doctor Harriet King.

The following week Peter Grant received a phone call from Doctor Gillespie.

"Mr. Grant, my office has received word from reliable sources that John Baxter is a member of the revolutionaries," she began.

Before their conversation ended, Grant learned his landlord was extremely dangerous and wanted for murder on several counts. The doctor suggested that Grant resort to his gun should Baxter return and pose a threat of any kind.

Even though she already knew, Doctor Gillespie asked the artist how his portrait was progressing.

After Grant admitted having a temporary painting problem, she told him about her colleague, Harriet King, the noted hypnotist. Doctor Gillespie suggested Doctor King could be helpful if his problem persisted.

Time was growing short and he believed somewhere there was an answer. There had to be a key or sign that would point the way. Three days after Doctor Gillespie's phone call, Grant made an appointment with Doctor King.

After another week at his easel, nothing had changed. His brushes felt clumsy in his hand.

The artist began to probe his past. He tried to think what it was that had propelled him through the storms. Where did he get his inner strength? He decided it had to be his faith.

He had recalled Doctor DuBreau's advice eight years earlier at his graduation exercises from art school. "Above all, have faith in your God," the doctor had said as he gave Grant the token of faith—the gold metal ring.

Kay had said to him on the recorded message: "Faith will be my source of strength and I pray it will be yours. God bless you and please keep the faith."

Grant turned to the Bible, thinking it may offer a clue. For several days he read it diligently, including Hebrews, Chapter Eleven, but to no avail.

On March 1, Grant phoned Doctor Davis for another session of hypnosis and she complied the following day.

His painting during the month of March was a total disappointment and he was about to give up.

During the first week of April, he made no attempt to paint.

On April 9, nine days before his deadline, Grant sat on his sofa and contemplated how he would inform others of his failure. Tomorrow, he would phone Ambrose Thorne and Monsignor Kelly with his deepest apologies. He would give the unfinished portrait to the parish, gratis. Perhaps Ambrose Thorne could commission another artist to paint the blood of Christ.

He would then inform Press before facing the most difficult task of all—telling Tracy and their son. He was counting on their love to help him through the crisis.

He stepped to the fireplace and leaned heavily against the mantel with outstretched arms as he gazed at the ceramic logs below. Darkness had fallen prematurely as a storm began to hit Cook County. A blast of thunder and pelting rain prompted Grant to secure the windows.

While at the front window of his studio, a street light below enabled him to observe a man on the sidewalk, bucking a strong headwind from the west. Bareheaded and with no umbrella, the drenched man paused near the staircase leading to Grant's apartment, then moved on. For a moment Grant thought the man was John Baxter.

After returning to the fireplace, his mind was still on his landlord. The artist tried to remember when and where he had last seen John Baxter.

After a moment, he swirled from the mantel. "My Lord," he said aloud, then hurried to the bedroom.

He pulled his blue serge jacket from the closet and removed the huge ring from the inside pocket. He sat on his bed and gazed at the ring with anchor encased, the anchor that symbolized faith.

"*The Anchor*!" he shouted aloud and pressed the ring to his lips.

The Anchor was the tavern's name. It was the tavern he had stumbled upon almost two years ago. It was the tavern with the sign of flashing blue lights that traced the shape of a huge anchor. It was the tavern where he had last seen John Baxter.

The anchor could be the sign he was looking for. It symbolized a faith that had provided him strength to overcome his obstacles in the past. Something or someone in the tavern held the answer to his painting problem. He was sure of it.

Grant knew the tavern was a den for cutthroats, perverts, and prostitutes. It could even be a hangout for revolutionaries. He wondered how this could translate to the blood of Christ but he was determined to find out.

He phoned a taxi, strapped on his shoulder holster, packed it with his Colt revolver, and grabbed his raincoat. It was seven o'clock.

Thirty minutes later his taxi pulled into the parking lot behind the tavern. Grant's first visit to the tavern was marked by curiosity. This time, he was apprehensive and hoped his body guard was close by.

Heavy rain pelted the cars that jammed the parking lot, as Grant paid the cabby and made a dash for the back door.

Once inside, talking, laughing, and occasional yells pounded his ears while smoke permeated the air. He hung his raincoat on a nearby rack and casually walked to the restroom. Not wanting to look out of place, he disheveled his hair, removed his jacket, unfastened the top buttons of his shirt and folded his sleeves to his elbows. His loosely fitted shirt provided ample concealment for his holster and gun.

Grant approached the bar and found an empty stool where he had sat on his earlier visit. He smiled and pretended to recognize someone across the room.

Grant quickly surveyed his situation. He knew the swinging doors behind the bar to his front led to the kitchen. He knew the kitchen had an outside door that led onto North Ashland Avenue. He had noted this on his approach to the tavern. Grant knew this information could be vital if he needed a quick escape.

The room was stuffy and he placed his folded jacket over his thighs. He ordered a beer and checked his watch. It was seven-forty.

A dark-skinned girl in her late teens suddenly entered the swinging doors to Grant's front. Her wet raincoat shimmered in the glow of the overhead lights. Her dark hair was pulled back tightly from her smooth forehead, clamped at the nape, and fell loosely down her back. Her face was attractive but cold. She caught Grant's eye and smiled faintly. When the bartender saw her, she waved and withdrew.

Possibly Portuguese or Spanish, thought the artist. Her heavy make-up indicated to him she was a house prostitute.

A frail man pushing sixty and wearing shabby clothing slid onto the stool next to Grant. He looked worried.

"Hi, Pops," said the bartender as he pushed a bottle of beer toward the little man.

"Hi, killer," he responded meekly.

"Kitty's here," the bartender said, gesturing toward the swinging door. "She came early. Better not keep her waiting," the bartender ordered with an air of superiority.

With a sigh and leaving his beer behind, the little man slipped from the stool and disappeared through the swinging doors.

Within minutes he returned, flushed, and breathing hard. He ran a dirty handkerchief over his forehead and around his neck before sitting again. He took a gulp of his beer and burped.

"You come here often?" Grant asked, considering the little man a safe source for information.

He grinned, exposing yellow teeth. "Sir, if I knowd you better, I might laugh, but I ain't laughin'. Truth is, I live here," he said.

Grant looked at him in a questionable manner.

"Got me a room upstairs. I work here," the little man explained with a grin.

Grant sipped his beer. It tasted flat and smelled like almonds. He knew two glasses would be all he could take. "Tell me, Pops," Grant said casually, "does anyone around here paint?"

"Paint?"

"I mean, do any artists ever come here?" Grant pressed on.

The little man grinned and nudged Grant with an elbow. "I could laugh at that one, sir. Easy to see you're an outsider. No sir, only one kind of person come here and they don't paint."

"I know what you mean, Pops."

"Yep. This is a high-class whorehouse. Never closes. Been that way ever since they licked the AIDS problem," Pops said proudly.

The little man took another swallow of beer and wiped his mouth with his shirt sleeve. "Everyone here is a sex maniac," he went on. "The gents always fight fir Kitty, mostly. The broads are worsen the gents, if you know what I mean."

Grant nodded. "I know what you mean," he said absentmindedly, as he considered his next move.

"Kitty's the best of the bunch. Each night she gives me a freebie!" Pops said, as he nudged Grant with a wink.

He took Grant's arm to get his attention. "To be honest about it, sir, I'm gettin' too old for this job but Kitty won't let me go. Honest to God."

"Yeah," cut in the bartender, catching the end of Pop's words. "That Kitty likes her men." He leaned toward Grant. "Beats the hell out o' me how she can be so young and so good."

"You mean the dark-skinned girl?" Grant asked.

"Naw. That's Nicki. She's new. Only eighteen. Kitty's twenty-five but she started young."

"Gotta go," said Pops, as he slid from his stool and pulled a yellow pad from his pocket. "I line up Kitty's customers and Buttercup, she handles the lesbians. I'll slip your name near the top of Kitty's list," Pops said, nudging Grant again.

"Not tonight, Pops," Grant said.

"See ya," said the little man and disappeared into the crowd.

Grant noticed that bouncers began to circulate the room to prevent free sex in the booths or restrooms. Also circulating were scantily clad teasers, or baiters, to encourage additional visits upstairs. A teaser approached Grant and took the stool Pops had vacated. She immediately applied her skills of seduction with soft words of smut and manipulating hands. When Grant cut her short, she kissed his cheek and moved on.

The bartender shuffled down the counter, picking up empty glasses and mopping spilled liquor, all with one arm and making it look easy. "They call me killer," he said to Grant.

"I'm Baxter," said Grant, using the first name to enter his mind.

"That sounds real. We don't use real tags around here. I'll call you Pistol."

Grant nodded. 'Your wife?" Grant asked, gesturing toward the fat lady at the cash register.

"Buttercup? Yeah," he said. He leaned toward Grant. "I call her Battleship, even to her face," he boasted.

He leaned toward the artist again. "You carry a tool?" he asked.

"You mean a gun?" Grant asked.

"Yeah. A gun or a knife. Say, haven't you been here before?"

"No, to both questions," lied Grant. "Do any artists come here?" Grant asked, changing the subject.

The bartender ignored his question.

"Not smart to come here without a gun," he said. "We have fights every night and shooting or knifings two or three times a week. That's how I lost my arm and got my name."

"You got shot?" Grant asked with concern.

"Twice. Shattered both bones in my arm. A drunk said I watered his drink. After he shot me, I grabbed him by the throat, drug him outside, and socked him onto the anchor hook, belly first!"

The bar crowd had fallen off as the rush for prostitutes was on. Grant decided to check out the wall paintings of nude lovers but they offered no clue. Still carrying his jacket, he casually transferred the gold ring from his jacket to his trouser pocket, thinking it would be safer there.

Grant had no sooner returned to the bar when he felt a blunt object pressing against his back.

"Don't move," came the harsh voice of a man at his rear. "Don't even blink or I squeeze and you are history. What you feel is a forty-five and it's achin' to shatter your spine."

Chapter 21
Tornado Alert

"Turn around...slow," demanded the man as he took a step backward.

A hush began to settle over the throng as people were alerted and passed the word. They eagerly closed in on the action and hoped for more.

Grant turned and faced a man who seemingly emerged from the woodwork. He was Grant's size but younger and his grin, like his gun, conveyed no hint of friendliness.

Grant's brain reeled as he attempted to grasp a situation that had the earmarks of a showdown. Foremost, he had to stall for time. Close to the surface of his mind was the thought that his bodyguard was possibly somewhere in the room. He couldn't imagine Doctor Gillespie's agents not having the tavern under surveillance.

"Stranger," said the gunman, his pistol leveled at Grant's midsection, "I think you're an outsider, an' outsiders ain't welcome here."

The man was wearing a loose T-shirt, cowboy boots, and tight jeans that hugged his spread legs. His blond hair was ruffled and his eyes held more than a glint of contempt.

Grant wondered what lurked in the man's twisted mind.

"Fact is," the gunman went on, "an outsider usually signs his death warrant by coming here." He glanced at the onlookers to his rear for approval and they responded with applause and urgings for hotter action.

Grant noted the man's rough hands, a nervous twitch at one corner of his mouth, and protruding upper teeth.

"Buck! What the hell you up to?" yelled the bartender.

"Shove off, Killer!" snorted the gunman. "This is my show!"

He turned to Grant and the artist could sense the man's patience was waning.

"Cody!" Buck yelled to one of his cronies standing nearby. "Check out the stranger's coat."

His friend complied.

"Coat's clean. No car keys neither," said Cody, giving the jacket to Buck.

The gunman's eyes never veered from the artist during Cody's search of the jacket and they remained there as he tossed the jacket over his shoulder, up for grabs to the crowd behind him.

"Cody, do you suppose the outsider is carrying a gun? Naw, he ain't that dumb," Buck reasoned, answering his own question before Cody could respond.

"On the other hand, let's play it safe. Cody, frisk him!" the gunman ordered.

Grant was ordered to stand and face the bar. Cody approached and frisked him, uncovering his gun and gold ring.

"I'll be damned, Cody, you hit the jackpot," beamed the gunman. "No wallet?" he asked.

"No, Buck," said Cody.

Grant realized the teaser must have picked his pocket. He slowly turned and faced Buck.

The gunman pushed Grant's revolver into his front trouser pocket and tossed the gold ring into the crowd. "It might be worth a couple bucks at a pawn shop," he yelled with a laugh.

The artist felt a sudden and deep sense of loss as the male spectators fought over the ring he had treasured.

Buck turned his attention to Grant with squinting eyes and a contempt that was reflected by his twitching mouth.

"Outsider, I want to know why the hell you are here and I want to know now!" he barked, stomping a boot to the floor.

Grant could feel blood rushing to his head as his mind groped for an answer. "I'm an artist," he finally said. "I came to observe the wall paintings."

The gunman broke into laughter and his followers joined him but the merriment was short-lived as Buck cut it off with a raised arm. "So, you're an artist," the gunman contemplated, pawing his chin. "Yeah…I saw you looking at our pictures and getting your jollies. Damn good pictures, wouldn't you say, outsider?"

Grant couldn't restrain himself. "They stink to high heaven," he said with conviction.

Buck's mouth twitched to the point that he had to settle himself before he could speak.

"Outsider, you've just signed your death warrant!" he finally roared as he leveled his gun.

Once again, a hush settled over the crowd.

"Buck," came the voice of Pops Sutton, who had broken through a wall of spectators. "Buck...it's your turn. Kitty...she's waiting'," he stammered apologetically.

Buck hesitated. He was like a kid trying to choose between ice cream and apple pie. He had two fires burning—Kitty upstairs and the outsider to his front, and he wasn't sure which fire he would extinguish first.

His hormones prevailed.

"Cody, your gun loaded?"

"Yeah, Buck. Loaded and itchy," said Cody.

"Cover this monkey 'till I git back. Remember, Cody, this outsider is mine. If he gits smart, shoot him in the knee caps. He's mine to kill, git that, Cody?" the gunman said, as he slowly pocketed his gun. He swaggered toward the stairs to the sounds of disappointment from a crowd who was thirsting for blood.

Grant's mind was working but he saw only a dead end. Somehow, he had to escape.

Cody pulled a chair from a nearby table and sat comfortably in front of Grant with his revolver hand resting on his knee. He was in his late teens and he tried to emulate Buck with a smirking face.

"Cody, mind if I sit and have a cup of coffee?" Grant asked.

Cody thought for a moment. "Okay, but don't talk to anyone. Jus' remember ol' Betsy here is pointin' at your spine."

"Thanks," said the artist with a slight smile. He enjoyed a deep sigh of relief as he turned back to the bar.

The bartender placed a beer before him and, as he did so, he leaned toward Grant and whispered, "Whatever happens, I'm on your side."

A blond teaser wearing black tights approached the bar. "Hey, Killer, someone told me we're under an alert—a tornado alert, I think." With that, she leaned against Grant and planted a kiss on his left ear, leaving a red smudge.

"Hey!" yelled Cody, "Git your butt away from him!"

She gave Cody a dirty look and moved on.

Using remote control, the bartender added volume and turned the television to a local channel to catch the news alert.

A weatherman, using charts and a scanner, was pictorializing several sightings of a tornado touchdown fifty miles east of Des Moines. He concluded his report with the following:

"Heavy rain continues to fall throughout the state with winds out of the southwest at sixty-four kilometers per hour and gusting as high as eighty. I repeat...the National Weather Bureau has reported a tornado alert-red is in effect throughout Cook County and is not expected to be lifted before midnight. Stay tuned to your local stations for further developments. Ritchie Richards, reporting from the windy city Weather Tower, returning you to the network program already in progress."

Grant checked his watch. It was eight o'clock.

When the local television station switched to the network program, Grant was jolted. On the television screen was an elderly man with a solemn face and compassionate eyes talking about Christ. The man wore a small brimless cap and a black robe, suggesting to Grant he was a bishop.

Grant was absorbed in the man's every word and movement as the church leader began to make references to the crucifixion.

Almighty God! Was this it? Would this be the key to solve his problem? Grant wondered. He suddenly realized the day was Good Friday.

Awareness of the Christian television program had spread through the tavern like the wind, causing rumblings of protest highlighted by cat calls.

"Who's the clown wearing the funny hat?" yelled a man from the rear.

"Looks like a monkey to me!" joined in another.

"Yea, he's a damn blabbering baboon!" shouted a man at the bar who had stood and faced the crowd with a toothless grin.

"Turn him off, Killer!" yelled a woman.

Meanwhile, the bishop had taken a piece of bread and a tumbler of wine from a table and had made preliminary remarks in preparation for the Eucharist. He replaced the tumbler as the camera zoomed in on his hand which held a small cube of bread.

By now, cries of protest had swelled to shouts of profanity and throwing objects at the television screen. A half-filled can of beer bounced off Grant's shoulder but he ignored it.

At that moment a bolt of lightning hit nearby with a powerful blast, bringing the house to a sudden silence.

"This is my body broken for you," said the bishop in a benevolent voice, clearly heard throughout the tavern.

Hearing the Christian's words sent the crowd into a frenzy.

Grant covered his ears with his hands, but couldn't escape the hysteria.

He instinctively jumped onto the bar and faced the mob. "Idiots! Idiots! Idiots!" he shouted.

Cody was caught off guard and nervously aimed his gun at Grant's legs.

Two shots rang out, silencing the crowd once again.

Buck was standing at the base of the stairs with gun in hand. His bullets had pierced a huge brace beam overhead.

During the lull and with his tumbler raised, the bishop spoke in a clear voice, saying, "This is my blood of the New Testament which is shed for many."

Buck leveled his gun and fired at the television screen, exploding it with glass spewing and a belch of smoke to the delight of his followers.

"Damn you, Buck! I'm gonna bash your head in!" Killer stormed.

The gunman crossed to the bar. "Shut up, you one-armed freak!" he retaliated, then gave a signal for his cronies, Bullets and Psycho, to disarm the bartender and his wife. "And you, outsider, stay up on that bar," Buck ordered.

Completing their mission, Bullets approached Buck. "Wh...what we do wit 'em now, Buck?" he asked.

"You and Psycho tie 'em and gag 'em. If they cause trouble, shoot 'em! Now, blow. I got business with this outsider," said Buck, impatiently.

The artist never felt so helpless as he stood on the bar. He had long since dismissed the thought of help from his bodyguard. Now he was thinking only about his wife and son. Aside from this, he could only hope and pray.

Buck turned to the crowd. "My friends," he bellowed, "if there's one thing worse than an outsider, it's a Christian outsider. Right?"

"Right!" The crowd roared in unison.

"This Christian outsider called us idiots," Buck continued, addressing the crowd. "My friends, I never saw a Christian who wants to die as bad as this here Christian. We treat him fair and he treats us like dirt. Know what? This damn Christian outsider will shed blood before this night is over. Right?"

Again, the crowd roared its approval.

Buck raised his arm for attention and it came quickly. "My friends, its time this Christian outsider put on a show for us. Would you like that?"

The worked up crowd was quickly becoming a blood-thirsty mob as they pressed forward, showering Grant with profanities.

"Bullets!" Buck blurted, "go upstairs and git Kitty down here quick."

"Sh...should she git d...dressed, Bu...Buck?" he stammered.

"Jackass! Just git her butt down here," Buck ordered.

Grant knew what Buck had in mind.

All eyes were on the outsider when Bullets and Nicki, the dark-skinned prostitute, approached the bar almost unnoticed.

Grant, however, noticed. He had caught the girl's eyes immediately and he thought she was trying to signal him. Twice, she waved a hand to Grant, then pointed to the pocket of the robe she was wearing. Grant was sure she was telling him she had something in her pocket.

Bullets and the girl approached Buck, who was sitting on a chair in front of Grant.

Buck jumped to his feet. "Bullets, you jackass, can't you do nothing right? Where the hell's Kitty?"

"Sh...she's sick, Bu...buck. Sh...she said you hurt her."

Buck pushed Bullets aside and looked at the eighteen-year-old. She was wearing a loose pink robe that reached her ankles with a belt tied at her waist. Her black hair was in disarray and her sweaty face, now free of make-up, wore a puzzled look.

Grant was looking at the right pocket of her robe and his heart was pounding.

It was obvious to him the pocket contained an object. It was clearly bulging and he couldn't understand why Buck or his cronies didn't see it. It had to be a small handgun but why would this woman want to help him, he wondered. His head was spinning. If it was a weapon and was detected, she would pay with her life. He wondered why this woman would risk so much for a stranger.

"Buck...what ees going on?" she asked, almost in tears.

"You naked under that thing?" Buck asked impatiently.

She nodded.

"Good. Git your ass up on that bar."

"Why for, Buck?"

"Dammit! You and the Christian are gonna give the house a free show, that's why for, you dumb foreigner," he answered with a sneer.

"No! I no like public display! Where is Keeler?" she asked, noting the bartender was missing. "I take orders only from Keeler."

"Git up there you little whore!" Buck blurted, then slapped the girl hard across the face, the blow knocking her to the floor.

Before the gunman could regain his balance, Grant instinctively dove at him, ramming his shoulder into Buck's stomach as they crashed to the floor. Grant's response to the slap was so quick and unexpected, those nearest the action were momentarily frozen.

Buck's pistol had been knocked from his hand and Grant was able to throw a fist flush against Buck's face before the gunman's cronies could put their gun barrels to Grant's head.

"Don't...shoot him. I...I want the Christian for myself," Buck said, gasping for air.

The struggle was over and the two men slowly regained their feet.

Buck's nose was bleeding and a protruding tooth had broken in half. He wiped the blood from his lips with his bare arm as Cody returned his gun.

He faced Grant eyeball to eyeball. His humiliation caused a rapid twitch of his mouth that momentarily rendered him speechless. While still glaring at Grant, he pointed at the bar.

The artist hesitated while five handguns were pointed toward him. He was down but he wasn't out. He was still alive.

As he slowly mounted the bar, Grant realized his right hand ached and the knuckles were bleeding.

He stood on the bar with the dark-skinned girl and the impatient crowd clamored for the sex show to begin.

Grant looked at the girl, who was trembling and still sobbing from the slap. He felt compassion for her in spite of his own predicament.

For some unexplainable reason, Grant's eyes strayed and fell upon a lone bottle of wine on a low shelf directly below. The wine reminded him of the bishop's words about Christ's blood being shed for many. Christ's blood and the wine. Was there a connection? He wondered.

Grant was also remembering the kitchen door that led onto North Ashland Avenue. The swinging doors leading to the kitchen were only about twelve feet from where he stood, straight ahead and behind the bar.

"Dammit, whore!" Buck yelled at the young prostitute. "Start doing your thing. Take off your robe!"

She smiled faintly at Grant and he felt she wanted to tell him something.

"Buck, ees it okay eef we kees first?" she asked, without taking her eyes off Grant's. "I must kees to warm up," she said.

Without waiting for Buck's response, she threw her arms around Grant's neck and pulled his head to her level, then smothered his lips with kisses.

The impatient on-lookers were yelling for her to take it off.

Nicki turned to the crowd, untied her robe belt and, for a brief moment, opened her robe to the delight of everyone. She turned to Grant and pressed her body against him. "You are han'som," she said.

She put her lips to his ear and whispered that she had the gold ring in her robe pocket. Her boyfriend had caught it when Buck tossed it away.

"You are beautiful," Grant whispered to her, thinking more of her kind heart.

Nicki stepped back from Grant, removed her robe, and tossed it to him.

In that instant of clamor, when all eyes were on the girl, Grant slipped the gold ring from the robe to his trouser pocket. Almost instantaneously, as the crowd continued to roar their delight, a sudden blast of thunder shook the tavern and momentarily left it in darkness.

Grant instinctively jumped to the floor behind the bar, grabbed where the bottle of wine was placed, and dove against the swinging doors, striking them with his left shoulder.

Shots flashed at the bar area.

"Shoot him!" screamed Buck, frantically. "Shoot him! Shoot him!" Landing on the kitchen floor with bottle in hand, Grant rolled to his feet, broke to his left, found the steps, and was out the door as a second volley of shots rang out. He was out of the building and into the rain in eight seconds.

When the lights returned in the tavern, Grant had disappeared into the back alleys and was running in a northeasterly direction. In his hand was the bottle of wine. In his trouser pocket was the gold ring.

When Buck and his cronies returned to the tavern empty-handed, they were met by a hostile mob who felt cheated.

"I shot him!" Buck lied. "The outsider is out there somewhere in the streets...dead. I swear it."

Buck's words fell on empty ears as the men, with guns drawn, began to box him in.

On the floor behind the bar counter lay the nude prostitute, Nicki. The hole near her left temple was the result of a stray bullet intended for Grant.

Chapter 22
Deadline

It wasn't until Grant had covered a half-mile of side streets that he was convinced his pursuers had been eluded and he could safely return to North Ashland Avenue. He was walking now, but his chest pained with each breath.

The wind and rain continued to pound his body, making progress difficult and the bottle slippery in his grasp. He was without raincoat and without money for taxi fare but he was alive.

Grant rested against a light post. As he did so, he closed his eyes and thanked God for the rainstorm, the dark-skinned girl, the timely blast of thunder, and the escape he had made from the tavern.

He felt an overwhelming urge to sink to the pavement, but he resisted. He had to go on. He knew there had to be a purpose for what he was doing. Somehow, it would all come together like the pieces of a puzzle. He looked at the bottle of wine he was clutching and wondered how it would fit into the scheme.

For more than two hours Grant inched northward, passing the Kennedy Expressway, trudging past McKinley High School, and on by Chase Park. The wind had eased and the rain stopped but he hardly noticed. He finally approached the intersection of Ashland and Fullerton, one-half mile from his destination.

As Grant started to cross the intersection, he stopped abruptly. Standing in the center of the intersection directly to his front was a man of massive size, silhouetted by the streetlight beyond. Like Grant, the man was bareheaded and coatless. Unlike Grant, he was holding a pistol in one hand, its barrel reflecting the light from above.

The man stood motionless.

Grant glanced to see if any cars were approaching. None were in sight. Due to the alert, the streets were almost empty of traffic.

He was exhausted and to run would be like committing suicide. From only twenty feet, the man would most likely fire immediately, pumping six bullets at him.

Peter Grant knew he would have to fight the man, even with the odds stacked against him. Earlier in the tavern, he had survived a showdown. Now he was being tested again.

He held up the bottle of wine in a friendly gesture, as an offering to the man.

There was no response.

Finally, the man pointed a finger toward Grant, indicating he wanted more than the bottle.

Grant quickly rubbed the palm of his hand on the inside of his pant leg in an effort to dry it, then firmly gripped the neck of the bottle.

His adversary confidently dropped his gun into a pocket and began a slow advance.

Grant's aggressive nature took over and he raised the bottle overhead in a threatening gesture.

The man lunged forward.

The artist attempted to side step, but his legs were too heavy. Knowing he would be struck by the man, he started to bring the bottle downward, aiming for the attacker's head. Again, he was too late, as the man's shoulder rammed his midsection, sending him sprawling backward onto the pavement.

Grant's back, shoulders, and head struck the hard surface, smashing the wine bottle, as the attacker landed on him with huge hands searching for his throat.

Still holding tightly to the bottle neck, Grant delivered it with one final thrust toward the man's face and its jagged edges found their mark.

The huge man lifted his head in momentary disbelief, as the glass had pierced both eyes, severing their superior oblique and recti muscles. He leaned backward with a wailing scream and jerked the bottle handle free, causing a gusher of blood to spurt onto Grant's face and chest.

The attacker's blinding distraction enabled Grant to free himself from under the man's huge frame, but he was too exhausted to immediately regain his feet.

The man sat there, bewildered. The severed eye muscles allowed the man's eyeballs to hang forward and slightly outward in a grotesque manner. With effort, he rolled to his feet, gave an agonizing cry, and staggered blindly down the middle of Fullerton Avenue.

It wasn't until the attacker's wails had faded away that Grant realized his head ached. He felt the back of his head and found blood, the result of his fall to the pavement. In addition, it wasn't until then that he realized his attacker was a black man.

The red wine was gone but the artist felt lucky to be alive.

Considering how the confrontation had ended, he could afford to feel sorry for the man.

His good fortune continued when he spotted the gun. During the brief scuffle, the man's pistol had fallen from his pocket, enabling Grant to arm himself once again.

With renewed vigor, he took a deep breath and moved on.

When his apartment finally came into view, the weary artist stopped short. He could see slivers of light under pulled blinds at the windows of John Baxter's first-floor apartment, telling him Baxter had returned. Furthermore, as he approached the building, he saw momentary flashes of light from his studio windows. An intruder was in his apartment with a flashlight.

When Grant saw lights in Baxter's apartment, he remembered Doctor King revealing Baxter as a revolutionist and was dangerous. Or was it Doctor Gillespie who had told him? He couldn't remember.

Grant rested momentarily at the base of the staircase. Beads of sweat rolled down his forehead and temples, mixing with the blood on his face. He checked his newly found pistol. It was a six-shot, single action weapon, and it was loaded.

He quietly ascended the stairs with the gun in hand and found the door ajar. He eased his way across the kitchenette to the studio door. Pausing a moment to collect himself, he gingerly opened the door far enough to enable him to reach inside and trip a wall switch. This activated the four floodlights near the base of the portrait.

The studio was flooded with light, revealing a surprised Baxter who was standing on the stepladder in front of the portrait. The sudden shock of exposure unnerved his landlord, causing him to drop his flashlight.

"Painter, that you?" Baxter asked, being temporarily blinded by the light.

Grant stepped closer to him.

"My God, what happened? Painter, you're a bloody mess! Were you in a fight?"

"What are you doing here?" Grant asked, ignoring Baxter's remarks.

"I must admit, curiosity got the better of me. Your deadline is a whisker away and I couldn't resist the temptation to check your progress," Baxter said, returning his attention to the portrait.

"Tell me, painter, are you having a problem painting the blood of Christ?"

Again, Grant ignored the intruder.

Still standing on the ladder, Baxter casually removed a switchblade knife from his pocket as he turned to Grant. "Tell me, painter, do I see a gun in your hand?"

"That's what you see, Mr. Baxter, and it's loaded."

"Ha! That's good, painter," Baxter said with a chuckle. "You're a Christian and Christians don't kill. It's against the will of your God," he said smugly.

Baxter snapped out the blade of his knife.

Grant stepped closer, raised his gun, and aimed it at Baxter's head.

"Painter, you're bluffing," Baxter said as he turned to the portrait and raised his knife.

Grant fired once. The bullet struck Baxter in the left temple, causing him to crash to the floor.

"But I'm a lousy Christian, Mr. Baxter," Grant said softly, lowering his arm. "You made that point clear to me on many occasions," he reminded his lifeless antagonist.

Peter Grant's eyes didn't stray from Baxter's body as he crossed the studio and slumped into a chair near his cot. Even as he placed his gun upon the adjacent stand, he didn't look away. He had taken a human life. His portrait had become an integral part of him and he couldn't imagine it being destroyed. Still, he was remorseful.

He looked up at this portrait and gazed at the red paint that so miserably represented the blood of a dying Christ. The hour was late and Grant was exhausted as he succumbed to the past six hours and three tormenting showdowns.

Now his gaze encompassed the entire portrait and, as it did so, the image of Christ became foggy and hardly distinguishable. He leaned back in despair with sprawled, heavy legs and half-closed eyes. Some time later the fog lifted and the portrait came into focus, but to Grant's dismay, the face of Christ remained distorted with deep lines of contempt. His eyes became wide and looked in Grant's direction. They were piercing, condemning eyes.

Stricken with fear, Peter Grant's urge to scream became a reality.

His sharp cry triggered a current of motion that sent the studio into a spin and he dug his fingers into the chair arms to avoid falling. The revolving room took on the illusion of circular streaks converging toward the motionless portrait at the center.

Grant's stomach churned and he began to dry heave. His head vibrated as the portrait began to counter spin and increase in size as though moving toward him. His grip finally failed and he slammed to the floor.

When Grant opened his eyes, the room was motionless and quiet, except for the soft rain tapping the black skylight overhead. He lifted himself to one elbow and became aware of the throbbing at the back of his head. He reached back and touched wet blood as the wound was aggravated by his fall to the floor. His face and chest were splattered with congealed blood and his clothes were still damp from the earlier rain.

He looked at the portrait and expected to be struck by the glaring eyes of Christ but he wasn't. The eyes were almost closed as he had painted them and Jesus' face was calm.

Grant's eyes moved down the figure of Christ to the easel base and to the floor. Baxter's body was gone. Grant scanned his studio. Nothing.

He knew his aim was good because he saw the blood spurt. He wondered if he was hallucinating. Yet, at this point, he felt it no longer seemed to matter.

Only the portrait had meaning and he was so close to its completion. Tonight he had beaten the odds more than once. The wine bottle had played its part. He had the gold ring. He would try once more to paint the blood of Jesus.

Grant rolled to his stomach. He was still nauseous and felt too sick to walk. With effort, he made the agonizing crawl across the studio to the portrait. He pushed the ladder aside and tripped the easel, bringing the heavy canvas crashing to the floor. Fortunately, it landed face up.

He was breathing hard and he rested for several minutes before he sat up and reached for the bottom drawer of his paint cabinet. He didn't realize how easy the drawer pulled until he saw it was empty.

Grant pulled the next drawer. Empty.

He tried to remember why he would have moved his oils and palettes. It made no sense. He quickly pulled the remaining drawers. His paints were gone. He scanned the shelving against the wall and discovered his brushes were missing. He had been burglarized.

It was obvious to Grant the thief was his landlord. Perhaps Baxter had done it earlier and returned to destroy the portrait.

Tears welled in Grant's eyes but he wasn't angry. He only wanted to die.

As he sat there, he became aware of the gold ring in his pocket. He withdrew it, kissed it, and placed it upon the cabinet top. From the same cabinet he removed sheeting and spread it over the portrait, covering the areas where he would lay as he painted. This done, he maneuvered onto the portrait near the head of Christ.

The artist was prepared to do with human blood what he was unable to do with paint.

He touched his right index finder to the cut at his head, picking up a small amount of wet blood and placing it to the portrait where the crown of thorns pierced the head of Christ. It adhered nicely to the canvas.

Grant knew it would darken as it dried. He touched his wet finger to a glob of blood on his shirt front and added this to the mixture. The result was a deep rich luster, causing his heart to pound.

He continued at a rapid pace, repeating the process of using his saliva as a lubricant and alternating a mixture of blood from his head and chest. He was painting with a mixture of his blood and that of the black man who had challenged him, but he was only vaguely aware of it.

Grant's mouth became a mass of blood as he continued to pick up saliva with his index finger which had become his brush. He found the results overwhelming and he stopped momentarily to thank God.

While hovering near the painted face of Christ, he lingered for a moment and tenderly examined the eyes and mouth. The eyelids of Jesus seemed almost to flutter. The slightly open mouth had a subtle quivering effect.

The artist carefully placed a mixture of blood where the huge nail had pierced the wrists and feet of Christ. The blood continued to reveal a rich velvety texture, containing its own highlights. Grant was confident it would retain this richness after it would dry.

His heart was pounding as the last mixture of blood became the last stroke to complete the blood of Christ.

The portrait was finished.

With renewed strength, Grant got to his feet and managed to prop the canvas against the wall. He stepped back to view his efforts and he was struck by its full impact.

His eyes were drawn to Christ's face, a serene and forgiving face in the midst of a dying agony. A wave of love struck to the core of Grant's being and he suddenly felt warm and comforted.

Grant dropped to his knees at the base of his portrait and lowered his head in reverence. "God, forgive me," he pleaded submissively.

He heard a voice speak low and clear. "Truly, I say to you, today you will be with me in paradise."

Darkness swiftly fell over the artist and he felt an easy floating sensation, as though being gently carried into immense space by strong arms.

Chapter 23
Revelations

Preston Thomas rolled out of bed Saturday morning expecting another uneventful day.

He was worried. Each day for the past month he phoned Tracy with nothing to report about Pete's progress at the easel. Press was hurting for a favorable word, any bit of news about his friend which would please her.

The portrait was scheduled for pickup in eight days and Press knew Grant's predicament would intensify with each passing hour. He decided if Pete didn't telephone him by noon, he would run down.

Shortly after nine his telephone rang.

"Good news, Preston!" said Doctor Gillespie. "I would prefer to tell you this news in person but time is pressing."

"Is it about Pete?"

"Yes! Mr. Grant has finished his portrait!" she said with a dash of excitement.

Preston Thomas hesitated. "Judith, would you repeat that?"

"It's true! Mr. Grant's portrait is finished! He did it!"

Press dropped into a chair.

"Preston, I'll bring you up to date later," she said hurriedly.

"Thank God. Pete beat the deadline," he muttered to himself.

"Please listen closely to what I say," Doctor Gillespie continued. "I'll notify Mr. Grant's wife. I'm asking you to contact no one, not even Mr. Grant. Kindly sit tight for two days and I'll get back to you." She hesitated. "Preston, are you with me?"

"Yes, Judith, I'm listening."

"Preston, the events that surround Mr. Grant's finished portrait are confusing to say the least. For this reason, I'm putting together a committee meeting for this Monday to sort out the pieces. Now I need a favor. For security reasons, your house would be an ideal setting for this meeting to start at 2:00 P.M. May I borrow your dining room?"

"My house is yours, Judith."

"Good. Preston, make note of this," she continued. "Report off work this Monday and give your house employees the day off. Also, I would like your presence on the committee, along with Mr. Grant."

"You can count on me," Press assured her.

"I must run. I'll phone you Monday morning about nine with the details," she concluded.

During the weekend, Press was a tangle of nerves as he tried to imagine what kind of confusion about the portrait would cause Doctor Gillespie's hasty meeting.

Meanwhile, he tried to pass the two days with walks, reading, and television. As it turned out, he couldn't concentrate on the media, except for a single news bulletin:

"White House Press Secretary James Fry announced the revolutionaries appear to have abandoned their aim to overthrow the federal government in favor of guerrilla warfare. The Devil's Corps continues to be the most feared branch of the revolutionaries. Citizens are advised to avoid large concentrations of people such as sporting events and church services."

On Monday morning, April 12, Doctor Gillespie phoned Press.

"Preston, every Monday a fleet of vans from the Rainbow Realty Agency tours the city to give real estate agents a firsthand view of listed and prospective properties for sale."

"At two o'clock today, a gold van with our agency marking will enter your driveway. All occupants, including myself, will be wearing gold jackets, emblematic of the agency.

"Our purpose is to conduct a meeting relative to Mr. Grant and his portrait. We will already have eaten and will be ready for conversation. There will be ten of us and your dining room table will nicely serve our purpose.

"I might add, Preston, clear away the ash trays. We want clean air as well as clear heads to prevail," she concluded.

Five hours later, the committee arrived.

When Press met Grant at the door, they hugged and their eyes were moist.

"I'm happy for you and your family, Pete."

"I got lucky," the artist countered with a grin.

Grant sobered quickly and placed his hands upon his friend's shoulders. "I feel like a different person in a different world, Press. It's strange and I don't understand it but you'll hear all about it in a moment."

After the committee was seated, Doctor Gillespie removed agenda papers, a recorder, and a notebook from her briefcase and placed them before her.

Looking her usual self with honey blonde bangs and wearing no make-up, Doctor Gillespie expressed gratitude to Preston Thomas for sharing his house and to the committee members for their willingness to respond on quick notice and in spite of heavy schedules.

She scanned the committee members and sat back. "My friends, when Mr. Grant completed his portrait three days ago, a number of strange developments occurred, including a disappearance of blood. Shortly after the portrait's completion, Mr. Grant was in a confused state and I admitted him at Edgewater Memorial for observation. On that occasion, I spoke with Mr. Grant and he explained the strange developments to which I refer."

"The purpose of this committee is to discuss these developments and make recommendations as to what should be done.

"As you can see, these proceedings are being recorded and copies of the tape will be available upon request at my office after tomorrow," she said as she distributed agenda sheets which included the following:

Agenda
April 12, 2027

Topics for discussion:
1. The artist, Peter Grant (afternoon session)
2. The portrait: *The Crucifixion of Christ* (evening session)

Committee members:
Doctor Harriet King, psychiatrist, Edgewater Memorial, Chicago
Agent Roger Davis, 340, Peter Grant's bodyguard
Cardinal Phillip Garmadio, Archbishop, Washington, D.C.
Doctor Matthew Mason, neurologist, Edgewater Memorial, Chicago
Reverend L. C. Reeves, pastor, All-Denominations Church, Chicago
Ambrose Thorne, art director, Nelson-Faust Advertising Agcy., N.Y.C.
Henri Goosche, artist, Ambrose Thorne's staff
Monsignor Kelly, priest, Saint Michael's Parish, Washington, D.C.
Preston Thomas, P.R. Department, Glick Publishing Co., Chicago
Peter Grant, free lance artist
Doctor Judith Gillespie, psychiatrist, Director of C. R. T.

"At this point," continued Doctor Gillespie, "the media is unaware as to what has happened and I remind you to keep your pledge of confidentiality until the committee has acted. We may decide to go to a higher level or directly to the White House."

Doctor Gillespie donned her reading glasses and opened her notebook. "To help you better understand the present, I'll give you three pieces of background information that led to the completion of Mr. Grant's portrait.

"First, for almost two years and without his knowledge, Mr. Grant has been suffering from a fatal disease known as the Flip-Flop Syndrome. Doctor Harriet King and I have worked on his case and, as you know, Doctor King is a member of this committee.

"We agonized over the question as to when we would tell Mr. Grant about his disease. Originally, we had planned to tell him after his recuperation from his hospital stay two Decembers ago, however, when he painted so effectively upon his release, we decided to hold off until the portrait was finished. Subsequently, his painting had turned sour, being unable to paint the blood of Christ to his satisfaction.

"A second piece of information," continued Doctor Gillespie, "deals with a microelectronic implant in Mr. Grant's skull.

"The implant is a security measure. Due to the religious theme of his portrait, Mr. Grant had become a target of the Devil's Corps and for us to know his whereabouts was essential. Until three days ago, the implant had enabled Mr. Grant's bodyguard, Agent Roger Davis, to do exactly that. The implant procedure was performed sixteen months ago by Doctor Matthew Mason, a member of this committee, as is Agent Davis.

"Even though John Baxter existed only in Mr. Grant's mind, the name had become known to the Devil's Corps. Consequently, we produced our own John Baxter, giving Mr. Grant's bodyguard that additional role.

"To enhance the safety of the artist, as well as his portrait, it was arranged for Agent Davis to occupy the apartment below the artist's studio apartment at 5210 North Ashland. In addition to credentials, Agent Davis was provided with a monitor which gave him visual tracings as to Mr. Grant's whereabouts.

"My final piece of lead-up information deals with a theory," continued Doctor Gillespie, as she turned a page of her notebook.

"The theory belongs to Doctor King, an expert in the area of hallucinations—their causes and effects. Simply put, her theory is this: *If Mr. Grant kills John Baxter, the antagonist who constantly haunts him during his hallucinations, he will be cured of the Flip-Flop Syndrome.*"

Doctor Gillespie glanced at her watch and leaned forward, resting both arms on the table.

"With that brief lead-up, we come to the day before the portrait was finished. That was three days ago, Friday, April 9 at 7:00 P.M. That was when we lost visual tracings of Mr. Grant. To account for his whereabouts from the point until the portrait was finished—about seven hours later—we pieced together the following time table:

7:00 P.M.:	A thunderbolt struck our transformer, cutting power to Mr. Grant's implanted detector while he was home.
7:05 P.M.:	Noting this on his monitor, Agent Davis phoned me to report the development. Shortly afterward, he phoned Mr. Grant to verify his presence, but the artist was gone.
8:00 P.M.:	The transformer was repaired. The monitor tracings had Mr. Grant at the intersection of North Ashland and Briardale Avenues. That area is noted for its lawlessness. The Anchor tavern, a hangout for thugs, is located there.
8:30 P.M.:	Under my direction, Agent Davis arrived at The Anchor tavern, only to discover Mr. Grant had been there but had departed.
11:30 P.M.:	The monitor traced Mr. Grant at the intersection of North Ashland and Fullerton Avenues when the monitor screen went blank again. Knowing the transformer was repaired, this told us the implant became impaired. Later, Mr. Grant told me he had fought a man at the intersection and had hit the back of his head against the pavement, explaining the implant's malfunction.
12:45 A.M.:	Saturday, April 10. By means of minicameras planted in Mr. Grant's apartment, Agent Davis saw the artist enter his apartment with bloody face, hands, and shirt front.
12:50 A.M.:	Agent Davis reported the developments to me and I arrived at his apartment in twenty minutes. Agent Davis and I decided not to intervene, as we observed the monitor. Mr. Grant looked a mess but he didn't appear to be seriously hurt. Mr. Grant went to his studio cot and appeared to fall asleep. I returned to my office while Agent Davis kept watch with instructions to notify me at his discretion.
2:10 A.M.:	Mr. Grant awakened. Agent Davis saw the artist crawl to the portrait and trip the easel, causing the portrait to fall onto the floor. Mr. Grant pulled out his paint drawers but they were apparently empty. He crawled onto his portrait and began to paint using blood from his head and chest.
2:40 A.M.:	Agent Davis saw Mr. Grant sign his portrait in blood, step back, drop onto his knees, and slump to the floor in an apparent unconscious state. Agent Davis contacted me.

3:20 A.M.: Three of my agents and I arrived at Mr. Grant's apartment and found the artist clean of blood. Let me repeat. We found no blood. Mr. Grant's face, hands, and shirt were clean. Agent Mossgrove and I took the artist to Edgewater Memorial for observation. Agents Davis and DeCamp remained to photograph the portrait. After using a blower to assure the painting was dry, the agents removed the portrait from its frame, and transported it to my headquarters for safekeeping."

Doctor Gillespie looked up from her notebook.

"That concludes the lead-up," she said as she took a tape from her briefcase.

"Yesterday, at Edgewater Memorial, before I began my contacts with each of you, I cut this tape. It's a conversation between Mr. Grant and me. I wanted Mr. Grant's version of those lost hours the previous day," she explained, as she slipped the tape into her recorder.

On the tape, Peter Grant revealed why he went to the tavern and the events that led to his escape. He revealed his encounter with the black man and his return to his apartment, where he hallucinated that he had shot John Baxter.

Finally, he explained how he was able to paint the blood and finish the portrait.

Doctor Gillespie removed the tape and replaced it in her briefcase.

"Before we get into discussion," she said, glancing at her watch, "Mr. Grant consented to tell you what he experienced from the moment he finished his portrait."

Grant stood and made a quick eye-to-eye scan around the table. The slight trace of a smile that usually greeted his associates was not evident. "If I appear to be nervous at this moment, it's because I am. I'm ill at ease because what I'm about to tell you is beyond my understanding."

The artist paused to pinpoint his thoughts.

"Two days ago," he began, "after considerable effort and improvisation, I made the last strokes of blood at the wounds at Christ's feet. The portrait was finished! However, as I signed the portrait, a hot surge rushed through my veins, leaving me with a strange sense of cleansing. But it was more. It was also a sense of well-being, strength, and awareness.

"With surprising ease I lifted the huge frame and leaned the portrait against the wall. I stepped backward and viewed my handiwork." The tempo of Grant's words slowed and his voice softened. "The portrait was...beautiful... overpowering... uncompromising. It was alive, personal, and touching me. I felt humble and ashamed. I found myself on my knees and felt an overpowering need to speak."

Grant noticed a glass of water had been placed before him and he paused to sip it.

"I begged forgiveness," he continued, "and I heard a firm voice accept me into the Kingdom of God."

The room was still and eyes were moist.

"At that moment, I apparently lost consciousness.

"Later, when my eyes opened, I saw Doctor Gillespie and three of her agents hovering over me. I thought I was dreaming because I felt no pain and I saw no blood on my hands. I reached back and felt no wound at the back of my head.

"I knew I wasn't hallucinating. My soul felt liberated, as if I were on the outside of my body and looking in. My mind was clear. I was aware of facts which heretofore were totally unknown to me.

"The last two years of my life had crystallized before my mind's eye. I realized I had been suffering from a mental disorder. I also knew I was now cured. I knew the nature of the disorder, how I had become ill and how I was cured. I knew John Baxter was a hoax. I knew when I had been hallucinating and when I hadn't. I could distinguish between reality and fantasy."

"Ladies and gentlemen, that's it. That's the best I can do to explain it," he concluded and took his seat.

The committee members stirred in their seats and exchanged glances.

Doctor Gillespie stood. "Mr. Grant, you handled a difficult assignment with courage. On behalf of the committee, I thank you for your contribution."

Doctor Gillespie glanced at her watch. "It's three o'clock. We'll break into groups of three or four of your choosing and have a one-hour discussion period. Feel free to spread out. At four o'clock we'll reassemble for a discussion period to conclude at five," she said.

That evening the committee gathered at Doctor Gillespie's headquarters where they dined and assembled at a huge table.

Doctor Gillespie stood.

"Before Mr. Grant tells us about the strange features of his portrait, I wish to remind you of three unusual features even before the portrait was completed.

"First, it is difficult to imagine how one could paint with such power, sensitivity, depth of feeling, and skill while suffering from such a depressing disease as the Flip-Flop Syndrome,"

"Secondly, how can one ignore the uncanny method used by Mr. Grant to paint the blood of Christ?

"Finally, our computers refused a negative print-out on the portrait even when fed negative data."

With that introduction, Doctor Gillespie gave way to Peter Grant.

The artist stood and loosened the middle button of his blue tweed jacket, letting the coat hang open. "I'll come to the point and give you two additional features of the portrait which must be classified as unbelievable," he began.

He scanned the committee. "Have any of you observed the portrait for about a minute?" he asked.

"No, I think not," asserted Doctor Gillespie. "We were reluctant to view the portrait in your absence," she added.

"If you had," Grant continued, "you would have witnessed a most unusual happening.

"Earlier today, I believe most of you had the opportunity to view the portrait. As you did so, you saw the plate I had painted on the cross upright above the head of Christ. The plate contains the four letters—I.N.R.I. As you know, this translates into *Jesus of Nazareth. The King of the Jews.*

"When a person observes the portrait for a brief period, the four letters will slowly disappear to the viewer. However, in seconds they will slowly reappear but not as the original letters. They will reappear as four different symbols—MM28—two letters and two numbers. These symbols will remain only for a few seconds before reverting to the original letters. This alternate change will continue as long as one views the portrait. My personal view is this: the symbols MM28 translates into next year—2028. The letters are Roman numerals."

The committee members were visibly shaken.

"My final observation is perhaps even more unbelievable," continued Grant. "It is simply this: *the portrait itself is capable of disappearing completely from view, depending upon who is viewing it.*"

The committee members shook their heads and slumped back in their chairs.

"After a few minutes of viewing the portrait," Grant continued, "with the exception of the smudge marks of human blood on the canvas, the portrait will slowly vanish before the eyes of a disbeliever, not to reappear."

"My God! What does this mean?" muttered Ambrose Thorne.

Tears welled in the eyes of Reverend Reeves and he nodded as if in recognition of God's mysterious ways. "Of course...you imply a disbeliever of the everlasting God...our Creator," he uttered softly.

"Yes," said Grant. "Of course all of this can easily be proven by any of you. You need only to observe the portrait and you'll see the symbols change and reappear. If an atheist views the portrait, his response will tell you it has vanished.

"Thank you, ladies and gentlemen," Grant said and took his seat as the committee members broke into a vigorous applause.

Grant stood again and the members became silent.

"Doctor Gillespie," he said, "before we go into questions and discussion, may I close with some personal remarks?"

Doctor Gillespie nodded. "Of course, Mr. Grant."

The artist stood tall. "All of you know nothing worthwhile is ever accomplished alone. If my portrait is of any significance beyond its intended purpose, I'm pleased.

"In which case, I would attribute this to those who have given meaning to my life, beginning with my parents. From them I inherited my skills. They taught me to succeed with humility. By example, they taught me to feel compassion for my fellowman, especially for those less fortunate than I. Finally, my parents taught me the greatest lesson of all—only by giving do we receive. My parents did this for me in but six years.

"I'm indebted to Doctor Ancel Dubreau for teaching me the meaning of faith. I view love as a composite of respect, understanding, and faith, with faith being the cornerstone. Simply put, it was faith that enabled me to paint the portrait.

"I accept your applause and appreciation of my efforts on behalf of my loved ones, including a special lady who is no longer with us."

Chapter 24
The Tribunal

Prior to the one-hour discussion period, Doctor Gillespie exposed the committee members to the portrait long enough to witness first-hand the alternate changing of the symbols painted upon the plate above the head of Christ. The experience was so overpowering, several members of the committee had to collect their composure before joining a discussion group.

Two general conclusions were reached by the committee during the first day of meetings.

The main thrust had centered upon the supernatural aspects with the clergy leading the way. There was a consensus of opinion the aspects transcended the realms of the physical and psychological sciences and entered the arena of theology. It was looked upon as a relationship between God and humankind.

Cardinal Garmadio had suggested the supernatural features were God's way of drawing world attention to His wonders and providing humanity the opportunity to renew and strengthen its faith in its Creator.

Cardinal Garmadio's remark served as an explanation as to why the supernatural features existed. But why now?

The world had recently entered a new millennium. It would be a fresh start of one thousand years. Just as Mr. Grant had experienced an awakening, the clergy suggested the time was ripe for a Renaissance in Christianity.

This thinking was reinforced by Grant's earlier observation: the four symbols—MM28—could signify the year two thousand twenty-eight, less than nine months away.

Monsignor Kelly, priest of Saint Michael's Parish, suggested the scheduled May ninth unveiling of the portrait be postponed until later in the year, allowing time for much needed preparation.

The second conclusion reached by the committee dealt with authority, as Doctor Gillespie suggested the discussions go to a higher level. She reasoned that once the findings were made public, international repercussions would likely occur. As a presidential appointee, she would be willing to contact the president on the matter. Meanwhile, the committee agreed to meet in one week, April nineteenth, and follow the same agenda.

Earlier, when Doctor Gillespie was organizing the committee, she had asked Henri Goosche to serve on the committee and also paint a quick replica of Grant's portrait to serve as a decoy.

Goosche agreed on both counts after learning he would be paid handsomely and have Grant's permission to use his studio and art supplies. Grant, in turn, would reside temporarily at Doctor Gillespie's headquarters.

The painting procedure would be relatively simple. Goosche would use a blown-up print on canvas of the photograph taken by Agent DeCamp shortly after the portrait was completed. Goosche would merely match some of the large area colors to make the canvas print appear authentic to the untrained eye.

On April 13, Goosche went to work on the replica. On April 19, he attended the afternoon committee session but elected to forego the evening meeting in favor of completing the replica.

When Grant's bodyguard, Agent Davis, returned to the artist's apartment that evening, he was disturbed to note the second floor apartment was in darkness and the door leading up the stairwell was ajar.

He approached the door and was further disturbed as the light at the top of the stairwell revealed smears of blood on the steps.

The agent withdrew his pistol and cautiously ascended the stairs. The door leading into the kitchenette was unlocked. He eased himself inside and crossed to the studio door. After a moment he opened the door far enough to put his hand through and onto the studio light switch at the wall.

With pistol leveled, he snapped the light switch and quickly stepped through the doorway to a bright studio.

The agent saw a trail of blood leading toward the portrait. The portrait decoy was in its customary position, resting upon the huge easel. A thick smear of blood marked the painting with a huge X extending from its four corners.

Agent Davis winced at the sight of it, knowing the X was the official insignia of the Devil's Corps, signifying its leader, Lady X. Worse yet, the head of Christ had been crudely cut from the canvas, telling the agent Henri Goosche had no doubt met a similar fate.

The agent's eyes finally dropped from the mutilated portrait to a brown, bloody bag at the base of the easel. Without hesitation, he crossed to the studio telephone and reported to Doctor Gillespie that Henri Goosche had been decapitated.

Doctor Gillespie had learned from the beginning Lady X was a vain woman who specialized in doing away with her enemy in a personal way. The doctor planned to exploit this weakness, as she firmly believed the vanity of Lady X would be her doom.

The unexpected tragedy raised some questions relative to security. Did a security leak attract the Devil's Corps to Mr. Grant's studio? Was Mr. Goosche tortured to reveal the truth about the original painting and its artist? Doctor Gillespie would assume the answers were yes. She knew the Devil's Corps would torture by knife or fire, until death if necessary, in order to gain information. She also knew beheading was the corps' *modus operandi*. The only relief from the tragedy was that Henri Goosche was a bachelor and had no living family.

Earlier in the day the committee had decided the portrait would be placed in a bank vault for safekeeping. Doctor Gillespie would make the arrangements and the move would be made that very evening.

After Agent Davis had phoned her the bad news, however, the circumstances that surrounded Henri Goosche's demise had gnawed at her mind, prompting Doctor Gillespie to alter the plan without committee knowledge.

She made several telephone calls, then summoned Agent Davis and Peter Grant for a private briefing on the matter. The artist would assist his bodyguard in moving the portrait to the Chicago City Morgue.

Shortly before midnight and using an agency van to accommodate the rolled portrait, Agent Davis and Grant entered a side door of the morgue. They descended steps to a cold basement with dim blue lights on a high ceiling. Some of the gray vaults were painted with a blue front to indicate corpses in frozen suspension.

On each blue vault was attached personal and maintenance data to assure proper periodic refueling of the corpses. Also, each had a date of resurrection. They placed the rolled portrait into a predetermined vault—number 50. It was a dummy blue vault with dummy data and a rebirth date of 2045.

Because of the beheading incident, Doctor Gillespie was able to have her presidential appointment moved up a week. On April 27, she and Peter Grant flew to Washington, D.C.

Armed with committee reports and a print of the portrait, the doctor made an impression that prompted the president to phone Attorney General L. Powers, authorizing her to present the matter to the secretary general of the United Nations.

When Attorney General Powers made contact, the UN secretary general suggested it was an internal matter and the United States should deal with the issue. The president assured Doctor Gillespie he would confer with top-level officials of the Internal Security Department within the week.

Before Doctor Gillespie and Grant returned to Chicago, they investigated leased apartments and found one with a lease to expire July 10. Grant would take the apartment on a temporary basis shortly after that date. Doctor Gillespie paid the short-term six month lease and Grant signed the necessary papers, using an alias.

Grant had agreed to the move provided he would be reunited with his family in the near future. Their separation had reached sixteen months and his patience was wearing thin.

Doctor Gillespie assured him the reunion would occur no later than early December and it would be permanent.

The president's meeting with the Internal Security Department planted the seed for the eventual congressional endorsement of the American International Tribunal.

As director of the president's Council on Revolutionary Tactics, Doctor Gillespie would continue to be responsible for the security of both portrait and artist. Once the tribunal was in place, however, that body would assume responsibility for the portrait's security.

By June 21, the tribunal was in high gear. Its thirty-three members were political, social, educational, and religious leaders representing ten nations. Sixteen members were women and twenty members were religious dignitaries representing each of the major Christian bodies—Protestantism, Roman Catholic, Eastern Church, and Mormonism.

Throughout the summer the tribunal held joint meetings with the world Council of Churches and the College of Cardinals. These mid-summer sessions served to give impetus to the religious implications of the portrait.

Enough of the secret proceedings had been permitted to leak, allowing the media to suggest something significant of a religious nature was underway in America.

It was an exciting and busy time, but Grant hadn't forgotten Mother's Day nor his practice of wiring yellow roses to Tracy in London. In early June, the artist was relieved that Tracy, Wes, and her parents had returned to Reading after the six-month lease had expired. Shortly afterward, Grant had moved into his temporary residence in D.C. It was July 13 and a sad moving day for the artist because it marked the second anniversary of Kay's death.

On August 15, the tribunal was solemnized and within a week issued its first public communiqué. Its message was brief but explicit.

The tribunal verified the existence of a painted portrait depicting the crucifixion of Christ, recently completed and possessing supernatural powers.

The tribunal acknowledged it was an American artist who painted the portrait, however, security permitted nothing more except the identity of tribunal members and its objectives.

The tribunal communiqué ended with the promise that a more comprehensive report would be forthcoming by satellite beamed television and wire service coverage the world over. It would include a description of the portrait's unique features and a color reproduction.

World reaction to the communiqué was mixed, ranging from apathy to bewilderment, with the majority being apprehensive, skeptical, and curious.

Anti-Christians scoffed with indignation and cynicism, labeling the tribunal a puppet machine designed to bulldoze fast-fading Christian believers with theatrics and hocus-pocus tactics.

On Sunday, August 29, the tribunal report was ready and would be televised from the tribunal office in the Pentagon Building. The speaker was tribunal chairman, Chief Magistrate Abdulla Theopolis, patriarch of the Ethiopian Orthodox Church. He sat comfortably before a battery of microphones while standby interpreters would translate his brief report into many languages.

The Ethiopian dignitary, wearing a black robe and a placid face, spoke softly and with eloquence as he described the characteristics of the portrait and artist.

Alone at his temporary apartment in D.C., Grant viewed the telecast with mixed emotions. His work was on display for the world to view, yet he felt an awesome responsibility for not knowing how or to what extent the portrait would influence.

By contrast, his feelings about his recent personal experiences were fixed. The artist was convinced his cure and his new awareness were God-given.

Finally, the Chief Magistrate spoke briefly on the potential of the portrait, referring to it as a "beacon of truth" and a "gift from God." Emotions choked his words and his aging eyes were moist as he began his closing remarks.

"We of the tribunal perceive a humanitarian vision. It is a vision that brings humanity to the breath of God. May this new relationship cause a reassessment of values and priorities in our relationship with God. May this new relationship enable each of us to identify more strongly with our fellow man. May this new relationship with God provide us with new insights into the integrity and worth of each human being. This is our vision.

"May this new relationship—humankind with God—enable us to overcome hate and prejudice in favor of love and understanding. May it help us rid this world of poverty, starvation, disease, illiteracy, greed, war, and self-annihilation. This is our vision.

"Our vision is a dawning world utopia. A life of man helping man and nation helping nation. A life that enables man to enjoy the fruits of this world and the beauty of God's creation.

"Every human being needs and deserves to be understood, respected, and loved. Only in this manner will we find joy, peace, and fulfillment. Only in this manner will we be victorious over death."

The Chief Magistrate lifted a photograph for all to see. "This portrait holds for each of us the kind of vision of which I speak. I challenge each of you to have the will, faith, and courage to accept this new relationship with God."

He removed his pincenez and looked up from his script. "To every person who would place credence in this, our vision, I ask you to pray for the deliverance of all humanity."

The tribunal elected to unveil the portrait with a Special Mass at Saint Michael's Parish in Washington, D.C., on December 31. Security for the Mass would receive top priority, even though the Revolutionaries had long since become disengaged and no longer a national threat.

Small pockets of fanatics still existed. The Devil's Corps had been humiliated for having missed some big targets but, even though this infuriated their leader, it only intensified their pledge to kill Christians by any means.

A growing fear of the unknown gripped the international community as the unprecedented unveiling neared.

Chapter 25
Family Reunion

Immediately following the tribunal report, Grant phoned Tracy. He wanted to talk about the report as it related to him. They would discuss it more fully when together, but they did agree his unusual experiences leading to the portrait's completion were of God's doing.

Doctor Gillespie also phoned. She wanted his reaction to the report and to assure him his move to D.C. proved a good security decision. From the Devil's Corps' perspective, his trail had cooled after they realized their blunder in his studio. The death was not publicized and Grant was never able to tell Tracy it was a mistaken beheading in his studio that had prompted his move to D.C.

Grant toyed with the idea of dashing to Reading for a surprise family reunion but the idea was quickly shot down. Tracy phoned that her friend Vicki Valentine was seriously ill. Tracy wished to visit her in Miami and suggested Wesley could stay with his grandparents and not miss the start of the school term.

Grant brought Tracy up to date on the latest developments, then wished her a safe trip and Vicki a quick recovery.

With the arrival of October, Vicki had recovered and Tracy returned to Reading where she was greeted with good news. Grant had phoned earlier in the day. The waiting was over. She and Wesley were free to join him in D.C. at any time.

On October 8 the day came. That morning, the artist and his family had the glorious luxury of being reunited after almost two years.

Grant apologized for the lost time they had endured as a family but Tracy would have none of it. Her love for her husband had transcended the temporary restrictions that had been placed upon their marriage. They were together at last and sharing a beautiful happiness. She was never more proud of her husband than at that moment.

Grant was amazed how Wes had grown and Tracy was more beautiful than ever.

Doctor Gillespie phoned Grant that afternoon with details regarding the special Mass and the role he would play. She would visit him in November with more information.

Grant and Tracy would never make up the lost time, but that evening they would try. While Wesley slept soundly in the next room, his parents would make love.

It wasn't exhausting because they were in no hurry. Tracy knew how to please her husband and Grant could satisfy, as well. He was tender and thoughtful and could be in control without appearing to be. This lack of domination on his part enabled Tracy to be relaxed as she responded freely and without inhibitions.

The artist's inventive approach and creative nature would never allow their intimate relationship to become mechanical or boring or a source of conflict as is the case with many married couples. Despite their special reunion, it was only a prelude to the special mass which lurked on the horizon, magnifying the level of expectation, apprehension, and fear throughout the international scene.

Grant tried to ease the tension by maintaining a jovial mood. At the same time, he made a point to devote every minute of each day with his family.

Wesley's eighth birthday on December 22 served to relax them. Christmas was also helpful and they treated it as usual. It included a decorated tree, gifts, a delicious dinner, companionship, and attending church services.

Grant noticed Wes was becoming more talkative than usual and full of questions.

While Tracy was busy in the kitchen, Grant relaxed in a comfortable tilt-back. He was remembering Christmas a year ago when Press had dined with them and the nation had been racked with time bombs. The artist felt confident no such bombings would occur this year.

Wes casually approached his father. "Dad, what causes wars?" he asked innocently, as he kneeled at Grant's chair.

Grant looked at his son and tousled the boy's dark hair. "Wars?" he began, putting the newspaper aside. "You see, Wes, leaders of one country may feel threatened by another country, usually a neighboring country. So, the leaders of the threatened country will make weapons of war to protect themselves. This causes the neighboring country to increase its weapons of war, also. And so it goes. This is called escalation.'

"I've never heard that word," Wesley admitted. "Dad, why does the neighboring country threaten the other country?"

"Because some countries have leaders who are greedy. By defeating another country in war, these leaders gain more wealth and power."

"That's a normal war, Dad," Wes jumped in. "I know civil wars are different," he added. "In school we learned civil wars are fought inside a country, like a country fighting itself...like a revolution," he said proudly.

"You're absolutely right, son," beamed the artist. "Like the revolution our country is having now, but ours is almost over."

"That's good. Dad, why are there always poor people in the world? That's not fair, is it?" the boy asked with concern.

Pride surged through Grant's veins and again he playfully tousled his son's hair. "That's a good question, Wes. Pull over a chair and we'll look for a good answer."

Wesley smiled and responded quickly.

"You see, Wes," Grant began, "life isn't always fair. Most people think it should be fair, but it isn't." Grant sat back and briefly reflected upon his parents' accidental death years ago.

"Wes," he finally said, "I'll tell you a true story about a man who found life to be very unfair. The man was born over fifty years ago into a large family that was poor and lived in the slums of Sacramento. Wes, do you know where the city of Sacramento is located?"

"No, Dad."

"California. Sacramento is the capital of California."

"I'll remember that," Wes said, almost apologetically.

"While this man was growing up," Grant continued, "he was called bad names and was treated badly by people."

"Why, Dad?"

"Because of the color of his skin. He was a black man, son," Grant lamented, as America's racial problem slipped into his thoughts.

"One day, as a teenager, this man was arrested for loitering," Grant went on. "He was sentenced to serve two days in jail. Then a strange thing happened. While in jail, he was visited by the chief of police who recognized the teenager as a good person and she told the man so.

"That was many years ago, son, and today the man and the chief are still friends.

"After serving his two days," Grant continued, "the teenager found a job, worked hard, saved his money, and finally enrolled in college. He was helped by receiving money from our government as a loan.

"When he graduated from college and got a job, he paid back the money he had borrowed. In college he had studied journalism. That's writing for magazines or newspapers. Later, this man got a job where I worked and he and I have been good friends ever since.

"The man I'm talking about is someone you know, Wes. His name is Preston Thomas."

"Mr. Thomas? Wow!"

"You see, Wes, even if life treats you unfairly, you don't give up. Mr. Thomas didn't give up."

"He sure didn't, Dad."

"Wes, did you ever hear me speak of Doctor Gillespie?"

The boy's eyes popped wide. "Sure! Isn't she a secret spy?" he asked excitedly.

Grant grinned. "Yes, in a manner of speaking. That's her job today. Years ago, she was the chief of police who spoke to Mr. Thomas in the Sacramento jail."

"Wow!"

Grant hesitated. "Wes, I have another story for you," he said uneasily.

"A true story?"

"Yes...it is," Grant said slowly. The artist looked into his son's inquisitive eyes, then he looked toward the ceiling.

"Just over two years ago," he began, "a lady died after putting up a tough fight against a bad disease. We were close friends, this lady and I."

"Why did she die, Dad?"

"I don't know, son...unless God wanted her more than I did. Anyway," Grant continued, "this lady was a photographer, Wes, but not just any photographer. She was little...not much taller than you, yet she took pictures of wild animals like jaguar and tigers. Of course, she didn't photograph them at the zoo where animals are caged. Instead, she went into the wild animal hunting grounds—the jungle."

"Dad, she really must have been something!"

"Yes, she was, son. She was a brave lady and she was also beautiful, just like your mother. While your mother has lovely blonde hair, this lady had soft reddish-brown hair."

"Dad, do you mean auburn hair?" Wesley asked.

The artist felt a tightness in his throat and he fought back tears. "Yes...she had auburn hair."

Grant ran a hand through his own hair and sighed deeply to break the tension. "You would have liked this lady, Wes, and I know she would have liked you. When she died I knew life wasn't fair because this lady deserved to live. She was a fighter and when she became ill, she fought even harder."

Grant cleared his throat. "Wes, there will be times when things will go badly for you. There will be difficult and sad times. This is when you must reach down deep within yourself and find strength to go on. The strength is there, son, inside each of us. It's waiting to be used when needed."

The boy was listening hard. "Dad, do you mean when the tough times come, that's when we must be *inside tough*?"

"Yes. That's good. Inside tough. That's what I mean."

"Time for a break," said Tracy, entering the room, picking up the newspaper, and flopping on a chair. "Wesley, I've just whipped up a batch of butterscotch cookies from a new recipe. They're on the kitchen table and just waiting to be sampled."

His eyes lit up. "Okay!" he enthused, and scampered off.

"Thanks, Mom," he said a moment later. "They were super!"

"You're welcome, dear." Tracy responded with a sigh of happy relief, knowing he didn't stop at one.

"Think I'll read some," Wesley countered, as he crossed toward his bedroom with a *Space Unlimited Magazine* in hand.

Within minutes, Tracy came to her feet. "Darling, did you read this?" she asked, giving Grant the newspaper and fingering the article for him.

It was a brief item on a back page.

A.P. New York City.

ART DIRECTOR DEHEADED.

Ambrose Thorne, Art Director of Nelson-Fause Advertising Agency, is dead at fifty-two. Authorities claim the murder is attributed to the Devil's Corps. It occurred December 26 at Thorne's agency office with burglary being the motive.

Tracy winced. "Isn't that awful! Darling, do you still carry your gun?" she asked.

"No, I don't. I still have the pistol that belonged to the black man I had encountered, but it doesn't fit my holster," he explained.

"Will you buy one that fits, for my peace of mind?"

He grinned and kissed her. "Sure, Tracy. I'll buy one today."

She returned his kiss. "Peter, I love you and I fear for your safety."

"I understand, Tracy," he said, soberly.

Grant changed the subject.

"Wes and I had a good talk while you were whipping up those cookies. We talked about life. I told Wes in every life there will be good times and bad times. I tried to explain the importance of accepting the tough times."

Tracy beamed. "I'm glad you and Wesley can talk about those things, Peter."

"He's very perceptive, you know. By the way, Tracy, have I told you recently how proud I am of my family? You've done a super job with Wes."

"Thank you."

Grant placed a hand on hers and he began to toy with her wedding band. "Tracy, there's something else I've been wanting to tell you," Grant said, seriously. "I don't ever want you to think you are in competition with the memory of Kay. Sure, I'll always remember Kay with love but I have a big heart and it's capable of much love, especially for my family. Tracy, you stand alone. I love you because of who you are—a thoughtful, kind, caring person, and my only desire in life is to help you and Wes find happiness."

Later that afternoon, Grant taxied to a local mall complex to buy a handgun.

During his absence, Wesley approached his mother in the kitchen. "Mom, was Dad sick?" he asked.

Tracy put a hand on his shoulder. "Wesley, let's go into the living room and talk, okay?"

They sat together on the sofa.

"Yes, Wesley, your father was sick for some time. It was a rare sickness. Neither he nor I knew about it until recently."

"How was it rare, Mom?"

"Occasionally, your dad would imagine things. He would see things that weren't there but he was still able to paint beautifully."

"Mom, Dad wasn't crazy, was he?"

"No, of course not, dear. Most of the time he was fine, just like you and me. Then, suddenly, a wonderful thing happened. Your father became well."

"How did that happen, Mom?"

"Nobody knows, Wesley. Your father and I think it was a miracle. We think God made him well."

"I believe in miracles," the boy said with assurance.

Tracy responded by kissing his cheek.

"Your father told me you and he had a talk."

Wesley nodded. "Dad and I talked about important things. Even about Kay."

"Yes, Wesley, I know about Kay. She was a brave lady."

"Dad told me she died."

"Yes, she did."

"Was she like you, Mom?"

"Perhaps in some ways but we were also different. I think Kay was more independent than I. By that I mean she could do a great deal without help. I need someone to rely upon...someone to share my troubles...someone who can provide a shoulder for me to rest my head upon."

They heard a car door slam shut.

"Dad's coming! I'll go meet him," Wesley said excitedly.

At the door, he turned to his mother. "Mom, you can rely on me to listen to your troubles. You can lean your head on my shoulder any time," he said before dashing out the door.

Tracy hurried to the bathroom and dabbed her eyes with a tissue. Her tears were a mixture of pride and love for her son.

Chapter 26
Affirmation of Faith

Doctor Gillespie had to postpone her scheduled November visit with Grant, finally arriving for a brief stay on December 27.

She wanted to review all the details she had covered earlier, beginning with the seating arrangement at the parish and how Grant would unveil the portrait. A taxi would pick them up the night of December 31 at precisely ten-thirty. Even should the weather be uncooperative, Doctor Gillespie was confident they would reach the parish within an hour. She also felt the sooner Mass began after Grant's arrival the better. She emphasized the importance of making sure their taxi was number seventeen.

All was set for the Special Mass, she had assured him. Only as an afterthought, and not in the presence of his family, did she reveal that Henri Goosche's remains had never been found. She believed they had been returned to Lady X as proof of the kill.

December 31, 2027, finally arrived. The weather was cold and snow was falling lightly as Tracy, Wesley, and Grant squirmed into heavy wraps and pulled on snow shoes.

Prior to the taxi's arrival, Grant crossed to his bedroom and opened the bottom dresser drawer. He gazed at the newly purchased gun. The Derringer was loaded and snugly packed into his shoulder holster. He touched the gun with his fingers before closing the drawer and joining the others, leaving the gun behind.

Δ Δ Δ

The taxi carrying Grant, Tracy, and Wes eased to the curb. Saint Michael's Parish was a short block away. Despite the late hour, Wesley was alert as he and his mother edged forward in their seats. Grant took a deep breath and let the air out slowly. He took Tracy's hand in his.

Grant noticed a black car parked a short distance to their front. Across the street, he saw a second black car parked at the intersection just ahead. The headlights of the second car flicked once.

The artist wondered why the taxi had stopped and he began to feel uneasy. Doctor Gillespie had assured him the parish would be ringed by security, yet, his instincts told him something was amiss.

The taxi transmitter-receiver began to beep.

The driver snatched it from the dashboard. "This is Big Bear twenty-two," he responded quickly.

"This is X one," came a woman's voice from the other end. "Abort A-bomb and initiate Bullseye immediately," she said in a low, raspy voice.

"This is Big Bear twenty-two. Wilco. Out."

The taxi driver replaced the transmitter, then reached under the dashboard, and withdrew a Beretta .45. He turned and leveled the gun at Tracy.

"Easy does it," Grant said, directing his words toward Tracy and Wes as well as the driver, while placing a protective arm over his wife's shoulders to comfort her.

"I'll be damned!" the cabby bellowed at Grant. "Did you think you'd reach the parish alive?" He shook his head. "Christian, this is the end of the road."

The cabby's face took on a deadpan expression. "Christian, if you do what I say, the wife and kid might live."

A series of heat waves raced through Grant's head and his throat became tight. Instinctively, he turned to Tracy and Wes. "It'll be okay," he assured them with unusual calm.

"Christian, open the door, get out, and walk slowly to that car up ahead," the cabby demanded. "If you make like a hero and run, your wife and kid are dead. Now, get out!" he roared.

Again, Grant turned to Tracy and Wes. "It'll be okay, I promise you. Wes, show your mother how brave you are. I love you," he said quickly, then kissed their cheeks.

He opened the door and stepped out.

Tracy began to sob softly.

"Dad!" yelled Wesley.

"Yes, son?"

"Dad, remember, inside tough?" he said almost with a sob.

"Yes, son, inside tough all the way," Grant said as he closed the door.

"Darling...." Tracy's hand went out toward him but he was gone.

Tracy hugged her son and they both sobbed as they watched the artist approach and disappear into the black car.

At that instant, the door of the second black car opened and a woman stepped out. She was wearing a black coat that reached her snow shoes and a floppy hat that covered hair that touched her shoulders. A handbag with a shoulder strap dangled at her side and she headed directly toward the taxi.

The woman opened the rear taxi door and slipped in next to Wesley. She turned to the driver. "Good work, Big Bear twenty-two. Very good work, indeed. I'll see that Council rewards you handsomely for your action. Now, you may further aid our cause by kindly disengaging the horn. This damn weather may cause it to stick and arouse the neighborhood." Without hesitation, the cabby disengaged the horn as Tracy and Wesley continued to sob.

The woman turned to Tracy. "Now, baby doll, you and the boy will get out and walk slowly to the automobile ahead. If either of you try something stupid, your Christian blood will quickly stain the snow and your folly will hasten the assassination of your husband. Now, get out!" she barked.

Wesley took his mother's arm and they walked slowly toward the car as instructed, while the woman and taxi driver watched.

Sitting behind the driver, the woman removed a handgun from her bag and released the safety switch. It was a Derringer DA-38 with a built-in silencer.

When Tracy and Wesley reached the car, a man stepped out and assisted them into the back seat.

"Big Bear twenty-two, do our cause another favor and kindly replace your gun," she said with a hard voice.

As the cabby leaned forward to replace his Beretta, the woman, with gun in hand, extended her arm until the gun barrel came within inches of the base of the taxi driver's skull. Without flinching, she squeezed the trigger and the huge man went limp without a sound, slumping across the steering wheel.

"That was your reward from Council. Sorry, Big Bear. You were on the wrong team," said Doctor Gillespie, using her normal voice.

The doctor quickly went to work. She pushed the dead man off the steering wheel and snapped on the horn switch. Next, she grabbed at her neck and, in one sweeping motion, pulled the mask over her head. With the mask came her wig and floppy hat, all of which she dropped into her handbag. She placed her gun into the handbag and removed a hat more to her liking. This done, she flicked the headlights twice.

Her signal drew agents from the second black car with guns drawn, but they were relived to find all was well when they reached her.

Doctor Gillespie joined a happy Grant and his family in the car and, as they were driven toward the back entrance of the parish, she apologized to the artist.

"That was cutting it close," she was saying, "and I'm sorry about the rough stuff, Mr. Grant. It was a gamble, I admit. I gambled your taxi would lead us to Lady X and it did. I was also counting on the toughness of you and your family and, indeed, you were. Big Bear is at rest. At the last moment, I went to plan B. I decided not to eliminate Big Bear before the eyes of your son," she told Grant on the side.

"Tracy and I appreciate that," said Grant. "And Lady X?"

"She's also at rest," Doctor Gillespie said matter-of-factly.

"Cyanide?" Grant asked.

"No, Lady X wasn't that clean. She was addicted to blood letting. It was a self-inflicted bullet to the forehead."

As they approached the entrance to the parish back door, they were met by a happy team of security guards.

Security helicopters hovered overhead.

"Praise the Lord! You've arrived safely!" greeted a parish official at the door.

Once inside, they shed their wraps and took assigned seats in the first pew on the left section. Grant sat closest to the wall, followed by Wesley, Tracy, Doctor Gillespie, and Press Thomas. The remainder of the pew seats were occupied by agents and parish officials. The tribunal members occupied a section of the second pew.

Soft organ music played to a quiet, meditating congregation. All eyes were closed or fixed upon the covered portrait hanging on the front wall. In this setting, Doctor Gillespie whispered the harrowing events of the past five minutes to Press.

The air was heavy causing Grant to ring his collar with a finger. For security reasons, it was not made public that he would be in attendance, so his introduction would be a surprise.

Tracy sat tall and proud. Wesley marveled at the huge gathering and wondered how so many people could be so quiet.

Grant glanced over his shoulder and viewed evidence of massive preparation for the Mass. The rear balcony had been enclosed with panels of glass, forming a series of soundproof cubicles which housed correspondents, newscasters, interpreters, reporters, electricians, and tele-operators.

The parish was overflowing. The front section was occupied by members of Saint Michael's Parish. The middle section held heads of state, congressional members, and a contingent of celebrities in different fields, while the back section was reserved for religious dignitaries.

The president and his cabinet would view the Mass from the White House, while the Pope's absence was due to a respiratory illness.

Four dozen television cameras were positioned on a smaller third floor balcony. Their operators had arrived the previous day and had been quartered in the parish basement.

To accommodate world coverage, three satellites had been steered into a 40,000-mile parking orbit from where they would send signals to relief stations at strategic points around the globe. A team of interpreters was ready to translate in thirty languages. Conservative estimates predicted three-quarters of the five billion population of the world would witness the Mass via television.

Rumors and predictions ran rampant. Even the Pope, during an audience prior to his recent illness, was reported to have suggested the possibility of a Godly response during the Holy Mass. Many reputed theologians predicted some kind of visual response from God. Less restrained prognosticators believed it would be the second coming of Christ. Others predicted doomsday.

The front of the sanctuary consisted of a two-step elevated platform with the pulpit positioned at right-front to accommodate the three spotlights presently directed upon the centered portrait. The portrait was veiled and hanging against the wall high enough for all to see.

The organ music abruptly stopped and an eerie silence fell upon the huge hall.

A nervous Monsignor Kelly, wearing a surplice over a black cassock and a biretta on his gray hair, entered from the right and stepped to the pulpit. After a brief moment, a lady entered and stood to the monsignor's left. She would interpret using sign language.

Due to the emphasis placed upon the portrait and the tightness of security, it was decided the portrait would be unveiled as early in the Mass as feasible.

Monsignor Kelly, feeling the pressure of the moment, opened the service with a shaky voice as he delivered a brief prayer. Following this, he spoke just as briefly about the portrait that had received international attention and had prompted the special Mass.

He looked in Grant's direction. "It is my privilege to introduce to you the artist who painted the portrait and who will unveil it at this time—Mr. Peter Grant."

During the applause, Grant quickly kissed Tracy and Wes, then climbed the two steps to the platform and crossed to the pulpit, while the monsignor stood to one side. The congregation rapidly became subdued in anticipation of his words.

"To each of you in this beautiful house of God and to those of you watching on television throughout the world, I say good evening."

"Before I unveil the portrait, I wish to comment about something you are about to see. Above the head of Christ, I painted a sign with the letters I, N, R, and I. You will see these letters only briefly before they change to four different symbols. This change will occur over and over again but it is nothing to fear. Please ignore it.

"Because this is a Christian gathering, the second unusual feature presented by the portrait is not likely to occur. However to those viewers who don't believe in God as your savior, expect to see the portrait disappear before your eyes within a minute, not to return.

"Whatever you see, my friends, please don't be fearful," Grant emphasized. He then crossed to the portrait and, without hesitation, pulled the draw cord.

A gasp echoed throughout the hall, as the sudden impact of seeing the portrait was usually the same. Chills would surge up the spine, followed by an overwhelming sense of humility, shame, and contrition.

Even as Grant viewed the portrait, he noticed the spot lights flicker and begin to grow dim. At the same time, the portrait began to slowly fade from the view of all individuals everywhere. A growing murmur swelled from the congregation. Monsignor Kelly's face paled and he was assisted to a nearby chair by the interpreter.

The portrait continued to fade and the congregation was on its feet. The turn of events had hit with unexpected speed and force. Murmurs had quickly turned to sporadic mutterings of prayer by many tongues.

The moment was laced with fear. Many dropped to their knees. Tears welled in eyes while some sobbed openly. Some fainted.

Within a minute the painting had vanished, except for smudges of red that had represented the blood of Christ. Finally, the flood lights went out.

Grant quickly withdrew his billfold and saw that his small copy of the portrait had not disappeared.

Guided by instinct, he sprang to the pulpit and raised his arms for attention and quiet. "Friends, don't be fearful!" he pleaded, speaking into the battery of microphones and megaphones. "Friends, listen to what I have to say...I beg of you."

The confusion was slow to abate. The artist turned to Monsignor Kelly. The priest anxiously nodded his approval of Grant's intrusion, sensing the intervention was spiritually inspired.

Again Grant faced the microphones and his audience of billions. Television camera spot lights from the upper balcony struck his face, revealing a glistening of sweat and strain. "Please be seated," he pleaded and the congregation slowly responded.

Grant leaned against the pulpit with straight arms. "My friends, I know why the portrait vanished. I repeat, I can tell you why the portrait has disappeared and you need not be fearful."

The congregation stirred.

"I painted the portrait and I understand it more than any living soul," Grant continued. "I also watched the portrait vanish and, as I did so, I suddenly understood why. You see, God is testing all of us. He is testing our faith."

"Also, my friends, we have failed the test. That's why the portrait vanished and has not returned. We came here hoping for a sign from God and it came. God put us to the test and we failed."

Grant leaned heavily against the pulpit, his voice growing unsteady. "We were a witness to our unfaithfulness...but...God is loving and forgiving. There is still hope."

Grant coughed and wiped his brow with the heal of his hand. His face paled and his breathing became labored.

"There's still time," he said, as he withdrew the gold ring from his jacket pocket and held it high for all to see.

The congregation was subdued.

"This ring is a token of faith. It helped me paint the portrait."

Grant coughed again and momentarily dropped his head. He winced as a sharp pain darted down his left arm. His hands felt numb and his throat was hot.

"There's still time," he went on. "Jesus said...*Oh ye of little faith*? I plead to the television audience throughout the world...people of every country...every continent. If enough of you will...with a contrite heart...accept God as your savior, the portrait will reappear. It will! But...if you don't...."

The artist felt a squeezing in his chest and the congregation became a blur.

Although it was after midnight, from somewhere a distant bell began to toll.

Grant stepped from behind the pulpit and turned toward the steps. He went to his knees. He fell forward and the gold ring slipped from his grasp, rolled down the steps and disappeared under feet. As Grant lay there, the last toll of the bell passed into history, but there's never an ending without a new beginning.

With the last toll of the bell came a startling revelation. The spotlights flicked and went on. Slowly, the figure of Christ began to reappear in all its clarity, beauty, and splendor. All viewers saw in the clutched left hand of Christ a painted gold ring. Faith in God had manifested itself.

A voice from each heart was heard, speaking words that were heard two thousand years earlier: "*Be thou faithful until death and I will give thee a crown of life.*"

In that hallowed moment was born the beginning of a new faith for mankind, and the portrait would stand as a beacon of that faith. It was a faith anchored in the knowledge that God's truth and love are everlasting. This was the truth Peter Grant learned, lived, and for which he died.

With the eagerness, energy, and tender promise of an adolescent, the earth unfolded to the dawn of a new era. It was an era free from wars, hate, greed, and bigotry. Man was free to live a better life.

In an early part of that new era, a sixth grader would open his notebook, take a pencil in hand, and reflectively jot a poem:

The Portrait

My Dad
My dad, painter of destiny,
Had to conquer insanity
And hang himself just so that he
Could paint the man from Galilee,
That faith in God would render free
Man everywhere…and Mom…and me.